I0692009

Magic in the Mountains

by

Donna Kunkel

Aspen Glen Series

Magic in the Mountains

Cover Art by *Kristian Norris*

The Wild Rose Press, Inc.
PO Box 708
Adams Basin, NY 14410-0708
Visit us at www.thewildrosepress.com

Publishing History
First Fantasy Rose Edition, 2018
Print ISBN 978-1-5092-2310-7
Digital ISBN 978-1-5092-2311-4

Aspen Glen Series
Published in the United States of America

This was unbelievable. "My boss isn't going to understand. This is just like my dog ate my homework. I'm stuck in the snow—for a month or more." Her mind raced through the possible ways of traveling. "What about a snowmobile?"

"Unfortunately, the road you came in on is the only way in or out. I wouldn't be surprised to find out that an avalanche blocked the valley pass last night. If so, it'll take a while before anyone can get through." He watched her. "Why did you drive out this way? Why didn't you stop at the hotel next to the highway?"

"What hotel?"

"If you had just driven under the highway overpass, you'd have been there. Why didn't you follow the detour sign?"

"Oh great. That's—just—great! The stupid detour sign blows away so now I'm stuck in the middle of nothing. I could have been tucked away in a nice comfortable hotel—with electricity and phones. But no—I'm stuck in no-man's land. I risked life and limb trudging through the snow for what?" She sighed. "Now what?"

Dedication

I want to thank Mary for all her help with figuring out how to fill holes in the plot. To Betty, Elizabeth, John, Joyce, Lori, Margaret, Tena, and Whendi for all your comments and ideas. My grandmother for the memories of collecting eggs with her. And to my husband, who is always there for me.

Chapter 1

Another blast of arctic wind seized her car in its frozen claws and shoved it maliciously. The little subcompact was no match for the ferocity of the storm. Alex Klein tightened her hold on the steering wheel. As soon as she'd headed into the mountains east of Grand Junction, Colorado, her little car had been buffeted by the unforgiving wind. Then the sky started dumping snow, reducing visibility to only a few feet at times. So far, the wind had cleared the road of most of the snow, but it still slowed her down.

"If I get caught in this storm, I'll miss my date with Jason." Alex thumped her steering wheel. All those days timing her arrival at work to ride an elevator up with Jason would be for nothing. And she'd finally gathered enough courage to ask him out. He was a normal, everyday, mundane guy. No magic, no freaky pets, no boasting about how much power he had. An accountant for crying out loud. An accountant wouldn't be caught in a snowstorm in the mountains of Colorado. She needed an accountant in her life.

She passed over another mountain ridge and encountered the full force of the storm. The lanes had disappeared as the snow piled up even deeper. She sighed. "Why did I pick this month to not use magic? I could have been back to Denver and home in minutes instead of driving for hours." Sick and tired of magical

1

men, she wanted to find someone normal, like Jason. She'd pledged to not use magic for thirty days to see if she could live normally. Just because she had magic didn't mean anything when it came to controlling the elements.

She checked her odometer again.

"Only a few miles to the next exit." She tried to remain hopeful, but those last few miles stretched on and on. An exit sign emerged through the blowing snow and the barricade had been lowered, closing the highway beyond. She eased her car down the ramp, following the faint tire tracks from other vehicles, then the tracks disappeared.

"Now which way?" There was always some type of hotel near an exit with a barricade. Something that would keep travelers from getting stranded. The weather in the Colorado mountains could be so finicky. It wasn't unusual to get thirty-six inches of snow in one storm system. That's how the ski slopes could end up with a ninety-six-inch base.

She looked left, right, and ahead, but no buildings, lights, or even signs were visible in the blowing snow. The mountains were closer on the left, but there seemed to be more room on the right. A hotel was probably there. She inched her car along the road that headed off to the right.

After several minutes, there still weren't any signs or even a single building and the road became a narrow channel between the looming mountains. "Damn it. I missed the hotel. It must have been the other way." She gripped the wheel even tighter. The road had now become impossible to turn around in, to say nothing about the steep drop-off on the right side of the road.

2

The only option was to proceed and look for any kind of building that might offer a little shelter.

"Shit. Why didn't I leave earlier?" People would find her frozen body out here and comment about how much of an idiot she'd been.

There were so few times when she could visit with her friends, and the storm wasn't supposed to hit until tomorrow. Of course, the weather forecasters were quite often wrong.

She had to keep going on. At least it should still be early enough that someone might be up watching TV. Snow now clogged her car's wipers. Her hands cramped up from gripping the wheel. She took a moment to shake them out to ease the stiffness. She had to go slow and steady. After several miles, the drop-off on the right side of the road started becoming less steep and the ground widened. This had to be a valley. Someone would surely live here. The road continued to hug the mountainside, but on the right side she caught glimpses of the valley getting wider.

She inched around a tight bend and spotted a faint glimmer of light. Did she imagine it or were her eyes playing tricks? She kept staring at the area. There it was again. *A light!* Definitely a light, slowly becoming more visible. At times the blowing snow would hide its location, but it was there.

"A driveway. Thank God!" She carefully eased her car off the road and headed into the narrow lane. After a few feet, the location of the driveway became unclear. She could barely make out some type of structure not too far from the road. The driveway had to head down the rest of the hill then angle toward the building. From the car she couldn't make out where it was. All along

3

I70, the road followed a river. There could be one at the base of the mountainside, or it could be farther out in the flat area. If there was a stream, could she take the chance of driving into it? It wasn't worth finding out. The house looked close enough that she could get there; but she'd have to leave the car and head on foot to the building. Eventually the plows would come through, so she pulled the car in as far as she could without heading down the slope. Hopefully the car wouldn't get too buried under a mound of snow.

She pulled her cell phone out. *No signal.* She stuffed the phone back in her purse and took a deep breath as she pulled on her bulky knit hat. Why hadn't she worn her boots? She twisted the matching scarf around her neck. Looking at her computer and purse, she grabbed them and slung the straps over her head so her hands would be free. There was no way she'd leave them behind. Her whole life was in those two bags.

The cold air hit her the second she opened the door. She pulled the scarf farther up across her face as she stepped out. The light represented shelter from the storm. It was close enough she should be able to get there, but too far away for anyone inside to hear if she honked. Knowing her luck, a crazy mountain man lived there, but it wasn't like she had a choice. She headed down the slope, determined to reach the light.

After taking only a couple of steps, her feet started sliding. Her arms flailed as she tried to remain standing. She hit the hard surface and sprawled on her back. Before she could manage to get back up, her body slid down the slope, gradually picking up speed. She managed to snatch a bit of bush, but it snapped off. She tried to grab something else to stop her descent. A tree,

4

rock—anything that might help.

Nothing there.

She dug her fingers into the snow like claws, anything to slow down. She slid into a low railing, stopping her at the edge of a bridge.

Lying there for a moment to slow her pounding heart, she looked around to get her bearings. She could barely make out the foot-high wooden railing that marked the sides. The bridge angled off to the left. If she'd tried to drive down, the car would have slid and probably missed the turn for the bridge and ended up...

She eased over to the bridge's edge and looked down, snow and black. There wasn't any way of knowing how deep it might be. A few snow-covered boulders mounded up here and there as the side sloped down. If she'd ended up down there, she could've been trapped in the car. No one able to see it. Alone in the night to freeze to death. She shuddered at the thought then looked up to the light. The light became her beacon in the dark.

She should be able to get warm once she got there. She stood up and shuffled slowly across the bridge. The moment she stepped off the other side of the bridge, the snow got deeper. It looked like a level trek to reach the building. Here the snow reached up to her knees, forcing her to lift each foot up high to take the next step.

After every few steps, she stopped and took several breaths. Each time she did this, it took more and more time to catch her breath. She pulled the scarf down, seeing the frost vapors pour out as she gasped. The cold air bit her lungs, but she needed more air and a few moments to rest. *Why didn't I leave sooner?* If she had left a couple of hours earlier, she would probably be pulling into her drive right now. Oh well, there was nothing she could do about it.

"No more dilly-dallying. Take some more steps. Keep moving before you freeze." Her voice disappeared in the wind's howling. She pulled the scarf back up and trudged on.

The harder she tried, the less progress she seemed to make. After fifteen minutes of fighting the snow, she felt like she hadn't gotten much closer. When she looked back, her white car had vanished and her footsteps were quickly disappearing. The only way left was toward the light.

She had to be getting closer. *Damn it*. She had to keep going—the wind was finding ways to get the cold in through her not-thick-enough wool coat. Snow had worked up her jeans' legs and her socks were soaked. *The light, I've got to keep heading for the light.*

She struggled on through the snow. The longer she took, the deeper the snow became. She paused.

Where's the light? She looked around and discovered it behind her. How long had she been walking the wrong way? So much for her resolution about not using magic. This was an emergency. She could create a light orb to show her the way. She patted the front of her coat to find out that her wand wasn't there. *That's right, it's in my suitcase. In the car*. She looked back, but there wasn't any way she could get back to her car. This was past the point of no return.

She turned around and pressed on. The bitter cold continued to seep through her coat. *I have to get there soon. It's so cold*. The light disappeared whenever the wind gusted. Now when this happened, she stopped and waited until the light reappeared. She couldn't risk getting turned around again.

Finally, the light started getting stronger. She had to be getting close. Then all of a sudden—darkness.

The light had gone out. *Now what? No. Stop and think this out. Do not panic.* Someone had to have turned out the light. That meant someone was inside—someone who could help. She stared into the swirling snow. There had to be a building there.

Once her eyes adjusted to the darkness, she thought she could see a dark shape up ahead. She took a few more steps closer. Then some more. Another whiteout. She stopped until the wind died down a little. The dark shape had gotten a little closer. *Just keep going.* She couldn't feel her feet or fingers now. *Get there.* She tucked her gloved hands in her armpits trying to keep them a little bit warmer.

The dark shape could always be seen now. *Must get warm. So frickin' cold.* She hit something with her chest. She had to pause and focus. A porch.

A porch.

To her right were some steps. *Four steps.* She grabbed the railing.

One—she used the banister to pull herself up.

Two—just keep going.

Three—almost there.

Four—must get warm. The porch.

She stared into the darkness.

A faint orange glow. *Fire. Warmth. Door?*

She looked around. Three steps to the door. *Three.* A small step. *Warmth.* Her teeth chattered. *Must get warm.* Another step. *One more.* She raised her shaking hand to knock.

7

Chapter 2

Her hand twitched. Warmth enveloped her. It was so cozy nestled under the covers. *Covers*? She needed to wake up. Her thoughts remained muddled; she couldn't focus them. *What happened? I need to move. But why*? Alex moved her hand. At least she could move.

Something licked her fingers. She snatched her hand back under the covers. Her eyes fluttered open, but everything looked fuzzy. Where were her glasses? Looking around, she could only focus on the big bed she was nestled in. How did she end up here? The last thing she could remember was being out in the snow. What happened? She ran a hand down her body to only find her bra and undies. Where were the rest of her clothes? Who removed them? She pulled the covers tighter around her.

A gray light filled the room. She couldn't tell if the light came from daylight or some kind of artificial source. Only the dog's panting disturbed the quiet. Slowly she stretched her limbs; at least they all seemed to work even though they were extremely stiff. A whine came from where her hand had previously been. Alex turned her head. A golden, shaggy dog had laid its muzzle on the side of the bed. The dog whined again, so she reached out to scratch its head. A happy pant replaced the whine. At least he was happy to see her, but would his owner be as pleased with uninvited company?

A large shadow moved into the doorway, blocking the light from the other room. "Mandy," a deep resonant voice whispered, "leave her alone. Maybe she wants to sleep some more."

"No." Alex moved slightly to get a better look at the stranger. "Where am I? What time is it?"

"You're in my cabin, and it's a little after eight. You needed sleep after trudging through the storm last night." He moved farther into the room and handed her glasses to her. "I need to check your hands and feet again for any signs of frostbite. Sometimes you won't see anything until the next day."

Alex extended both hands to him. She had expected to see a lean, sinewy man bent over from hard work and age. Instead, he had a well-developed solid frame, a full beard and mustache. She guessed he was in his twenties like her. His height and wide shoulders created an intimidating presence. The golden retriever kept nudging their hands, trying to get some more attention.

"I don't remember knocking or coming in," Alex said. The second he touched her hand, a surge of electricity shot through her fingers, like shaking hands with another wizard. Her body instantly responded, some basic instinct calling out for satisfaction. This was new, nothing she'd ever sensed before. Could he be a wizard? What were her chances of accidentally stopping at a wizard's house?

"You didn't." He thoroughly examined all of her fingers, not appearing to notice anything.

The skin on his hands was tough, but he handled

9

her fingers as if they were china.

"Your hands look okay. Now stick your feet out so I can check your toes."

She slid her feet out to him. "How did you find me?"

"I didn't. Mandy did." He carefully moved each toe. "I'd just gone to bed when Mandy started whining and scratching at the door. She wouldn't quit, so I got up to look. Imagine my surprise to find a woman collapsed on my front porch. All clear."

She slid her feet back under the blankets. At least he was willing to assist a stranded woman. "So you brought me in?"

He nodded.

"Thanks for helping me," she paused. "Where are my clothes?"

"Everything was soaking wet. I took them off so you could warm up."

He didn't even look embarrassed. Like it was the most natural thing to do. Alex shifted a little farther toward the middle of the bed.

"I examined your hands and feet for frostbite. I didn't know how long you had foolishly been walking. Don't you know that you're always supposed to stay in your car?"

"Of course I do. I only walked from the end of your driveway. I would have driven in closer, but I couldn't tell where the driveway was. I didn't want to take the chance of rolling my car into a ditch—or worse, a partially frozen pond." *Lucky me. I picked some backwoods hick who thinks that women have the common sense of a toad.* "If you would give me my clothes, I'll get out of here."

"You walked all the way in from the road?"

She nodded. "My clothes?"

"Sorry. They still aren't dry, and more importantly, the storm hasn't let up yet."

"Why don't you toss them in the dryer?"

"No electricity."

"You should get your power back once the storm's over."

"No." He hesitated. "It doesn't work like that out here. First, I have to take my snowmobile into town to let them know that my power is out. Then they have to come out and fix the problem. But they can't get out here until the plows have a chance to get through."

"And the plows come out when?"

"If we're lucky, they get out here several weeks after the storm ends. If we get multiple storms, the delay can be even longer. It takes them so long to clear the main roads that they usually rest for a few days before starting on the little ones." He moved back and leaned against the doorjamb. "We've had a lot of snow this season. I'm surprised an avalanche hasn't already closed the pass."

They had been getting a lot of snow this season. The skiers were in seventh heaven. But she didn't ski and had a job to get back to—as well as a life, such as it was. "So about how long am I going to be stranded out here?"

He hesitated again, "Last time we had a storm like this it took a month."

"A month!" She sat up, clutching the blankets to her chest. "I can't stay here for a month. I need to get home." What was she going to do about work?

"There's been a couple of times when it was longer

than a month before we could get through the pass."

"How do you survive that long without power?"

"I have a propane tank and a backup generator that I can only use sparingly."

"Then I can get my clothes dried?"

"I only have a washing machine, no dryer."

No dryer. Did anyone live like that these days? But then…she knew several wizarding families who lived without any electric. She needed to know more about him. "How do you get them dry?"

"I hang them up."

"I assume you hung up my clothes. Are they dry now?"

"Yes and no. The fire dies down overnight so they're still wet, but they should be dry later today."

"You at least have a phone, don't you?"

He looked away.

More bad news.

"Most of the time, yes."

"Don't tell me. The phone is also out."

"Unfortunately, yes."

This was unbelievable. "My boss isn't going to understand. This is like 'my dog ate my homework.' I'm stuck in the snow—for a month or more." Her mind raced through the possible ways of traveling during winter. "I know. What about a snowmobile? Could you drive me into the nearest town?"

"Unfortunately, the road you came in on is the only way in or out. I wouldn't be surprised to find out that an avalanche blocked the valley pass last night. If so, it'll take a while before anyone can get through." He watched her face intently. "Why did you drive out this way? Why didn't you stop at the hotel next to the highway?"

"What hotel?"

"If you had driven under the highway overpass, you'd have been there. Why didn't you follow the detour sign?"

"O-o-o-h-h, great. That's...just...great! The stupid detour sign blows away so now I'm stuck in the middle of nothing. I could have been tucked away in a nice comfortable hotel...with electricity and phones. But no-o-o...I'm stuck in no-man's land. I risked life and limb trudging through the snow for what?" She looked up at the wood paneled ceiling, then took a deep breath and released it. "Now what?"

"You can stay here for now. When the storm lets up, we can decide more." He ran both hands through his long, shaggy, brown hair and shook his head. "I'll fix you a late breakfast. You must be starved."

She watched his hair settle back down to his shoulders. "If you can't get out, what do we do for food?"

"I should have enough to get us through, but we'll have to be careful. Eggs and milk aren't a problem, but if the storms last a month, we'll probably run out of some of the staples."

"Run out of staples. What about—Do you have any diet sodas by any chance?" *Please, please, please, let him say yes. I need my caffeine.* For some people it was their morning cup of coffee, for her it was a soda.

"Only three, so you'll want to ration them out. I have enough tea for several days, otherwise you'll be drinking milk and water."

What else could go wrong? She shifted. "Your water pipes don't freeze up? Do they?"

13

"No. They won't freeze."

"What about hot water?"

"Only limited amounts. No long showers, only short rinses. We need to conserve the propane for cooking and washing clothes. I'm not a fan of doing those chores over a fire. Now get out of bed and get moving before everything stiffens up."

"I don't have any clothes on."

He walked into the bedroom and headed to what had to be a closet. He pulled a thick pair of sweatpants and a hoodie out and tossed them to her. "You can use some of my clothes until yours have dried out."

"After we eat, I could go out and get my suitcase out of the car."

"I'll get your suitcase, but not until this storm lets up some. I hope you're not shy. This is a small cabin. Last night I slept in a chair so you could get a good night's rest. Tonight, I plan to sleep in my own bed. You can either sleep on the other side, or sleep in a chair, or on the floor. The bed is a lot more comfortable and warmer." He pulled out a thick pair of socks and tossed them to her. Before he left the room, he added, "Get dressed so you can come out and eat."

Alex watched him leave, then looked at Mandy and whispered to her. "What am I going to do? He's a complete stranger. All that hair. I sure hope he isn't some type of weirdo. I don't know if I could find some way to get to town if I had to." She glanced at the shelves full of books. "He must like reading. That's a good sign." She reached out to scratch the dog's head. "He must not be too bad or you wouldn't be so friendly."

She pulled the clothes closer. They smelled like

14

cedar and man. She took a deep breath—no cologne, no bad BO, evergreens, and maybe a hint of summer grass. An interesting mix.

But how could she get in touch with her family so they wouldn't worry? After she'd been out of touch for a while, her mom would probably use a crystal suspended over a map to scry for her and see where she was. Then she'd send a pigeon with a message. That was her mom's preferred method of communicating with other wizards. A little outdated, but then so was her mom. The problem would be that pigeons were common in the cities, but out here they'd be noticeable. If so, she'd have to intercept the bird without him seeing. Somehow, she'd find a way to get in touch with them.

Chapter 3

Steve strode out to the kitchen to start breakfast. *Crazy woman. She could have killed herself.* He plunked the skillet on the burner and grabbed some eggs from the basket on the counter. *When the storm lets up, Peter will check the pass. If it's clear, we'll get her to the hotel. If not, I'll send her over to Peter's house. He won't mind taking in an attractive woman.*

I live out here for a reason. I don't want guests— even ones as interesting as her. Besides, she'll be more comfortable at Peter's. He has all the modern conveniences. A woman like her won't be able to cope in a cabin that doesn't even have central heat, let alone electricity.

****

Alex slid over to the side of the bed and dressed. This was the first chance she got to notice the room. There was a window on the opposite wall, but the window was covered with heavy, wooden shutters bolted shut, like you'd see in the eighteenth century to keep out wildlife. On the interior side of the room, was an open closet. She poked her head in. The left walls were covered with shelves, whereas the right side had hang-up rods and more shelves. It actually extended quite a ways back. A trace of cedar filled the air. The rest of the bedroom wall and adjoining wall were covered from floor to ceiling with bookshelves loaded

16

with all types of books. She quickly scanned the spines, nothing magical.

Alex scratched Mandy. "I guess we'd better go see what's for chow."

She stopped in the doorframe and looked around clockwise. Four large sash windows with shutters opened into the room and bracketed a river rock fireplace, flooding the room with diffused light. There wasn't a sofa, but two brown leather chairs with ottomans and a small rectangular table were centered in front of the fireplace. A couple of books as well as a pewter Aladdin lamp filled the table. The lamp had a clear chimney that extended through a pale green glass shade. Almost the same make and model of kerosene lamp her grandmother had. Only her grandmother's had a red glass shade and hung from the ceiling. Aladdin made lamps famous for the amount of light they put out as long as the mantel was in good condition. The room should be well lit up at night.

Most of the opposite wall was covered with bookshelves and books. A clothesline stretched between the shelves and the rough timber mantel. Her missing clothes were hanging up, but still sagged with moisture. Past the bookcase was a door, water heater, refrigerator, stove, and sink. He had his back to her as he moved pans around on the stove. She did a quick scan down his body. He couldn't be carrying a wand, she would see it in his formfitting jeans. He might be normal after all. Why did she get such a strong reaction to him? She continued looking around the room, to a simple table and four chairs, with clean lines, which separated the spaces. Everything was on the older side but looked like it had been well cared for.

This wasn't unlike some of the older wizarding families' homes. Except now they would have a lead-lined room so they could use their electronics. Magic and electricity refused to co-operate; magic loved to fry nearby electronics. She had to keep replacing phones because of accidentally using magic nearby.

The only sounds in the room were the fire, the rattle of pans, and sizzling bacon. The storm must have died down. She edged over to the closest window and swiped some of the frost away. A glass-enclosed porch ran across the back of the cabin. That's why she didn't hear the wind. In general, the cabin appeared to be clean and neat. Maybe he was simply a normal man who liked to live out among the mountains instead of a crowded city.

"Bathroom?" she asked.

He pointed to the right.

She headed for the open doorway to her right, looked at the front door, and stopped.

The door was made out of heavy, wooden planks bound with black iron straps, a lot thicker than the average door. Two large, black, iron brackets were on the door as well as one on each side of the doorframe. A two-by-six plank rested in the brackets stretching from one side of the doorframe to the other as a brace. The deadbolt set in the door was inconsequential compared to the bar plank. It reminded her of the medieval castles in movies where there were doors like this that used the crossbar to keep the marauding hordes out. She glanced at the back door. It was exactly like the front. What could possibly be big enough to require this kind of protection? A large bear or elk? *Yeah, right, a large bear.*

She turned to the open doorway, went in, and reached for a door. "Where's the door?"

"No door. Just pull the sheet across the opening," he answered while he continued to cook.

"Great," she mumbled. "I'm in a strange house, with a strange man, and there isn't even a door on the bathroom. What kind of place is this?" She looked around the small space. At least it had all the usual fixtures, even if they were almost on top of each other. He appeared to have running water. A definite plus. Maybe she could manage being stuck here a while. She'd find some way to make it work. After all, he had taken her in and kept her from freezing to death.

She desperately tried to not make a sound while peeing, but it sounded like a waterfall in the tiny space. She shifted her seat which only made it a little quieter. She washed her hands, then took a quick look at herself in the bathroom mirror. Even with the faint light, one side of her hair looked like rats had invaded, balling up her brown strands into knotted clumps. She snatched a comb off the side of the sink and did a quick untangling. This at least made her look a little more presentable. After all, her hair was one of her better assets. She continued to stare at her reflection. She wasn't too tall, short, thin, fat, ugly, or beautiful—absolutely average. Her whole life had been about being average. Even her magical powers were average. That's why she was trying to live in the normal world with normal people. People with no magic. Her younger brother had the magical talent and her older sister had the looks to land a successful wizard husband. If she had to listen to her parents asking when she'd get married one more time, she'd scream. She placed the comb back on the sink. Being out here with a normal man, for a day or two, would give her the chance to make sure she wouldn't use any magic. The number one rule in the wizarding world was that normals couldn't know about magic.

"Hurry up in there. Your eggs are ready," he called.

"This might be good for me after all," she said to her reflection. She could hear the plates and dishes rattle as she pushed the curtain back across the rod. "How do you get by without doors?"

"Why do I need doors? So Mandy can't watch? No one else is here."

"You're right. You wouldn't need any." She took a seat at the table. "I have to warn you—I'll probably be really crabby when I withdraw from caffeine." She admired the polished tabletop with the plain tan stoneware. It fit the rest of the space.

"Then make sure you keep tapering down on the tea. By the end of the week, you'll be down to only one cup without having too many withdrawal symptoms. Just remember to keep drinking a lot of water."

Most days she didn't eat much breakfast, but this morning she devoured the eggs. Once finished, she was left with thinking about her situation. "How long is this current storm supposed to last?"

"The forecast was for between two to three days. Then another storm front is expected. The first break we get, I'll make a trip to your car."

She toyed with her fork. "I can walk out to my car. You don't have to." After all, she wasn't completely helpless.

"Have you ever used snowshoes before?"

20

"No, but I got from my car to here without any."

"And Mandy found you collapsed on my porch. Without snowshoes, it would take about twenty to thirty minutes each way. With snowshoes, I can probably make the trip in ten minutes. We won't get a long break with these storms, and I don't want either of us caught outside when one builds up again." For the first time, he looked directly into her eyes.

She returned his gaze. "I see your point." His eyes were a light steel gray with flecks of blue. They pulled her in with their intensity. "There has to be something I can do?" She stopped playing with her fork as she watched his eyes.

"Every morning and evening, I have to milk the cow. In the mornings, there are eggs to collect, the cow's stall to clean, feed to be dispensed, and water bowls to change. Then there are dishes, cooking, washing, and cleaning to do. After everything is done then I usually sit down and enjoy a good book."

"What about TV? Oh yeah—no electricity." She again started playing with her fork while thinking. "I don't know how to do the milking, but I should be able to help you with some of the other chores." Again, she looked at him. "But, I'm lousy at cooking."

"That's okay. I enjoy cooking. I'll be glad for your help with as much as you can manage. I have some spare boots that you can use, but they'll be big. The morning chores still need doing. I didn't want to leave you for very long in case you needed help, so I only got the milking done."

"Show me where the boots are and we can get to work." She got up and put their dishes in the sink.

"I'll leave the boots inside the barn door. But I'd

21

recommend putting on one of my flannel shirts instead of the sweatshirt."

"How do you get to the animals in weather like this?" After adding some water to the dishes, she turned and leaned against the sink.

He pointed to the wall with the bookshelves. "Do you see the doorway next to the fridge? That door goes to the pantry where there's another door leading directly into the barn. This makes life a lot easier during the winter. The animals are in a warm barn instead of being outside. I keep the chickens penned up, and during the summer I keep the cow in a tall fenced enclosure. I only have one cow and a limited number of chickens, which I can't afford to lose to a predator. This makes it easy for me to get my milk and eggs."

"By the way, I'm Alex Klein." She moved closer and extended her hand.

He stood and gently enclosed her hand in his. "Glad to meet you, Alex. I'm Steven Davis, but my friends call me Steve."

A charge tingled her fingers. Was he a wizard or not? She'd have to find out, at least figure out why she wanted to touch him so much. "Nice to meet you, Steve, and thanks for helping me out last night."

"The least I could do for a damsel in distress." He smiled and released her hand. He went to the bedroom, laid a shirt on the bed for her, then headed out to the barn.

She took a few minutes to do a quick search of the bedroom and closet, no wand or hidden books. She replaced the hoodie with the flannel shirt, then headed out of the bedroom. At least she was alive and safe. She looked around the cabin again, at the fireplace and the simple furnishings. Alive maybe, but living in the nineteenth century. Why would a normal person choose to live like this? He must have an interesting story.

Mandy had stayed at her side. Her brown eyes followed Alex's movements, while her tail swished.

"What are you waiting for?" Alex asked.

Mandy walked toward the door, stopped, and looked back to Alex.

Was the dog actually waiting to show her the way? "Okay, girl. Lead on."

Mandy walked the rest of the way to the door and stared at the handle.

"I'm coming. Hold your horses," Alex said. "Are you reading my mind?"

Mandy barked.

"At least when I talk to you, I can say what I want. Do you mind?"

Mandy shook her head.

"I swear. It's as if you understand me." No more delaying, she had to face the barn. Would it be as old as the cabin? Maybe about to fall down? *Just open the door*. Alex followed Mandy through the door into the fully enclosed storage area that had shelves running along the wall next to the cabin. The shelves were piled with all kinds of canned goods and box mixes, anything that wouldn't spoil. Not a single herb was hanging up. He had to be normal; what she felt must have been from static electricity. Three cans of soda stood out. She moved closer and ran her fingers down the cool surface. "I'll have to save you for a special occasion." She moved back to the other door across from the one she'd come through.

Mandy pawed at the concrete floor in front of this

door. Alex shut the cabin's door and opened the other one, which opened into a large barn. The scent of fresh hay and warm animals filled the place. She was surprised that the storage area and barn weren't overly cold. He had to be heating the areas to keep them above freezing. Even out here with the animals, the barn was neat and organized. *Nice.* This man obviously took pride in his possessions.

Mandy bounded in and headed to the stall to take care of her business.

No wonder she didn't smell wet dog in the cabin. By coming out to the barn, Mandy didn't have to plow through the snow drifts. Alex had to give Steve credit, he took good care of his animals. She almost tripped over the boots he'd left by the door. She slipped the large rubber boots on and her feet swam in them. By only lifting them a little bit or else shuffling could she keep them on.

Steve was already at work trying to clean out a stall. The cow kept nudging his arm making his job twice as difficult. As he picked up a shovelful, the cow nudged his arm again, making him drop half of the shovel's contents. Alex couldn't help but break out in laughter at the cow's antics.

At the sound of her laughter, the cow turned then started walking toward her. Her laughter immediately stopped and her eyes widened as the cow continued approaching her. *Shit. Now what?* What would this big animal do?

Steve looked up. "Alex, this is Anna Belle. Don't worry, she's extremely friendly. Maybe even too friendly. Scratch her behind her ears and she'll be your friend for life."

Alex relaxed some as the large animal strolled toward her. Anna Belle moved up against her. Alex took a step back. Anna Belle moved up again.

"Stay still and let her lean up against you. If you keep moving, she'll keep following." Steve snorted with laughter, then turned away.

"I'm not used to animals this big."

He turned his head back in her direction. "You could really help by keeping her out there so I can finish cleaning her stall."

She finally got the courage to reach up and scratch the cow. Anna Belle. He had named his cow. But then, so would she. After all, the cow acted like an over-sized dog. Anna Belle leaned so hard against her she almost got pushed over. In the time it took her to get used to the cow, Steve had finished with the stall.

He exited the stall carrying two metal buckets. "Here, take the water bucket. I'll show you where the water is so you can take care of watering her from now on." As they walked toward the cabin, Anna Belle followed them contentedly.

"Won't she make a mess out here walking around?"

"I don't care. I'll simply clean it up if she does. She enjoys the chance to stretch her legs so I let her walk around the barn. When it isn't snowing she can go to the outside pen." He showed her the sink by the barn wall where she could dump, clean, and fill the water bucket. She carried a half-full bucket back to the stall while he carried the full feed bucket. Anna Belle continued following their every move.

Was the bucket filled with rocks instead of water? Her arm could pull out of the socket by the time she got to the stall. He carried buckets around like nothing. No wonder his shoulders were so wide, and his body was so large. If he did this all the time he would have to be in good shape. She sure wasn't. What did she expect? Her day usually entailed sitting at a desk. She didn't carry buckets of water or feed.

After Steve spread some fresh straw around for Anna Belle, he headed over to a door near the corner closest to the cabin. He removed a wooden peg and flipped the latch back. "You're new, so don't be surprised if some of the hens are skittish." He pulled the door open and waited for Alex to go in first.

A long narrow room ran along the side of the barn. There were all colors and varieties of chickens: white, black, brown, and combinations of colors. Birds were sitting in boxes along the barn, perched on bars, or wandering around. Two all-white ones flew off to the farthest perch, but the others continued searching for food on the floor or sitting in their nesting boxes.

Steve showed her how to fill the feeder and waterer. "Why don't you collect the eggs while I clean up the floor?" He handed her a wicker basket then started sweeping the floor and dumping it in a wheelbarrow he'd brought in with him.

Alex headed over to the boxes. First, she picked up the eggs from the empty slots, then she gathered the eggs from all the black birds who appeared to be the friendliest. She then went to the buff colored one. All the while, a brown hen with white speckles strutted around, following her. Several headed down to the feeder, so she emptied those boxes. Now this was a job she could do. She moved on down the line to the noisy red and black hen. It watched her every movement. She reached in under the bird and it pecked her arm. Thankfully she'd already had the egg in her hand when she yanked it back. She rubbed the back of her arm.

The two brown hens, sitting in the neighboring boxes, clucked loudly. They turned their heads to keep a beady eye glued to her hand. The second she headed toward them, they attacked. This time they nailed her good. "Shit," she pulled her arm back and rubbed the sore spot. She tried the black and white striped birds. They also attacked. "What am I doing wrong?"

Steve stopped spreading the fresh hay and walked over. "You can't show any fear. Just reach in. The eggs are ours, not theirs." He removed the eggs from the black and white birds. The brown ones ruffled their feathers and continued to watch her, ignoring Steve. "If they keep defending their nest"—he shooed the birds away—"get them to move." He placed the last eggs in her basket and went back to take care of the wheelbarrow. He made it look easy.

They left the henhouse, put away their tools, and he looked at Alex's arm. "They got you good." He got a paper towel and wiped off the places where they'd hit her hand hard enough to draw blood. "I've never seen anyone as skittish as you. They're only chickens." He showed her where to leave the boots in the barn, and they headed back inside.

The chores might have been finished, but she was exhausted. How did he do it every day? She'd used muscles she never knew existed—well, at least, she didn't have them. At least he only had one cow and around a dozen chickens. Thankfully he kept the hay, straw, and various feeds inside the barn so they didn't have to go out into the storm. She wanted to go back to

27

the cabin, get cleaned up, and relax.

Before she even got a chance to do any of those things, Steve said, "We still have one more job to do."

Chapter 4

Alex wandered into the kitchen. "Now what?"

"The storm has let up a little. I need to get your clothes out of your car before it picks up again. In another day, I'll have to dig a path out, the way this snow is accumulating. If we have several more days like this, it'll be impossible to get to the road. Where are your car keys?"

"In my purse, wherever that is." She turned in a full circle as she searched the room.

He walked over to the bookshelves and tossed her purse to her. "I need you to wait outside on the porch. If I lose sight of the cabin, I'll call out."

"What do you want me to do?"

"If the storm gets bad again, keep shouting so I can follow your voice back. How many bags do you have and where are they in the car?"

"I have one small suitcase in the trunk, one toiletry bag behind the driver, and a small bag of food and drinks on the front passenger seat." She tossed her car keys to him and pulled out her cell phone. No signal. Again.

"I'll get as much as I can."

"Get the suitcase, at least." Her magical talent for reading people's intents made her trust him, but she'd feel safer with her wand nearby.

He walked over to the front door, removed her coat

and hat from a series of hooks by the door, and tossed them to her. She put on her still damp shoes, coat, and gloves. He donned a heavy, denim coat and placed a dark brown, furry hat on, pulling the edges down to cover his ears and neck. He lifted the door brace, set it next to the door, and headed out onto the front porch.

Alex slipped her phone in her coat pocket and followed him out. The cold air bit at her face and neck. A light snow was still falling, but she could see a ways out. Snow covered everything. If she'd been at home, she would have been enjoying the white-covered landscape.

Mandy pushed out between them. She went to one end of the porch, stuck her nose up sniffing the air, shuffled to the other end, and sniffed again.

Alex pulled her phone out and held it up, trying to catch a trace of a signal.

"Any signal?"

"Nothing." She put the phone back in her coat pocket. "But I thought I'd try just in case."

Steve pulled a pair of snowshoes out of a storage box that was tucked up against the cabin's wall. He walked off the porch, sat on the steps to lace up the bindings on the snowshoes, and pulled on his thick gloves. "I'll be back as soon as possible."

Mandy wandered back to the middle of the porch and leaned up against Alex.

Alex watched Steve trudge off through the snow. He gradually became fainter and fainter the farther out he got, until he melted into the landscape. *Please let him be safe.* How would she find him if something happened? The snow was significantly deeper than last night. She would never have been able to cross it

30

without snowshoes today.

All of a sudden, the sky opened up and dumped. The snow muffled all sound and absolute silence reigned. Even with Mandy leaning against her, giving her a little warmth, the frigid air cut right through her wool coat. The wind started blowing, showering her with snow even under the porch roof. After what seemed like forever, Mandy pricked up her ears. Alex listened carefully but couldn't hear anything. Before she could make a move to stop her, Mandy bounded off the porch, jumping through the deep snow. A couple of minutes later, Mandy jumped back up on the porch and shook, flinging snow everywhere.

Alex called out to Steve every fifteen seconds or so. Several minutes passed without any sign or sound from him. "I hope he gets back soon," Alex said to Mandy.

Mandy gazed up at her, then turned back to continue her vigil, ears pointed straight forward.

What will I do if he never returns? Could I venture out to help or would I get lost? What else can I do? She continued calling out his name.

Mandy leapt off the porch and disappeared in the falling snow. Now they were both out in the snow. Within a couple of minutes, Mandy came back. Good. Mandy must have headed straight to Steve and come back. He had to be close for her to return so quickly. Sure enough, a solid white blob appeared in the snow. A couple of minutes later, he hefted her luggage on the porch, removed the snowshoes, and knocked the snow off them before he stored them back in the box. Alex dragged the luggage inside while he tried to shake some of the heavy snow off before coming in. No matter how hard he tried, snow clung to his coat like Velcro.

"I guess that's all I'll get off."

"Did you have any problems finding everything?" She hung up her coat and hat and cleaned the fog off her glasses.

"No, but the end of the driveway was a pain in the ass. I slid on it coming and going."

"I did that last night too."

"I could hear you faintly, but I got disorientated on my way back." He slipped out of his coat and hat. "When I saw Mandy, I followed her trail back. But then her trail started to disappear. So I yelled to her. I sure was glad she came out again to give me some fresh tracks. At least I got everything in one trip. Any more snow and I'm not sure if I could have made it up the slope to the car." He took their coats and hung them up on the line to dry. "I want to get all this sweat rinsed off. Maybe you'd better warm up a little first before getting your shower. I'll only need a few minutes and the bathroom will be all yours."

She went over to the fire and stretched out her hands toward the warmth. The fireplace had a good pull; there was only a trace of pine scent in the cabin. By the time he was done showering, her hands had become nice and toasty. She couldn't help but look over when he came out. If she'd seen him in a bar, she wouldn't have looked twice. But something about him drew her attention. *Boy I must be losing it to find a man attractive in a flannel shirt and sweat pants.* She continued to look and had to admit, *he is attractive in an off-beat sort of way. I wonder what he would look like in a nice suit.* Watching him warmed her whole body. How had he avoided being claimed by some woman?

"Is something wrong?" He moved to the kitchen.

"No, I'll go get some clothes." He headed to the kitchen sink while she took her suitcase to the bedroom. He had no clue how he could affect a woman. She selected a shirt and underwear. *No clue at all.* She'd have to try and give him some space. He probably wasn't used to sharing his cabin. She couldn't afford to tick him off, if she had to spend a month here. But then…it could be a good month being stuck here with a nice man like him. She shook her head. No, she needed to give him his space.

He called to her while she was still pulling out some clean clothes. "You'll probably want to use a clean pair of sweatpants and a clean hoodie for around the cabin. Set the others aside for doing chores in. I'll fix us some lunch while you get your shower. You need to wash down first and then turn the shower on only long enough to rinse off. There's only a limited amount of propane for heating water. We don't want to run out before the roads are clear enough for a truck to get out to refill the tank."

She took the clothes he'd laid out and some of her underwear into the bathroom. By the time she finished cleaning up and strolled out of the bathroom, he had the breakfast dishes done and had placed two bowls of soup with crackers on the table.

"Feel better?" Steve asked.

"Definitely. But I could have enjoyed another fifteen minutes under the hot water."

Steve's nose twitched and he sneezed. His eyes started watering. He moved toward the door to the barn.

Alex stopped, "What's wrong?"

"I forgot something in the barn. I'll be back in a little while." He continued to the door, sneezing as he went.

Alex looked around then headed toward him.

"Just stay inside," he said.

"Why? What's wrong?"

"I can't handle perfume or strong fragrances."

"What fragrances?" Then it came to her, "Oh, my creams and deodorant. I never even thought about them."

"That's okay. I'll go out in the barn until the air clears."

"Are you sure?"

He dashed over to the table and picked up his food. "Don't worry about me."

Alex watched him leave then headed back to the bathroom and inspected her toiletries. Apple shampoo, rose hand cream, mystery scented face cream and soap. Then there was the deodorant, toothpaste, and a couple of other scented items. She was used to them, but he obviously wasn't. She picked up his soap and sniffed, almost no fragrance. Then she opened his medicine cabinet and looked at the contents. Everything was unscented except for his lime shaving cream. By the length of his beard, he hadn't used this for a while. No wonder all her stuff bothered him. She'd have to use as few as possible. He shouldn't have to leave. It was his home, and she was only a guest. She closed the cabinet and went back to the living room. There wasn't anywhere she could go in this small cabin to stay away from him. She'd have to wait for the fragrances to dissipate.

Mandy wandered over to her and sniffed her all

over.

"I know girl. You're not used to all these smells either." She stroked the dog's head. "His nose must really be sensitive. I'd just walked into the room and he ran. I'll do better from now on." She set her fingernail polish remover and a couple of tissues on the table. After he came back in, she'd have to go out to the barn to remove her polish. That way the odors would be someplace else.

****

Steve sneezed all the way to the barn. *Damn woman. Wasn't it enough to let her use my bed last night? Now she's chasing me out of the cabin with all those strong, conflicting fragrances.*

Anna Belle strode over to him and leaned against his shoulder.

"I know. It's not her fault. She doesn't know how sensitive my nose is." He shoveled his soup in before it got cold.

As much as he'd like to take her to a neighbor's house, he couldn't. Touching her fingers stirred something deep inside. For some weird reason he wanted to protect her and keep her close. Maybe the storms would continue and he'd get a chance to know her better and figure out why he was so damned attracted to her.

****

Alex sat down and played with her vegetable soup. As soon as she swallowed her first spoonful, she couldn't stop until the bowl was empty. She had just finished drying the last dish when Steve came back in. "Sorry about that," she said. "I'll avoid using as many fragrances as I can tomorrow." She picked up the polish remover and headed toward the barn. "I'll be back in a few minutes. I have to get the chipped polish off." She held up a hand and waggled her fingers. "And even I hate the way it stinks."

Once finished, she came back in, tossed the tissues in the fire, and washed her hands.

"We can read for several hours before we have to do the late afternoon chores." He kept his face turned to his book, but his eyes would flick over to her every so often.

His frame fit one of the leather chairs perfectly. "What chores do you have in the afternoon?"

"I milk Anna Belle, and you can make sure the water buckets are full. We also need to clean up any messes in the barn. It won't take nearly as long as the morning chores. After we're done, I'll fix us some dinner."

"If you show me what needs to be cleaned up, I'll do that so you can start dinner sooner."

"Deal. I hope you like to read."

"Love to, but I can never seem to find enough time."

"Look around and find something. The mysteries are in the bedroom, action stories out here on the left, and the right side contains everything else."

Alex walked over to the mantel. There were several large crystals placed here and there on the wood timber. She looked over to the shelves. Bookshelves ran the length of the wall from floor to ceiling, covering all the available wall space. The shelves had been packed full and books were squeezed in above the vertical novels filling up the available spaces. She scanned the shelves carefully, half-expecting to see a cat balancing along the front edge or wedged between some books. Every good library needed a cat.

No cat.

She scanned the titles looking for something interesting. Almost everything here was fiction except a few reference books near the door. Then she spotted a book about chickens. Maybe this would give her some insight that might help. She curled up in the chair. The soft, supple leather cradled her body. It felt good to sit down, relax, and read, although she'd probably fall asleep in minutes. Now all she needed was a bowl of popcorn and a tall, cold soda. She wouldn't get popcorn or soda until she got home. Oh well, she sighed.

She relaxed and started browsing. There were sections on raising chicks, designing a coop, daily care, and several others that weren't useful to her. She finally got to the section about the different breeds. As she paged through, she identified some of the breeds he had. According to the descriptions they were all supposed to be friendly, except for the brown Rhode Island Reds, which could be aggressive. *No shit.* No wonder they'd gone after her.

She identified the speckled hen that followed her as a Speckled Sussex, and the black and white striped ones as Barred Plymouth Rocks. They were supposed to be docile, so why did they go after her? Could they have been mimicking the Reds? Some sort of gang mentality?

Tomorrow she'd see if by collecting the eggs from all the other birds before the Reds would help. The book also talked about grabbing the bird by the tail and lifting it so you could remove the egg if the bird was brooding. She'd give that a try, if she could bring

37

herself to grab a chicken's butt. On cleaning, the book talked about sweeping the whole floor. But Steve had only cleaned under the perches and one corner, the rest of the floor had been free of poop. That was strange. Why would his birds do that? It wasn't like litter-box training a cat. Could you train a bunch of hens to do that?

Enough about chickens. She re-shelved the chicken book and pulled out a Sherlock Holmes novel she hadn't read. She turned the book around and was surprised to find it dust free. After checking out several different locations, she still didn't find any dust. He obviously cared about his collection of books to spend time dusting all the shelves. But then, his whole cabin was clean.

Not like her apartment. She hadn't seen the top of her dining room table in years. Mail migrated to the horizontal surface regardless of how hard she tried to throw it away. The end table near her favorite chair was almost as bad. She at least managed to keep the rest of the apartment clutter-free. How could she keep everything else so meticulously organized, but let her mail get so out of hand? She ought to make an effort to do better in the future—when she finally got back home.

She settled back down in the comfy chair. The fire crackled and popped. Her head drooped and she fell asleep before even getting to page three.

****

Steve tried to concentrate on his book, but he kept looking over at Alex. His thoughts wandered all over the place as he watched her sleep. Her fingers twitched and the book started sliding. He jumped up and grabbed the book before it could hit the floor. After sticking a bookmark in, he placed it on the table. Her fingers, eyes, and mouth continued to twitch as she slept. Her lips shimmered in the firelight. *Kissable lips.*

How was he going to co-exist with a woman? He lived out here so he could be alone. He visited his neighbors whenever he wanted to, but not every day, all day long. At least a woman should be easier to get along with than a man might be. He'd never lived with a woman before.

She snorted and curled up in the chair.

Would she get on his nerves? If so, could he convince his neighbors to let her stay with them part of the time? The chores would be easier with another pair of hands. She'd eventually build up enough muscle so she could handle the buckets more easily.

He had to admit she was attractive, even in his clothes. Her hair shimmered in the flickering light. Maybe he'd enjoy this after all. No—he needed to keep his distance and keep her safe. Maybe treat her like a sister. He could take care of a sister until the roads reopened. *Concentrate on the book, not her.*

After reading for a couple of hours, he decided to rearrange his closet so she could have some space. As soon as he entered the bedroom, he caught the faint fragrance of roses and apples. Her scent. Now his clothes would be picking up this fragrance. For some reason he didn't mind. He cleared off several shelves and emptied some space on the rod next to the door. A few pieces of clothing sat next to her open suitcase on the bed. He picked up the items and a soft, delicate fabric slid through his fingers to fall on the floor. A pair of pink underwear. He imagined how it would feel to have something this soft against his skin, or to run his hands over her with these on. *No. Keep thinking of her as a sister, not an attractive woman.* He snatched up the garment and tossed everything in the hamper.

He went back out, sat down again, and picked up his book. His thoughts kept straying back to her scent. Only with great effort was he able to concentrate on his book. After another hour or so it was time to do the evening chores. He got up and brushed some of her wayward hair off her face. His fingers barely grazed Alex's soft skin; she stayed asleep. He clasped her shoulder and shook her awake then headed back out to the barn.

Anna Belle followed him to her pen. As he milked, his mind strayed back to Alex. *This is going to be more difficult than I originally thought.*

Over dinner they talked about bits and pieces of their past, about the pets they'd had, including his childhood turtle and her white rabbit. An hour had passed before they cleaned up the dishes. He was surprised about how easy she was to talk to. After finishing, they sat in front of the fire and watched the flames dancing across the logs.

He broke the silence. "I cleared some space for you in the closet and tossed the clothes that were on the bed in the hamper. I figured you wouldn't want the creases to set in, even if you're only here for a couple of days. You should get everything unpacked tomorrow morning and add the rest of your dirty clothes to the hamper. I can loan you some t-shirts to wear under your sweaters, but I don't know if what you have will be warm enough. Sweat pants and my flannel shirts might help keep you warm."

"Sorry I slept through the afternoon. I should have emptied my suitcase instead of sleeping. Thanks for giving me some closet space."

"No problem." *Except for the pantie thing.* "I'm sure you were worn out."

"Yeah, I'm not used to doing physical labor." Mandy moved to Alex's side and leaned against her legs. Alex absentmindedly stroked the furry head.

"I usually turn in early since I get up so early."

"I know. When your light went out as I approached your cabin, I nearly freaked."

"Sorry, but I didn't know I was expecting company." He broke his gaze from the fire to her, to enjoy the way the firelight lit her face. "Where do you plan to sleep tonight?"

She squirmed in her chair as she debated her answer. "I'll curl up on the floor and stay close to the fire."

"It'll get really hard."

"That's okay, I don't want to impose on you any more than I have to. I'm not used to sharing a bed with anyone else."

He got up and retrieved several blankets and a pillow for her. "If you need anything else, just let me know." He made a quick stop in the bathroom then went to bed. Even he was tired tonight. The trip to the car and lugging her suitcase back through all the deep snow had exhausted him. He thought of Alex's face as he drifted asleep.

****

Alex was still restless. She never went to bed this early and her afternoon nap had helped. Nothing to do but read some. At least the book was an interesting

41

story. But still, she'd never imagined she'd be reading by candlelight. The twenty-first century and he still used candles. Okay, maybe it wasn't candles, per say, but a kerosene lantern. Thank goodness the fireplace still flooded the room with heat. She couldn't believe someone fairly young would choose to live like this. Maybe an old hermit, but not someone in their early twenties or thirties.

She couldn't function without the Internet or her cell phone. How could she live for several weeks without visiting on Facebook? And to think she lugged her computer through all that snow for nothing. Could their lives be any more different? Oh yeah. He had livestock to take care of. She hadn't seen a cow since her school years. Even then, she'd never spent much time with one up close—or chickens. The wizarding school she'd attended had classes in animal husbandry, but they'd only spent a little time with regular livestock. Most of their coursework had been on magical animals. Could she live like a pioneer?

She got up to get some more water, and Mandy wandered out of the bedroom to join her. Only after listening to Mandy's slow breathing for a couple of hours, did Alex's eyes droop. She placed her glasses on the side table, nestled down in the blankets, and Mandy stretched out next to her, warming her up all over. She eventually drifted off to sleep by listening to the fire's crackles and pops.

She felt like she had just fallen asleep when Steve was shaking her to wake up. She cracked one eye open. "Whass up?" she mumbled. "It's still dark."

"Time for morning chores. Anna Belle won't wait. She's used to being milked at six." He bustled around the kitchen making breakfast. "Come on and get up. The sooner we get started the sooner we finish."

She dragged herself up off the floor and went to the bedroom to put the work clothes on as best as she could. Her hips ached from sleeping on the hard floor. After a quick meal they were out in the barn getting the chores done. Today the buckets of water seemed even heavier than yesterday. Anna Belle kept following her around while she finished up. When she walked in the henhouse, the birds went about their business. She swept the floor and gave them food and water. Then she started collecting eggs.

The brown hen cocked its head then turned its head so that one beady eye was locked on her. The eye followed her every move. As if a silent message had been sent, the rest of the birds in the boxes mimicked the brown hen. Now she had six beady eyes tracking her. The birds that had been wandering around stopped when the speckled hen sounded. The speckled hen flew up into one of the nesting boxes and the others followed suit.

Silence filled the coop. Now all the birds were watching her. Had she entered some kind of horror movie? Would the birds all swarm her and peck at her arms and head? So the chickens were going to be holy terrors. The first birds kept their eyes fastened to her as she retrieved the eggs. A black and white hen hit the back of her hand at the last second. The red bird didn't wait but went for her hand the second it was close enough. The speckled hen fought her the whole time. *The biddy actually drew blood.* That bird had to have some vampire blood in her somewhere. Even so, she only got impaled three times. Alex eased her way back to the door. The hens stared. She slipped out the door and latched it shut.

The only redeeming fact was they were done a lot quicker today. Alex headed back to the bedroom to unpack. She laid her clothes out in piles, tossing anything dirty into the hamper. She started to toss her underwear, bras, and socks on a shelf, but stopped. At home she'd toss everything in a drawer and root around until she found what she wanted. But he had all his clothes carefully arranged by color. He was either obsessive compulsive or had too much time on his hands. Living out here it was probably the latter. She carefully organized everything on the two shelves.

As she hung up her shirts, she glanced around the top shelf. A polished turtle shell lay along the right-hand side. She pulled it down and traced the patterns on the shell. It had to have been the pet he'd talked about. She used the bottom of her t-shirt to polish it and eased it back on the shelf. Yesterday, as she was looking for a book, she didn't see any knives or guns sitting around. There had to be some kind of weapon around for protection, but there wasn't anything she could see in the living area.

Why would he have such a heavy door but no weapons? She did a basic search of the closet. Only clothes, no weapons. He had to have something. You wouldn't live out here without some sort of protection. She listened. Steve was still in the shower. Time to check the rest of the bedroom. The shelves only held books. She dropped to her knees and lifted the bottom of the blankets.

A rifle. With a large diameter barrel. She pulled out a small box and found tranquilizer darts. Guess he didn't want to kill any wildlife that got too close. She knew he had to have something, but as dusty as it was, it meant he rarely used it. The shower shut off. He'd be done in a few minutes. She pushed the box back, got up, and brushed off her pants.

The only thing left in her suitcase was the black satin, padded bag with her wand. To her it almost glowed with a light of its own. She had to wonder if it looked this way to someone else. She picked it up and slowly loosened the black cord drawstrings. She took a deep breath and slid her wand out. The dim light flickered across the cherry wood. A warmth and tingle passed through her fingers as the magic reached out to connect.

It was so tempting to use her magic to get the chores done. But that would be taking the easy way. No. She was going to remain strong and not use any magic as she'd promised herself. This would be the perfect time to go without using magic. No accidental slip-ups. She'd bury the wand in her suitcase so she wouldn't pick it up without thinking. At home she kept catching herself using her wand for simple things.

"Shower's free," Steve called out from the living room. "Is everything okay?"

She could hear his tread approaching. "Everything's fine. I'm finishing unpacking," she answered, trying to give herself a few more moments. She slipped the wand back in the satin bag and pulled the top shut. Then she slipped it back in the suitcase's inside pocket as Steve's shadow fell across the doorway.

"Did I give you enough room?"

Alex zipped the suitcase shut. "Plenty. Thanks."

She carried the suitcase into the closet and buried it under her shirts. After re-emerging, she picked up her clothes and headed to the bathroom for a shower. She would have given anything to have been able to let the soothing water massage her sore muscles. But after a quick rinse, she dressed, went back to the living room, curled up in the chair, and immediately fell back to sleep.

She didn't wake up until she felt someone gently stroking her hair off her face. Her head leaned into his touch, wanting more.

"Alex. It's time for some lunch," he whispered.

She gently touched his fingers as they brushed more hair back. "Okay, I'm getting up," she mumbled. She took his hand to help her stand, shuffled over to the table, and plopped into a chair.

Steve pushed a warm cup of tea into her hand. "Drink this, it should help." He closed her fingers around the cup.

After finishing one full cup, she was able to eat lunch. It took eating lunch and drinking two cups of tea before she finally woke up.

After all the lunch dishes were put away, she asked, "Mind if I familiarize myself with your kitchen?"

"Have at it," Steve said.

She went from cabinet to cabinet. A partial package of tea was tucked behind some spices. She placed it on the table, along with any other tea packets she came across.

"If you need any help, holler." Steve carried his glass of water over to his chair and sat down to read.

Mandy plopped down in front of the fire.

Alex finished inspecting the kitchen and took the tea out to the storeroom. She searched the shelves. There were cans of vegetables and fruit, but no chips or other junk food. She'd be eating healthier than she usually did. Another partial tea box had fallen behind some of the cans. She placed all the tea and a partial container of hot chocolate next to the soda.

On the bottom, she found a bag of sweet potatoes and noticed a slight reflection. She pulled the potatoes out and looked back under the shelf. A heavy-duty chain attached four steel shackles together. The gear reminded her of stories she'd heard about using something like this to hobble an animal so it couldn't run away. It would be a big animal with cuffs that large. Placed here, in such an out-of-the-way spot, must mean he rarely used them. But then with a tranquilizer gun, why would he even need the chains? She shivered. He took care of and loved his animals too much to be dangerous. She shoved the potatoes under the shelf and headed back to the house to read.

Tonight after dinner, she quickly curled up in the blankets and fell asleep.

The third day of chores was hard. None of her muscles agreed to do anything she wanted them to and they hurt. She filled the bucket half full and had to use both arms to lift it out of the sink. She'd take two steps, then set it down to shake out her arms, and take two more steps. Alex finally reached Anna Belle's pen and dumped the bucket into the cow's drinking pail. She spotted Steve leaning against his shovel, watching her.

"You do know that whenever you set the bucket down water slops out?"

Alex smiled as she headed back for another bucket

47

of water. "Guess I'd better not carry the milk bucket then." She watched him shake his head and get back to work.

She finally finished her tasks except for collecting the eggs from those demon chickens. The speckled hen had it out for her, but she was prepared today. That hen wouldn't be able to draw blood through an oven mitt. Alex made sure the mitt was pushed all the way on her hand to cover her wrist and lower arm. Before opening the door to the henhouse, she turned to the middle of the barn. She saluted with the mitt covered hand and entered the henhouse.

****

Steve looked at the place where she last stood. *She was losing it. The chores and lack of sleep had gotten to her. And why was she wearing the oven mitt? Somehow he'd have to make sure she got more sleep tonight.* He watched until she emerged from the henhouse. She was grinning from ear to ear. He could have sworn she said, "That biddy didn't get me today." She strode back into the cabin carrying the basket of eggs.

He finished brushing Anna Belle, "We're going to have to keep a close eye on Alex. She isn't used to doing farm work. I think she's going to need our help." He gave Anna Belle a last pat before heading back into the cabin. And for once in his life, he couldn't wait to see what tomorrow would bring.

Chapter 5

Alex struggled to wake up. Was it even morning? A piece of log broke in the fireplace, shooting out a few sparks. The room had a definite chill to it, so it must be morning. She put her glasses on and squinted at the mantel clock trying to see what time it was, six o'clock.

It was morning, but the room was still dark. Alex wrapped the quilt around her body and shuffled over to the window. After clearing off the layer of frost, she saw heavy clouds and blowing snow. *More snow.* She shuffled out to the barn and waited until the door clicked shut. No one could hear her out here.

"ARGHHHHHH!" she yelled. "Won't this snow ever stop? It's been four days. Enough already! How much longer can this continue?"

Anna Belle watched Alex then resumed chewing her cud.

"Sorry, Anna Belle." Alex moved over to Anna Belle's stall and reached out a hand to stroke her head. "I didn't mean to disturb your peace and quiet."

Anna Belle nudged her hand for more attention.

Alex leaned against the wooden planks. "Why did I come out here and talk to you? You can't understand me." She scratched Anna Belle's ears some more. "At least you always listen." The barn door opened and Mandy bounded into the barn.

"What are you doing out here? It's freezing," Steve

said.

"I was talking to Anna Belle." She rubbed the cow's nose.

"Come on back in. I'll fix you a hot chocolate."

Alex shuffled toward the cabin. She was a sucker for chocolate, any way, shape, or form.

Steve checked on Anna Belle. "Was she really out here in the cold talking to you?" He gave her back a pat. "Now she has me doing it." He turned and rushed to open the door for Alex. "Talking to a cow," he muttered and shook his head.

She giggled as she pulled the quilt closer.

Alex got dressed while Steve fixed breakfast. She savored her cup of hot chocolate before heading out to the barn. When Steve had finished milking and cleaning, he headed back into the cabin. Alex had already cleaned the henhouse and fed the birds; she only needed to gather the eggs. She tried to open the door to the henhouse. She pulled and pulled on the door. *Maybe I don't have the strength to open it.* She pulled harder, but it still didn't budge. But she'd opened the door only minutes earlier. She grabbed the knob with both hands, braced her feet, and yanked hard. The door flew open, sending her sprawling on the floor. The door swung partially closed without shutting. Alex got up and started toward the door when a loud squawk erupted. She dashed behind a bale of hay just as the speckled hen hopped through the door.

Anna Belle shifted. Alex glanced back as Anna Belle quietly moved deeper into her stall.

Mandy whimpered and started to crawl toward Alex.

So even Anna Belle and Mandy are afraid of the

hen. Alex peered around the hay bale to check on the bird's progress.

The hen was high on its feet, with its neck feathers ruffled out. It let out a loud cluck.

Mandy changed course to Anna Belle's stall, then peeked around the edge of the stall once she was tucked inside.

Life was too short for this. Alex started to rise to shoo the hen back but stopped. She watched the hen's head jerking this way and that—looking for a subject to torture. Alex didn't doubt for a minute that if the hen saw her move it would give chase. The hen strutted farther into the barn, rustling its wings and squawking as it moved.

What kind of bird would do this? Was it possessed by a demon or just plain mean? Alex tried to remember back to the hens at school. They'd never acted like this. Those birds had been gentle and liked attention. One hen even liked to be hugged. Not this bird. Steve never had any problems with any of the birds. He was always at ease and comfortable around all the animals. How did he do it?

Mandy whimpered faintly.

Alex would have to do something to get the hen back into the coop.

The hen spied something against the wall and made a beeline for it.

Alex dashed over to the door and cracked it a little wider, then rushed back behind the hay bales.

The hen snatched at some spiders, devouring them. One spider made a dash toward the henhouse and the hen pounced. She looked like a bird of prey the way she attacked.

Alex almost felt sorry for the spider. And to think she could have been home enjoying a coffee or tall soda, watching TV in her warm room. But no, she was stuck here. Up at the crack of dawn trying to deal with a demon hen. She'd even miss her birthday, not that she got many gifts, but still. Daylight shone through a window. *A break in the storm.*

After spending a few more minutes searching for bugs, the hen hopped back through the door. Alex dashed over and slammed the door shut. She made sure the latch was engaged, keeping the hen inside. She brushed off her hands and wiped her brow. The light dimmed. So much for the sunshine. She looked at the henhouse door. *No way in hell am I going in there! Not with that demon hen.*

She tried to brush the hay off her clothes. "I can't even do the simplest of jobs. Just collect the eggs. Yeah, right, easy for him."

Once the door shut, Anna Belle strode out of her pen. She leaned against Alex, knocking her over again.

Alex sat on the floor. "I give up." The cow put her nose down to Alex. She rubbed the cow's muzzle. "It's not your fault. I'm not any good at doing farm chores. I live in a big city." She rubbed the cow's ears. "You're the first cow I've seen in ages."

Alex levered herself up and brushed her pants off again. She patted the cow's back. "And now I'm talking to the cow again. I'm pathetic." She gave Anna Belle one last pat and headed into the cabin.

"Where's the eggs?" Steve asked when she entered.

"I'll get them later. I wanted to get cleaned up." Alex motioned to the hay sticking out of her pants, shirt, hair—everywhere. She could tell that he was working hard to cover up his laughter.

"Guess…you'd better…at that," he finally managed to get out.

As she headed to the bathroom, she could barely hear him say to Mandy, "I wonder what happened now?"

By the time the afternoon chores came around Alex tried to act confident. Whenever one of the hens even looked like it wanted to attack, Alex would shove the bird out of the box. At least she was able to collect all the eggs. But the demon hen bit her leg when she went to leave. That bird refused to go down without a fight.

****

As on previous mornings, when Mandy curled up next to her, Alex cracked an eye open. "It's still dark," she whispered to the dog.

Mandy maneuvered her head even closer and licked Alex's cheek.

"I'm not going to get up before sunrise."

"Sunrise has already occurred," Steve said as he strode out into the kitchen and began pulling pans and dishes out.

Alex struggled up, grabbed her glasses, and wrapped the blanket around her. She waddled over to the front window and scraped some of the frost off. The dreadful changelessness. "Is it ever going to stop? I have to get home sometime," she mumbled. She could imagine the mound of snow that enclosed her car. It would take days to dig the car out and then there were the roads. They wouldn't be passable for weeks.

If she had counted right, today was the fifth day, and it didn't seem like anything had changed. *If it would only stop long enough so I could walk out on the porch and breathe in some cold, crisp mountain air. But no. I'm stuck inside again.* Steve might be right, she could be stranded here for a month or more. There had to be some way to get a message to her parents. Her mom's pigeons couldn't get through all this snow. Her family had to be worried sick.

She could make a piece of paper fly, but only as long as she could see it. Nothing that could make it all the way to Denver, especially not her. Her specialty was picking up on people's feelings, nothing strong enough to help in this situation. Magic couldn't solve all problems, and she couldn't do any magic in front of Steve. Magic had to stay secret, the number one rule. Break this rule and she could lose her powers forever. She might be trying to live as a normal, but she wanted the option to change her mind.

Bacon was sizzling in the skillet. Bacon always made everything better. She turned away from the window and slowly moved to the kitchen table, keeping the blanket tightly wrapped. Her hips hardly moved from sleeping on the floor, but sleeping in the chairs had been worse. Her neck had kinked up and stiffened to the point of being painful. The floor was really hard. Now, every muscle hurt, even some she never knew existed. "When will I be able to get a message out?"

He placed the meal on the table and sat down. "Once the snow stops we'll start digging a path out from the cabin. Then when we get a clear day, my neighbor, Peter, will check on the pass. If it's open, we'll be able to get you to the highway by snowmobile. If there's been an avalanche, Peter can get a message out for you." He laid a hand over hers. "At least you're safe, warm, and getting food."

She pushed her eggs around the plate with her fork. "I know. I could have been stuck out on some road by myself. It's not that I don't appreciate your company, I would just like to get outside for a change."

"It shouldn't be too much longer before we get a break."

"I keep hoping," she mumbled. She finished breakfast so she could get the chores over with. After slipping her work clothes on, she stopped in the bathroom. As she started to walk out, she glanced in the mirror. Her hair stuck out in weird angles and her shirt was buttoned wrong. "No wonder he kept looking at me this morning." She tugged on some strands sticking up. "What a mess."

Steve was already in the barn by the time it took her to get straightened up. Mandy paced back and forth by the barn door, but Alex hesitated. She looked at Mandy. "It wasn't bad enough yesterday. What am I going to do today to make a fool of myself?"

Mandy thumped her tail and barked.

"I know. You like having someone else to throw your balls."

Mandy barked again.

"All right. Let's get this over with. But if I see that speckled, demon hen coming toward me, I'm outta there."

Alex eased the solid, wood door to the barn open and peered through the six-inch gap. "It's okay, Mandy. No hens in sight."

She opened the door the rest of the way and strolled in. Steve was busy cleaning Anna Belle's stall. He hadn't seen her peeking through the door. Now all she had to do was get the eggs. She wasn't going to let a stupid hen get the better of her. By again donning an oven mitt, she was able to shoo the hens away and retrieve the eggs without bloodshed. But the demon hen sure did try her best to get her hand. It would wander around until Alex turned her back. Then the bird would fly at her, startling her. One time, Alex almost dropped the basket of eggs.

Today the water buckets were almost impossible to carry. She wouldn't let them win. Everything hurt, even her hands. If only she could take a couple of days off to rest. Anything to quit the hurting. She'd never done this much physical work, at least not without using magic to help. How could so few animals make such a mess? And it never ended. *How could Steve do this day after day, year after year?* After only a week, she wanted to quit. And he was lifting all the heavy bales of hay; she only had some easy chores to do.

She might be dealing with TV withdrawal, caffeine withdrawal, and muscles aching, but she wasn't going to complain. He'd taken her in, was feeding her, and providing her with a warm place to stay. If she'd still been out in the winter storm, she'd be dead.

"Get moving," she told herself. She rubbed her legs and arms trying to get her limbs loosened up. Even after moving around for a few minutes everything still hurt. When would her muscles get used to the work? It didn't matter. She had to help him as much as she could. It was the least she could do. She owed him big time.

Anna Belle must have been feeling some cabin fever today too. She pushed against Alex again and again. Anna Belle gave a hard shove.

Alex flailed her arms trying to keep her balance but

ending up falling right into a large cow pie. She tried to get up and her feet slipped out from under her. The more Alex tried to get up, the more she kept slipping. The crap was going everywhere.

Steve started laughing so hard tears started rolling down.

Alex shouted, "Well, don't just stand there. Help me up."

He got his laughter under control, walked over, and held out a hand to help her up. "I've never seen anything so funny."

"That's just great. I've become your entertainment now."

"Even you have to admit, it was funny."

She took his hand and he pulled her up. If only she had some of his strength. He made everything look easy. "I guess you're right...it had to look funny."

He pulled her in close to his chest, smearing cow crap on his clothes. He smiled. "Why don't you go on in and take a shower. I'll finish up for you today."

She should be angry, but she was too busy watching his eyes twinkle. And his smile was priceless. Maybe her disgrace was worth it. After all, she had made his day. At least this had broken up the monotony. "Thanks."

He held her arm as she stepped away, then released her. Just before she reached the door, he yelled over. "Leave your dirty clothes in the hallway. I promise I won't look while you undress. Much."

She could have sworn she heard him laughing again.

****

By the end of the week, she was still completely

exhausted, and every bone and muscle continued to ache. She kept looking out the window hoping for a change in the weather. *A week of snow.* The windows were coated with intricate lace patterns of frost. She traced the outline of a crystal, then swept her hand over the glass until she'd cleared a spot in the middle. The white landscape looked flat, everything blanketed with snow. The pine boughs hung down under the snow's weight. Only bits of green needles were still visible. Each day the continuing snow had covered up more and more of the green branches. Gray light cloaked everything. She looked at the clock again. It was only two in the afternoon and it already looked like twilight.

Alex finished making her cup of tea and clutched the warm mug between her chilly hands. She took a sip, savoring the aroma and tang of the black tea.

Heaven.

She took another sip, trying to make the drink last as long as possible. This would be her only cup for the day.

The caffeine trickled in as she sipped more.

God how she missed her morning caffeine fix. One mug a day wasn't enough. It was a shame he didn't have more tea bags. Even with only one a day, she'd run out before two weeks, then she'd have to go without. She could deal with everything else, but she wanted her caffeine.

She trudged over to curl up in the chair and enjoy the fire's warmth. She longed for a glimpse of the sun, even if for only a few minutes. Or even a chance to leave the cabin and breathe in the clean, cold, crisp air.

But no, even getting out would mean hard work. They'd have to shovel out the doorways. She was trapped, literally. What had been a couple days visit with her friends had ended up becoming something else. All day long, day after day, for all week the snow seemed to keep falling. This was getting ridiculous, she didn't care what the weather was going to be tomorrow. She was going to get out the cabin door and feel the wind on her face. At times she enjoyed being here, but all she could do was wait and wait some more. She sighed and tried to read. Her eyes refused to focus on the words, drifting shut every time she finished a paragraph.

Thankfully, the sun peeked out by late morning. Six days with only snow. She bundled up in her warmest clothes and forced her way out the door to the front porch. The air was crisp and the snow sparkled, a wonderland. She wanted to sit on the top step to the porch, but the snow had already buried them in a deep drift. The covered porch only had six inches of snow so she could walk across it. Instead of tromping through the snow, she stood there and enjoyed the clear air. She had to get word to someone. Her family, friends, and employer would be worried by now. At least she got the chance to inhale some fresh air before she went crazy. Within ten minutes a new storm front moved in dropping more snow and bitterly cold air. She reluctantly returned to the cabin.

On Sunday, her seventh day there, she was so exhausted she could hardly function. She crawled into the blankets right after dinner.

Steve strode over to her. "You can't keep doing this. For the last two nights, I've watched you toss and turn. You have to be miserable sleeping on the hard, wooden floor."

"It is pretty hard." Alex rolled onto her back and looked up at him.

He leaned over, picked her up off the floor, carried her into the bedroom, and laid her down on the bed. She tried to object, but he interrupted. "You can't keep going on without a good night's rest. I promise that I won't come near you. I might accidentally touch you with an occasional stray arm or leg, but that's all."

She snuggled under the fluffy covers and immediately fell asleep.

Chapter 6

The next morning, she woke up a lot more rested. He'd kept his word and stayed on his side of the bed. With the extra sleep, she wasn't nearly as exhausted. As she did every morning, she looked out the front window. At least now they were getting a few moments when the sun peeked through the heavy, gray clouds. Snow blanketed everything. Only splotches of dark green proved there were fir trees scattered around the valley. She knew her car was out there, but all traces of it were obliterated, buried under the days of snow. In the direction of the road, only the tops of the fence poles still managed to poke through, the rest of the fence buried. Past that, the mountains towered, their granite faces sparkling in the bright light. Absolute quiet filled the valley, not a single bird called out. There was a softness to the scene creating a sense of peace. She'd pondered why people would choose to live in such a desolate place. Now she started to understand. There was a peacefulness here that she'd never felt in any city.

With all the snow, it looked like she'd be stuck here forever. How would the plows ever manage to clear the road out? And if they did, her car would be buried until spring. Steve had mentioned that she'd come through a pass before entering the valley; the pass was probably also buried. By the looks of the mountains the brutal winds had kept the snow from accumulating on the peaks, dumping everything in the valley. It was hopeless.

Steve had said that he'd be able to get her back to the highway if there hadn't been an avalanche. Unfortunately, her car wouldn't be able to get there for several months. She had to have faith that he knew what he was talking about, but she couldn't get him to commit to any date. He kept avoiding giving her an answer. *When* had become the biggest question.

Today she tried to use the ax to chop some firewood. Chips flew everywhere, but each time she struck the log the blow hit in a different place. This was another job she figured she'd never learn. She could hear Steve trying to cover up his snickers. Of course, when he did it, his blows hit the exact spot every time. She gave up trying when her arms ached. After finishing the rest of her chores, she went inside to get cleaned up. How she had managed to get so many wood chips in her hair and inside her clothes was a mystery. Only after shampooing her hair was it wood-free. As she brushed her hair out in front of the fire, she listened to the wind whistling down the chimney, causing the flames to flicker. At least she was warm. She watched the dancing flames until lunch.

The next morning Steve woke her up when he said, "Um, Alex. Can I get up?"

Alex stirred and realized that she had her arm draped over his side. She jerked it back and slipped out of bed. "Sorry, I didn't know what I was doing."

"That's okay," Steve said as he slipped a jacket on.

He tried to keep his face averted, but Alex caught a glimpse of a smile. At least he wasn't upset. She went on out and looked out the front window. Sunlight filled the valley, with only scattered clouds.

"Look. Sun." Alex pointed out the window.

They quickly donned some warm clothes and boots to get outside before the weather changed. Steve wrestled the front door open and they both stepped out onto the front porch. The snow drifts obliterated the steps and porch railing, but that didn't matter. The frigid air almost made her go back inside, but she took several more steps out onto the porch. *Fresh air*. After having to stay inside so much, this felt like heaven. Snow blanketed and drifted around everything like a fondant icing. The branches on the nearby fir trees were bent almost to breaking under the snow piled up on them.

She took a few minutes to admire the snow. It didn't matter how many times she'd seen the white fluffy stuff, she was still awed by it. Sunlight hit the snow crystals and prisms of color flashed purple, green, and blue throughout the surrounding white, as if glitter had been tossed across everything. The world had been transformed into a fairy's winter wonderland. Maybe being stuck here wouldn't be too bad after all.

Ice stalactites hung from the edges of the roof, thanks to the bright sunshine. Last night the wind had died down leaving snow on the sides of the looming mountains. She pulled in a lungful and coughed from the frigid air. *At least I'm not alone for once*. She had a wonderful selection of books to read in front of a merrily crackling fire. Mysteries were obviously Steve's favorites, being the most prevalent, followed by spy thrillers. He did have groups in other genres as well, although there were only a couple of romances, probably left by some old girlfriend. Tomorrow they'd start digging a path out from the porch. Within a day or two, she'd be able to finally contact her family.

She turned to go back inside and ran into Mandy. She stumbled and fell forward. Steve instinctively reached out to catch her. Alex's hands splayed across his chest, while he firmly held her upper arms. He pulled her closer and they both paused. Her heart pounded as she leaned into him, her fingers curling into his coat. Their eyes remained locked together, hardly blinking. Puffs of vapor expanded around them as they took long, deep breaths. Steve whispered, "Are you okay?"

"Never better," Alex whispered back.

They stayed immobile for a minute before Steve moved away. "We'd better get some breakfast. Anna Belle is probably waiting."

Alex nodded and followed him inside. During breakfast, they didn't speak, but kept stealing glances when they thought the other person wasn't looking. During chores the demon hen escaped as Alex left the coop. Alex dashed over to Anna Belle's stall and hid. Alex jumped when Steve nudged her.

"What's up?" he asked.

Alex pointed to the speckled hen. The hen strutted back and forth in front of the door to the henhouse like an attack dog. "Why in the world would you ever buy a hen like that?"

Steve leaned on the shovel's handle and watched the hen. "It isn't like I picked the hens out. I bought some fertilized eggs, hatched them, and that's what I got."

"Why do you put up with her?"

"I don't have any problems with her, and she lays a lot of eggs."

Alex slipped out of the stall to get the bucket filled with feed. *That hen sure would be good for dinner. I could see her in a large pot with a bunch of potatoes, carrots, and spices.*

The hen raised up high on its feet, squawked, and started running toward her.

Alex took off for the door to the cabin. Her feet danced across the floor, slipping and sliding in the loose straw.

"Better move faster or she's going to catch you." He doubled over laughing.

The bird jumped up and grabbed Alex's pant leg, sinking its claws into the fabric.

"You little—" Alex fumed. "If I get a hold of you." Alex yelled as she stabbed at the hen with the empty bucket.

"I think that hen enjoys tormenting you." Steve shooed the hen back into the coop and walked back to Alex. He clasped her arms and kissed her cheek. "You sure do make my days brighter and more interesting." He headed back to the stall, whistling.

Alex stormed off to the cabin. She'd only been inside a minute when Anna Belle nudged her. "What the—" She looked over to see both doors partially open. "You can't be in here." Alex pulled on Anna Belle's halter, but the cow wouldn't move. Alex pulled and pulled. "Come on, girl," she coaxed.

Anna Belle gazed around the room ignoring Alex's attempts to get her to move.

"This is not my day." She headed back out to the barn where Steve was still whistling.

"Um…Steve…Anna Belle's in the cabin." Alex looked down and toed some hay.

Steve stopped and turned to face Alex. He pointed to a spot behind her. "I swear, that cow follows you around like a dog."

Alex turned to find Anna Belle standing a few feet behind her. She put her hands on her hips. "All that pulling and coaxing. All I had to do was walk out to the barn and you would have followed?" she said to the cow.

Anna Belle moved forward and shoved Alex with her head.

Alex gave Anna Belle a pat and headed back to the cabin, making sure the doors were completely engaged. How was it she couldn't seem to do any of the jobs without messing up? She was such a dork. Had she really been using magic to do even the simplest of chores? She sat down at the kitchen table and went through her typical morning. She never used magic for fixing breakfast, too many electrical appliances. But getting ready, that was another story. Her wand was always lying on her bedside table. She would pick it up to pull her clothes out and put them on in seconds, or use it to make her bed and put the laundry away. She used it without even thinking.

Being stuck here was turning out to be beneficial. It was breaking her from using her wand for all those simple tasks. If she wanted to act normal, then she'd have to avoid using her magic. If she couldn't function here without using magic, then she'd never be able to live as a normal. In time, she'd get better and quit messing up as often. She needed to slow down and avoid rushing. That's when she'd screw something up.

Steve walked in still whistling, Mandy trailing behind. He looked at her and smiled. She could see him shake his head as he headed to the bedroom for some clothes. Mandy wandered over to the fireplace and plopped down. Steve continued to whistle as he headed to the bathroom.

"I'll show him. No more mistakes. I'll prove to him that I'm not completely useless." Mandy turned her head to look at Alex.

At lunch, Alex looked at Steve again. Now she knew why he'd taken so long getting cleaned up this morning. He'd trimmed his beard to an inch long. Up until now, his face had been fuzzy and scruffy. But today, he actually looked distinguished.

"I like your beard. It looks so much better shorter," Alex said.

Steve placed the food on the table.

"Why'd you trim it?"

Steve shrugged and sat down. He fussed with his fork before answering. "I thought you might like it better shorter."

"I do." She pushed her food around her plate and kept her eyes down. "It looks a lot neater."

"I'd trim my hair a little shorter, but that's something I can't do by myself."

Alex continued to stare at her food. "I could give you a simple cut…If you want…I owe you so much for letting me stay here. This is the least I can do to help. I'm not much help with the chores."

"You're a big help. I get tired of dealing with those hens." He chuckled and looked at her.

She looked up. "So you do have problems with them."

"A little, but nothing like you. I swear that speckled hen is out to make your life miserable."

Alex nodded and started to eat.

Steve took a couple of bites. "Maybe after lunch you could trim my hair?"

Alex nodded. She'd get the chance to run her fingers through his hair. His long, silky locks that weren't straight as a board or curly, but kind of flowed around his face in gentle waves. She dug into her meal before she could say anything embarrassing.

****

After the lunch dishes had been cleaned up, Steve said. "What do you need?"

"Scissors, towel, and your comb."

When he returned, he sat on one of the kitchen chairs. "My hair isn't in good shape right now. I should get some conditioner, but I always seem to forget when I'm at the store," Steve said.

"Actually, I know an old-fashioned concoction you could try," Alex said.

"Go ahead and try it. It's not like I'll be seeing anyone soon."

Alex went over to the fridge and pulled out the pitcher of milk and took an egg out of the basket. Steve turned to watch what she was doing. She poured a little cream into a bowl, broke the egg into it, and beat the mixture.

"Are you going to put that on my hair?"

"Sure. It actually does work, but it takes a couple of shampoos to get all of the smell out. And it doesn't have any fragrances in it."

"Yeah, but—"

Alex placed a hand on his shoulder and turned him

68

away from her. She draped the old towel around his shoulders. "I need to cut your hair first before I treat it. Do you trust me?"

"I guess so." Steve straightened in the kitchen chair, still wondering if this was a good idea. Maybe Alex couldn't cut hair worth a damn, and he'd end up with a whack job. She said she could do a good job with a simple cut and how hard could it be to shorten his long hair.

"How much do you want off?"

"At least several inches, enough to get rid of the bad ends."

She slid her hands around his locks and pulled them back.

The second her fingers brushed his neck, a tingling spread out from the point of contact. The skin on his neck felt alive. He inhaled deeply and slowly breathed out. It didn't matter if he got a whack job, this was worth whatever she'd do.

She slid her hands under his hair, her fingers spreading up across the back of his head.

Wherever her fingers touched his skin, a warm current reached out. He stopped breathing for a moment. From somewhere within his chest, a flame of something stretched out. Something he'd never encountered before. The flame was warm and alive. He took a deep breath and held it. The flame radiated out from his chest, spreading out into his arms, flowing on toward his fingers. His heart pounded as his blood warmed. He exhaled, then started breathing steady and deep.

Her fingers gently slid up.

The flame reached up through his neck. He closed

his eyes, experiencing the sensations to their fullest. The flame slowed and tentatively reached out toward the current emanating from her finger tips.

Her fingers froze in place.

Her current and his flame touched, slipped back apart a second, then touched again.

His nostrils flared as he inhaled. Her scent was rich and vivid, filling the space around her. His hands clutched the chair and held on as his jeans got tight. The flame slowly wrapped around her current. Her current responded and curled to intertwine with his. They curled and twisted together.

She pulled her fingers out through his hair, separating the strands.

Her current quickly dissipated and his flame slid back down to his chest. His pulse slowed.

She picked up his comb and ran it through his hair. After several passes, she set the comb back down on the table and picked up the scissors. The soft snips of the scissors were almost buried under the sounds of their breathing. He savored her apple scent mingling with his cedar and grass. It reminded him of warm fall days. A log popped and broke apart. The sections of wood crackled. He could enjoy a life like this, being with her, but he couldn't. He would never forgive himself if something happened to her.

"Maybe you should put the conditioner on," she said.

He never heard her lay the scissors down. His voice broke when he started to speak. "You'd better do it. I'd make a mess." Besides, he wanted her to touch him again—to see if his flame would reach out to her again.

She paused before starting.

The cool mixture made him gasp.

"Sorry, I guess I should have warmed it up."

"It's okay, keep going."

She dribbled some more on his head then started working it in.

This time his flame raced straight up and started to twist and play with her moving current, teasing and taunting the current to reach out even further. The play was comforting while still being invigorating. He couldn't keep from smiling.

"You're enjoying this, aren't you?"

"Yeah. Maybe you should do this again in a few weeks. My hair is in pretty bad shape."

She worked the mixture on down his hair.

His flame lingered, waiting for more, then slid back down. He'd have to convince her to do this again. Never had he felt this before. Who knew a simple haircut could be so erotic.

"You need to wash the egg out." Alex went over to the sink and washed her hands.

While her back was turned, Steve dashed to the bathroom before she could see how much of an effect she'd had on him.

****

What the hell was that? That was something new. She could feel her magic reaching out to him...calling him. Her fingers tingled from touching him. And she hadn't wanted to stop. She sat down in the chair he'd vacated. It had taken all her willpower to pull her hands away to pick up the scissors. She'd never sensed this before by simply touching a man's neck. *I wonder if it would happen again?*

Maybe she'd have to find out. If touching him felt this way, what would happen if they kissed? She heard the water turn off and Steve came out rubbing his hair between the towel.

"I think that conditioner helped. You'll have to do it again next week." He headed back to the bedroom humming.

So he sensed it too. Would she really want to experience this again? *Hell yes*. She jumped up, got the broom, and started sweeping up the hair clippings. She needed a distraction before she did something she'd regret later.

Steve came out still smiling. "Thanks for the cut. It feels a lot better now."

Alex watched him saunter over to his chair. Mandy followed on his heels, circled a couple of times, and lay down in front of the chairs. Alex finished cleaning up the hair, picked up her water, and headed toward the other chair. At least this had been something she did right. She settled into the chair and opened her book.

I'll show them tomorrow, no more mistakes. She quickly glanced at them. The man and dog were alike in so many ways. Good or bad, they were always there, especially today. For some reason Steve had been watching her more and paying more attention. *Could it be because of this morning*? This morning when he woke up with her arm draped across him, or when Mandy knocked her into him? *Could Mandy have done that on purpose*?

Mandy lifted her head and looked at Alex.

Alex could swear the dog was smiling. All afternoon, she stole glances at him. He definitely looked a lot better. She kept wanting to run her fingers through his newly trimmed long hair.

Chapter 7

The bright sunshine that afternoon was such a blessing. Tomorrow she'd be helping dig out the porch in addition to the regular chores. It had been a day without howling winds and continual snow, even though it was still bitterly cold. She'd never gone this long without talking to her parents. Her boss would have contacted them when she hadn't shown up for work. Twelve days and she still hadn't been able to contact anyone.

Did Steve have any family outside the valley? Surely he had someone out there who worried about him. But he'd avoided talking about his family so far. He had to have some way to get in touch. She had to find out tonight.

As they ate dinner she spoke up. "How do you get in touch with your family when the phone lines are down?"

"I use my snowmobile and go over to Peter's. He has a shortwave radio that can get messages through."

She dropped her fork. "So why haven't you mentioned this?"

"I knew it would be several days before the storm cleared enough so I could get there safely. I didn't want you to worry more than you already are."

"When can we go? I need to let my family know that I'm safe."

"Tomorrow we'll get the doorways and front steps clear. And then if it's still sunny the next day, we'll leave as soon as chores are finished. We have to travel while the sun's out or it'll be too cold."

"So what does Peter do so he can live out here?" Alex picked up her water and started to drink.

"He's a wizard—"

Alex spewed the water out. She jumped up and got a towel to mop up the mess. "Sorry about that. You were saying."

Steve paused for another moment. "He's a computer programmer. He writes computer games that become famous. It's like magic the way he can work."

"But he can get a message to my parents?"

"Should be able to."

"How?"

"His roof is covered with solar panels. He almost always has electric."

Electric, long hot showers, Internet, heavenly. Her breathing increased.

"Alex, what's wrong?"

"Nothing, I was just thinking." She picked up her glass and took another drink. She couldn't wait to meet this neighbor.

****

The next morning, Alex's arm and leg were draped across Steve when he woke up. His chest tingled where her open hand was lying on it. Every now and then her fingers would curl and open again, making his skin burn from her touch. Oh, how he'd enjoy feeling her hand stroking his chest and her leg wrapped around him. He stayed as still as possible, wanting this moment of contact to last. Her hand and leg tensed, tightening up against him, almost as if she was snuggling up to him. She murmured something unintelligible. He couldn't not touch her any longer. Ever so gently, he eased his hand down her arm, savoring how soft her skin was.

She jerked. "I'm so sorry," she said. "I don't know what keeps making me do this."

Steve stretched out, putting his hands behind his head, grinning. "Actually, I don't mind."

"I'm not too heavy for you?" Alex struggled to get unwrapped from the sheets then slid out of bed to get her warmer clothes from the closet.

Steve gazed from her toes to her head, taking in her shapely bare legs extending down from her shorts and especially how her soft t-shirt clung to the curves of her breasts. He had to take a moment before forming a coherent thought. "You, too heavy? That'll be the day."

"I try to wrap myself up in the sheet so I won't encroach on your side." She hurried out of the room, clutching her clothes.

Mandy and Steve looked at each other.

"Actually, I don't mind when she ends up against me. She could do it more often." He quickly threw on some clothes and headed out to make breakfast, just to keep her in view.

****

The day was cloudy, but at least it wasn't snowing. After breakfast, Alex wandered out into the barn and noticed an intricate web stretched between the side of the barn and the nearest post of Anna Belle's stall, a silken maze. During the night, Anna Belle's breath had created tiny drops across all the web's fibers that sparkled like diamonds in the lantern's light. Alex moved the lantern and watched pieces of rainbows dance across the barn's walls. She hadn't realized she'd been doing this for several minutes until Steve cleared his throat.

"Do you mind? I'm trying to get some work done."

"Look at this. It's beautiful."

Steve moved close and leaned on his shovel's handle. His warm breath grazed her cheek.

"Look at all the rainbows." She moved the lantern around some more, trying to ignore her body turning on fire by his presence.

Steve sighed. "Yeah. Now can we get back to work." He moved back to the pen he was cleaning out.

"I got distracted." She carried the light over and hung it up on its bracket.

"Sorry." He looked up at her. "It is beautiful. I see it every day, so I've taken it for granted."

"I know. It's stupid. It's only a spider web." She picked up the water bucket and started getting to her chores.

Steve mumbled, "Next she'll be talking about dragons, or pixies, or heaven forbid, unicorns."

Mandy shoved into his legs, knocking him off balance.

He said to the dog, "Taking her side now? You ole redcoat, you. Aren't you supposed to be man's best friend?"

Mandy shoved him again.

"Okay, okay. I get your point."

Mandy sauntered away, tail wagging.

Alex kept her head turned away, trying not to laugh at Steve's comments.

They finished the normal chores, and then she

started to shovel the front porch and steps, while Steve made a path to the barn's shed. When he finished, he walked around to the front and found Alex making a snowman.

"What are you doing? Didn't you have enough work for one day?"

"I wanted to do something that was fun for a change." And exhaust herself physically so she wouldn't get hot whenever he was close.

"Need help?"

"Sure, you can make the middle ball and put it on this one." She continued to roll the large ball.

He finished a medium sized ball and placed it above her bigger one. She walked over and placed the smallest ball on top. "All done." She bent over to brush snow off her pants.

Mandy charged into her, knocked her into the drift near the porch, then dashed off around the cabin.

Alex struggled to get up. Steve held out a hand for her. "Here, take my hand," he said.

She clasped his hand. When he jerked her up, she fell against him. He kept her one hand tightly clasped in his and touched her cheek with his other. They stared at each other, as he moved toward her, so close his breath warmed her face. Heat flooded her core and her breathing became heavy. His lips touched hers briefly. He stayed within inches for a moment, then kissed her again. This time the kiss was insistent and hungry, his tongue asking to come in. Alex opened her mouth to him and moved her body closer until their chests touched. They took their time exploring each other. He tasted like cinnamon and bacon. When he started to withdraw she moved closer, not wanting the kiss to end.

He responded to her silent request and re-engaged. When he finally broke apart, he leaned his forehead against hers. Her lips still tingled and her body was hot from her desire. She wanted more, a lot more.

He pulled back and released her. He gently brushed the snow off her coat as she stood there. She couldn't move, her body aching to savor his touch, even with the heavy coats and gloves. "We'd better get some lunch," he finally said.

Oh how I want to keep kissing him. Instead, she nodded and followed him up the front steps. Mandy sat on the front porch watching. Alex gave the dog a thumbs up, and Mandy's tail started wagging. Steve placed a hand on her back until they'd entered the cabin. He helped her out of her coat, brushing her shoulders as he did. He paused and took a deep breath, as if he was smelling her. After hanging up their coats and hats, he hurried to the kitchen to fix lunch.

All during lunch, he remained silent with his head bent over the table. Occasionally he would look into her eyes and smile. She couldn't stop thinking about how wonderful his kisses had been. It took all her self-control to keep from leaning across the table and pressing her lips against his, or to slide her bare hands along his neck and curl into his hair, or give him something to really smile about.

They'd finished clearing the lunch dishes when a snowmobile could be heard approaching. Steve headed out onto the porch as it drove up to the cabin.

"What's with the snowman? Never seen you make one before," Peter said.

"I have company," Steve answered.

"Company? How?" Peter got off the machine and

headed up the porch.

Steve opened the door the rest of the way and they headed in.

"I just checked the pass. It's closed. It'll take a while before anyone can get out," Peter said as he walked in and removed his hat, gloves, and coat. He hung them up as Steve walked back to the table.

Steve swept a hand in Alex's direction. "Peter Robertson, meet Alex Klein. Alex, Peter."

Alex stood and held out a hand. "It's a pleasure to meet you." Peter was average height, lean, with brown hair and a beard.

Peter shook her hand. He looked at Steve. "I thought you were kidding." He looked back to Alex. "How'd you get here? The pass is buried."

Alex sat back down. "I came two weeks ago, before the pass closed."

Peter whistled and sat down at the table. He listened as Alex told how she got stranded. "What can I do to help?"

"I need to get a message to my parents. Steve mentioned that you have a radio."

"I'll see what I can do," Peter said.

"Peter usually checks on the pass and all the neighbors after a big storm. He sees if they need anything," Steve said.

"Give me the numbers and messages for the people you need to reach. I'll see if they can be available in a few days so you can talk to them," Peter said.

Alex wrote down the numbers and messages for her parents and boss. "How do you do this without a phone?"

"I use my radio and contact another ham radio,

pass the message along, that person calls and relays the message. Hopefully they'll let the people at the other end come over so you can talk to them directly." Peter looked away from Alex to Steve. "Need anything else?"

"I'll probably need some more canned goods," Steve said.

"Sure thing, and I'm dying for some fresh eggs."

"We'll bring some eggs and milk with us. Do you want a few now?"

"No, I've still got to check on everyone else." Peter stood and started for the door. "I'd better get going or I'll run out of daylight." He looked back to Alex. "I'll see you tomorrow."

Steve walked Peter out. The snowmobile started and pulled away. Steve walked back in. "I bet we start seeing him a lot more often, you being the only single woman in the valley." He refilled his water and sat back down at the table.

"How many other people live in this valley?"

"I'm the closest to the pass, then Peter. Past him there is the Gibson family of four, another couple, then a gay couple."

"That's not very many."

"It's a small valley that ends against a mountain. That's why we're one of the last places a plow gets to, as well as having to deal with the pass."

"So what do you do about the pass?"

"When the pass has an avalanche, we're left with only getting through by snowmobile. Peter is the best supplied, so he helps the rest of us out when we get trapped."

"Can we get out on your snowmobile?"

"Not for a while. The snow has to settle and

81

compact before it's safe to traverse. Before then, a snowmobile would sink."

Alex stroked the side of her water glass. "What do the other residents do when they can't leave the valley? How do they get by without electric?"

"The gay couple are wealthy, so they enjoy their hobbies. The other couple has some money and earns some extra by selling oil paintings. The Gibsons are both writers with a young girl and boy. Peter is wealthy."

"So why out here?"

"They all wanted to get away from a large city and all its problems."

"What about you?"

"Me? I do some prospecting during the summer." He got up, walked over to the fireplace, returned, and set several crystals on the table. "This is what I look for, aquamarines." He picked one up and handed it to her. "This is one of the better pieces that I've collected."

Alex took the crystal and ran her fingers along the stone's facets. "It's beautiful. You find these?"

"Yeah, up on the mountain at the end of the valley. That's why I located here. What about you? What do you do?"

"I'm a technical writer, if I still have a job."

"Do you like it?"

"It's okay, but I've become dissatisfied the last couple of years. Writing technical journals is boring; they lack variation. I took the first job I could get after college to pay off my loans. They're all paid off now. I can pay my bills and take a nice vacation occasionally, so I've been reluctant to go out and look for something else."

"What will you do if you're stuck here for two months?" Steve asked.

"I don't know. I have some savings that will get me through a few months, but after that…"

"What will you do about paying your bills?"

"My parents will probably do that for me. My brother is living in my apartment so he can take care of Vladimir for me."

"Who's Vladimir?"

"My chocolate lab." Alex set the crystal back down on the table.

"What were you doing that made you travel that night?"

"I was visiting with some of my college friends. They're all in relationships, involved with their careers, settling down, growing up. I probably won't be seeing them as often now. They're all getting too busy." Why hadn't she looked into getting a career? Instead, she was passing time not going anywhere. It was as if she'd been waiting for something to happen. Maybe this was it, especially if she had to find a new job. "What about you? Why'd you stay here?"

Steve picked up the crystal Alex had set down. "Me?" He looked into the depths of the stone as he rotated it. "I found a serenity out here that I've never had before. I bought the land and buildings. The cabin was rundown so I fixed up the interior and added the barn. I rent out part of the land to the other residents to cover the mortgage. For the rest, I find these," he held up the crystal. He got up and put the crystals back on the mantel with several others. He collapsed into his chair and picked up his book.

She was surprised he'd said so much. He had been extremely quiet so far. Maybe he was just shy. For whatever reason they'd opened up to each other, trusted each other with their feelings, and had kissed. Given their close quarters, she couldn't imagine not ending up close to him so they could kiss again, maybe this time without the coats and gloves.

Chapter 8

The next morning Alex woke up even more entwined than before. She loved how Steve made her warm all over, like a sexy, living teddy bear. As much as she wanted to stay wrapped up around him, she gently untangled herself, slipped out of bed, and got dressed. Alex poured some honey into her mug of weak tea. Using the same bag for a third cup had produced unsatisfying results, but it was the last one. Maybe the honey would add a little flavor to the colored water.

They had gotten a light snow last night so they'd have to re-shovel outside. She savored her caffeine, anything to delay shoveling. She still ached from all the work yesterday, and those damn chickens still gave her problems. Maybe a chicken dinner would be just the ticket tonight. That speckled hen, the hen from hell, looked particularly plump. But she knew they couldn't do that, the hen gave them some of the eggs they so desperately needed. She sipped the rest of the tea visualizing the chicken's demise.

Steve wandered out. "You should have awakened me."

"I knew you'd be up. I wanted to savor the last of my tea."

Steve nodded and fixed breakfast. Once finished, he headed out to the barn.

No more delaying, she had to get busy with her

morning chores. At least today was a little warmer. Maybe the storms were finally clearing out. Today she took her time and didn't make any mistakes. Finally, she only had to collect the eggs. She put the oven mitt on again and paused for a deep breath before facing the hens.

Steve walked up to her and pointed to the mitt. "What are you doing?" he asked, shaking his head.

"I just thought..." Just thought what? Thought that the hen would let her take the eggs. No, this was her defense. The oven mitt worked great. "Those brown hens and that demon hen hate me," she finally answered.

"I know the hens can be a pain. You need to reach in with confidence. They can smell fear."

"I fear her all right. She's pecked my hands raw. The mitt keeps me safe." She showed him the back of the mitt. "See. Look what she's done."

He looked closer. The stuffing poked out all over the back.

"See what I mean. I might be stupid when it comes to chickens, but at least with the mitt on I can get the eggs." She opened the henhouse door and strode in. Alex had made some progress. Half the hens would willingly let her collect the eggs, all but those brown birds. They refused to co-operate. With the mitt, she could get the eggs. Now that she'd gathered the eggs, she removed the mitt to spread some corn kernels.

She dug her hand in the grain bucket and scattered a handful. She reached in again to get the last handful. As soon as she pulled her hand out, a pop shushed the hens. A piece of popcorn fell to the floor. Another kernel popped. She dropped the grain before any more changed. How hard could it be to scatter grain? She should know by now, nothing had turned out easy here. She'd adjust to one thing then something else would happen. What would go wrong next?

****

Alex left the coop, rushed over to him, and pointed to the blood. "What happened?"

"It's nothing." Steve pulled his arm back.

"It might be; let me clean and dress it for you. You don't want to get blood everywhere." Alex strode into the cabin. Steve followed her in and found her waiting by the sink. She held out her hand to him.

Steve started rolling up his sleeve as he headed over to her. "I'm only doing this so you'll quit buggin' me." He held his forearm under the faucet while she washed it. He patted the wound dry with a paper towel and headed over to the table to sit down. He kept pressure on the slice while she went to the bathroom to get bandages.

Why was he letting her fuss over him like this? It wasn't that big of a cut, he'd barely noticed when he did it. He watched her every move as she cut some strips of tape and stuck them to a non-stick pad. She nudged his hand away, replacing the paper towel with the dressing. Her fingers slid across the strips of tape. The tape would be a bitch when he had to pull it off, but it was worth it. Her touch was electrifying. He'd have to get her to touch him more often. Her fingers strayed farther up his arm and she traced one of his scars with a light touch.

"What made this scar? It's so big," she said as she continued to finger the mark.

"A bear," he quietly answered.

87

"You got this from a bear? It was that close?"

He inclined his head. "She didn't want to go away."

"And you were able to chase it away even after this?"

He shrugged.

"Is that why you have such heavy doors and shutters over the windows?"

He paused. "Yeah, to keep bears out."

"Do you also use those shackles in the storage area?"

"If I have to." He shifted a little in his chair. "I can shoot an animal with a sedative, then use the shackles as a safety measure, while I relocate the animal."

She trailed a finger over the scar one more time before she yanked her hand away. "Sorry." She got up and headed to the bedroom.

He smiled as he watched her retreating figure. She embarrassed so easily. He would gladly trade dealing with her fragrances for all the times he could watch her move. But why did he always react so strongly to even a simple touch? Her staying here might end up being enjoyable after all. She was good company. Sometimes he regretted his lonely lifestyle.

Mandy pushed up against his leg and he ruffled her fur. "She's one tough broad. She doesn't give up. You know it isn't safe for her with me. But it's a shame she can't stay longer, I'm beginning to like her."

Mandy shook her head.

****

Alex headed into the bedroom to the closet. She reached into her suitcase and felt around for her wand. After pulling the bag out, she sat down on the floor and slipped it out of the bag. She ran a finger along the wood. She could heal his cut in a minute. *No.* She swore she wouldn't use magic. She slid the wand back into the silk bag. There wasn't any way she could explain magic to him and couldn't. *I can't break the rule—magic must remain secret.* It was a shame though, when there was something she could do to make his life better and couldn't. She stood up, put the bag back in her suitcase, zipped it all the way shut, and shoved the suitcase back under the clothes. She took a couple of deep breaths and swiped her hands down her clothes.

No more delaying. All she did was touch him. *No big deal. Right.*

She paused.

It felt like so much more. Why couldn't she figure out why? She wandered out to get a quick shower so she'd be ready for lunch.

They'd finished lunch when they heard a snowmobile approaching. Steve let Peter in and took his coat.

"How's everyone?" Steve sat down at the table next to Alex, facing Peter.

"They're all dug out and are doing fine. You were the only one to get a surprise visitor." Peter filled a glass with water and leaned against the counter. "They all commented that they were glad it was you."

"Why me?"

"You know they'd all be willing to find someone for you if you'd let them. They're all a bunch of matchmakers."

"Then why haven't they found someone for you? You're looking a lot more than I am."

"You know they've tried. No woman in her right

mind wants to be this far away from the shopping," Peter said.

"Not all women are interested in shopping," Alex said.

Peter snorted. "Wanna bet?"

"I don't, and some of my friends don't," Alex added.

"Then I'd like to meet them," Peter said.

There was only one problem with that—they were almost all wizards who liked to use their magic. Alex took some sips from her water to avoid answering.

Peter watched her. "Yeah, that's what I thought. No one comes to mind, do they?" He walked over and took a seat at the table. "You know I had a woman tell me that she'd only go out with me when pigs flew."

Alex snorted, spraying water across the table. "Sorry about that." She jumped up and got a towel while Steve and Peter watched. She started wiping the water up. "A woman actually said that to you?"

Peter looked at Steve. "That's an idea. You know that game I've been wanting to do, I'll have a woman say that."

"Then what?" Steve asked.

Alex picked up the lunch dishes and carried them to the sink.

"I'll have the man make the pig fly with magic so she has to go out with him. I know…I'll make the whole game about witches and wizards."

Alex almost dropped the dishes in the sink. "Witches and wizards?"

Peter looked over at Alex. "Yeah, I've been wanting to write a fantasy game for a couple of years. I just didn't want to spend the time doing the research I'd need to do to be convincing."

"Did you get hold of my parents?" Alex came back to the table and slid into a chair.

"Your parents and your boss. Your parents said they'd take care of everything until you get back. But your boss could hardly believe it; it took a while to convince him I was telling the truth. I told them that there had been a big avalanche and it would be a while before we can get you out."

"Were you able to set it up so I can talk with them?"

"They've all agreed to go over to my friend's house in two days, Thursday, so you can talk."

Alex nodded.

Peter said to Steve, "I brought some canned goods with me. Thought you might be running low."

They both got up, put coats on, and headed out. Within a couple of minutes, Steve returned with a bag full of cans.

Alex got up. "I'll put those away for you." She took the bag and went out to the storeroom. It only took a couple of minutes to shelve them, but she stayed. Hearing about her parents brought tears to her eyes. They'd never gone this long without talking. But she was torn between leaving before she'd learned more about Steve and seeing her family. She took several slow, deep breaths to calm herself and swiped the tears away. Only two days and she'd be able to talk with them. She walked back in the cabin and visited some more with Peter before he left.

The next morning, she woke up curled against Steve's back. If she kept this up, she'd be lying on top of him in a couple more weeks. What an intriguing thought. She inhaled her breakfast so she could get the chores over with. With all her hurrying, she only made a couple of small mistakes. She cleaned the henhouse out, left to fill a bucket with corn, and headed back in to feed the chickens. She dug her hands into the kernels and tossed them across the floor. Pop, then another pop, followed by a bunch more. *Could chickens even eat popcorn?* As the rest of the kernels popped, all the hens became silent and tilted their heads to eye the popcorn. None of them moved or made a sound, just watched.

Alex dug out another handful and tossed these across the floor. The kernels clattered across the floor then pop, then a lot of pops, as these kernels all changed. Alex didn't move. *What now?* She flipped a piece off her boot and watched it land among the others. The demon hen flew down to the floor and eyed the popcorn. Alex froze. The hen pecked at one piece and watched the remainder bounce away. She pecked again, watched, then started pecking more intently. Another hen hopped down and started pecking. The demon hen started gobbling up the pieces. The other hens all hopped down to get in on the action. They all started gobbling up every piece. When they'd finished, they all worked their way over to Alex and stared up at her.

Alex looked at the bucket. She reached in and grabbed another handful. As soon as the kernels popped the hens were pouncing on them. Alex threw handful after handful until the bucket was empty. All the hens were busy so she went around the boxes and collected the eggs as fast as she could without stepping on any of the birds. The moment she'd finished, she dashed out and slammed the door shut. She leaned against the door. *What happened? I've never done that before. What if Steve sees a piece of popcorn? How will I explain that?* She took several deep breaths. At least they all seemed to enjoy it. She looked at the eggs in her bucket. This was the easiest she'd ever had getting them. But could she do it again, when she didn't know how she'd done it today?

Chapter 9

Alex couldn't settle down enough to read so she took Mandy out to the barn to play fetch. Tomorrow she'd go over to Peter's. This was the first time she'd had to think back about where her life had gone over the years. The farm animals reminded her of her high school years at the wizarding school, Aspen Glen. Then, everything seemed so important and life changing, but now those days seemed so easy and carefree. Her other problems had become minor, compared to her being stranded in the mountains. In one day her life had changed. Was it for the better?

College had taught her one very important lesson—never give up. No matter how long it takes, keep trying. The old adage "if at first you don't succeed, try, try again" had become her motto. Especially now. She would get her life put back together. Tomorrow she'd get to talk with her parents and her boss.

She tossed and turned all night, worrying about whether she'd still have a job. In the morning, they hurried through breakfast and chores so they could get over to Peter's early in the day. Alex wrapped each egg to make sure none of them broke as they rode and tucked them into the snowmobile's saddle pack. Steve and Peter used an exchange system of milk and eggs for canned vegetables. The day was sunny at the moment, but more storms were predicted for later in the day so they couldn't stay too late.

But it would be an afternoon away. She'd been going stir crazy the last few days with the frequent snows and looked forward to getting out of the cabin. To make matters worse, Steve had been keeping his distance. She was curious if Peter's cabin was basic or if he had more modern features. They loaded up the snowmobile and Alex climbed on behind. Steve had shown her the basics of how a snowmobile worked yesterday. She'd lived all her life in Colorado but had never ridden one before; today would be her first. Steve took off across the open field heading straight down the valley. After a few minutes they went down a hill and Alex could see a large house. It was a two-story brick building with porches and balconies on each level. The roof was almost completely covered with solar panels which sparkled in the sunshine. Beyond, she could see three other structures stretching off down the valley. Behind them another mountain loomed up. On the far side of the valley a line of pines and firs ran along the bottom of another wall of rocks. She spent so much time looking around, they were at Peter's before she realized it. Steve parked, helped Alex off, and carried the saddlebag up to the house. Peter came out as soon as they reached the porch.

"You need to stop by some day," Peter said. "Come over and take a long leisurely shower and enjoy using electric for a change."

When they entered the house, Alex stopped mid-stride and stared. She'd never imagined anything like this. There were curtains, puffy chairs with pillows, area rugs, a big screen TV, and modern appliances. She wandered around taking it all in.

"How do you run all this?" she asked.

"Did you see my collection of solar panels?"

Alex nodded.

"They power everything here and even provide some power for the other three houses. I also have a satellite dish for TV and Internet. I can't work without them," Peter said. He took the milk and eggs and headed back to his storeroom to get some canned vegetables. He screamed, ran out of the storeroom, slammed the door, and leaned against the door, trying to catch his breath.

"What happened?" Steve headed toward Peter.

"A spider. A big, hairy spider."

"You big girl." Steve headed out to the kitchen and returned with the flyswatter. "You should know by now to take this with you." He waved the flyswatter.

"Yeah, but it was so big." Peter moved away from the door.

Steve entered the storeroom and they heard several loud smacks. A few moments of silence passed, more smacks, silence, another round of smacks. Steve reappeared.

He was holding the biggest spider Alex had ever seen.

Steve looked at it a moment, turning the mangled body this way and that. "You were right. It was big." He started to act like he was going to fling it at Peter, and Peter made a run for the other part of the house. He smiled and looked over to Alex. "It always amazes me how a man who writes battle games can be so afraid of spiders."

"Why haven't we come over here sooner?" Alex asked Steve.

He was dumping the spider body in a trash can. "I only have a limited amount of gas so I only use it for important trips."

Peter poked his head around the corner of the hallway. "Is it gone?"

"All gone," Steve said.

Peter looked at his watch. "We'd better get to the radio then; it's almost time. Sorry we have to use the radio, but the Internet reception is iffy right now, and I haven't gotten a satellite phone yet."

Alex followed Peter back to one of the other rooms while Steve settled into one of the chairs. The first call was to Alex's boss, Tom.

Tom asked, "When can you get back?"

"I don't know for sure, but it could be almost a month or more before I can get out," Alex said.

"I couldn't believe it when I first heard. If it was anyone else, I would wonder if they just wanted some time off. I know you wouldn't do this." He paused, "I put you on sick leave for a week, then put you on vacation, but even that's running out in a couple of days."

"I appreciate it. I'm so sorry this happened."

"I really like you as an employee, but I can't keep your job open that long. I'll have to hire someone else."

"I understand." Alex gripped the microphone tighter. This had been what she was afraid would happen.

"I'll give you two weeks termination pay, that's the best I can do. When you ever get back be sure to stop by in case there are some openings. I'm sorry, that's all I can do."

"I'm sorry too. I'll have my parents come by and

clean out my desk." She paused to get her voice under control. "Thanks for all your help."

"I'll pass the microphone to your mom now. Good luck," Tom said.

Some indistinct voices and rustles came across the air-waves.

"Alex dear, is that really you?"

"Yes, Mom."

"I couldn't believe it when I got the call a few days ago. I'd been worried out of my noggin. No call, nothing. I scried…I could tell you were alive at least."

"I know, Mom, but it isn't like I could pick up a phone and call."

"I know, but you could have sent me a bird."

Peter looked at Alex like he wanted to ask what she meant.

"Mom, be careful. You know I couldn't do anything like that here. Did you hear what Tom said?"

"Yes. I'm so sorry for you, but you know how I felt about that kind of work."

"Can you clean out my desk for me?"

"Of course, dear. You know I'd do anything for you."

Alex squirmed in the chair. "How are Joseph and Vladimir doing?"

"He's spoiling that dog rotten. He can only afford to pay three quarters of the rent for now though."

"That'll at least slow down the drain on my money. You know where all the accounts are, don't you, Mom?"

"Of course, but you needn't worry about that now. We'll help you out, just keep yourself safe. Don't be taking any risks to get here a little sooner. We'll take care of things for you."

"I know you will. Thanks."

"Can we talk again next week?" her mom asked.

Alex looked at Peter and he nodded.

"I should be able to. Love you, Mom, and give my love to Dad."

"Love you, honey. Take care and stay safe. Bye."

Alex mumbled bye and handed the microphone to Peter. He talked to his friend on the other end for a minute then disconnected.

"We arranged for another call with your parents next week," Peter said.

"Thanks for doing this for me."

"Anytime, just glad I could help." Peter pulled open a desk drawer and pulled out a half full bottle of whisky. "Take this. I think you need it. Let me show you around."

Alex took the bottle and followed Peter as he showed her the rest of his house. There were several bedrooms on the second floor with only a couple of them furnished. "If you ever want to, you could stay here."

"Thanks, but I'm okay for now. I've been trying to catch up on some reading." *And kiss Steve again.*

Peter nodded. They headed back to the first floor. He showed her the rest of the rooms which included a theater decked out to look like the bridge of a spaceship. His study was an explosion of sticky notes and papers. The walls were covered with dry erase boards, which had writing and sticky notes filling all the space. One large desk was covered with computer equipment while another desk was heaped full of papers. Manuals lay scattered around the floor.

Then she spied it, a diet soda can. She dashed over and picked up the can. "Do you have any you could give me?"

"Sure, I've got some in my pantry, come on." They headed back out through the living room. He went through a door off the kitchen but paused and looked around the floor. "Just checking. I don't want to find that spider's brother."

Alex walked into a large narrow room. There were two freezers and wall-to-wall industrial shelves packed with all kinds of supplies. "No wonder you can share with others." She walked around looking at everything.

"Yeah, we've arranged a pretty good barter system. Steve provides milk and eggs, I have canned goods, and one of the neighbors has a greenhouse where they grow fresh vegetables. Here's the soft drinks." He handed her a couple of cans. "I'll bring more the next time I come over."

"You don't know how much I've missed these." She pulled the cans close to her body.

"Don't need to tell me. I couldn't live without them."

"Do your panels always provide you with enough power?"

"Most of the time. I only have problems when we get a lot of snow and they get covered."

"Like these last two weeks? Then what do you do?"

He pointed to a large cabinet at the end. "My batteries get me by for quite a while if I'm careful, then I have to resort to my generator and fireplace."

"I guess we'd better get back before it snows again. Thanks for the supplies." She held up a can.

Peter walked with her back through the house. "Have faith. Everything will work out."

Steve stood up when they came back out. "Ready?"

Alex nodded and they headed out. She tucked her supplies in the saddlebag and got on. Alex thought while she rode back to the cabin. *Why hadn't I left earlier? Even one hour would have made a major difference. One hour earlier and I would have made it home. How could something that seemed so minor have such devastating consequences? Here I am, I've lost my job, and can't even predict when I might be able to get home. Just one hour earlier.*

What if I'd turned left instead of right? I would have found the hotel. I'd have had to stay for a couple of days, but I wouldn't have lost my job.

No. I turned right and got marooned in this mountain valley. With no idea of when the road will be passable even on a snowmobile. She would find a new job, maybe something even better, and for now just enjoy every day more fully.

Oh well. At least she had a roof over her head. She'd even been able to get a call out to let her family know that she was safe. After all, tomorrow might not ever come. And when it did, who knew what it would bring.

Chapter 10

When they got back to the cabin, Alex said, "I need some time to think. I'll be in the barn."

She grabbed the bottle of whisky out of the saddlebags and a box of tissues from the bathroom, tucked both items under her arm, and went into the barn. Tears started to creep down her face. She grabbed the milking stool and carried it into Anna Belle's stall. She set everything down and unscrewed the cap. "Here's to my disaster of a life." She held up the bottle toward Anna Belle then took a swig out of the bottle.

Anna Belle moved close.

The liquid burned as it slid down her throat, making her cough. "That's strong stuff. I've never had it without a mixer before." She took another drink.

Anna Belle leaned against Alex's shoulder.

Alex rubbed Anna Belle's side. "I lost my job today. It wasn't like I loved it, but it was work. It paid my bills." She took another drink. The tears came faster. "Then there are people like Peter who love what they're doing. Why couldn't I have a job like that? Everyone says you should work at what you love and then it won't seem like work. Boy do I wish I knew what that was." She grabbed a tissue out of the box, dabbed her eyes, and blew her nose. "This is the first job I've ever lost. It shouldn't matter so much...but it does."

She'd reached a crossroads. If she continued on the path she'd been raised up with, she would have to find some way to fit in the magical world. Could she ever find a wizard who wasn't obnoxious about how much more power he had? So she'd decided to look elsewhere. For months she'd ridden an elevator at work with Jason, a normal, simply nodding to each other. They progressed to "good mornings" or the weather. The last few weeks they actually talked for the short ride. Then she got the nerve to ask him out for a Friday dinner, something she'd never done before. And he accepted. He had even smiled when he said yes.

If she picked someone normal like Jason or Steve, she would have to give up magic forever. Did she really want to go to this extreme? Regardless, she made the pledge to go thirty days without using any magic. If she couldn't go thirty days how could she ever completely exist in the normal world. Trying to function well in both was wearing her down. There were her college and work friends that she had to continually be on her guard with.

The magical world had to remain secret.

It was the law.

Then there were her childhood friends who remained only in the magical world. She couldn't figure out why she didn't fit in. To give up the fight and fit in would be so much easier. But she wanted more. There was a whole world out there. Then she made the stupid pledge and ended up here. One advantage to being here was getting the time to find out what it was like to live without magic. She took some more drinks and blew her nose.

"You know, Anna Belle, now that I'm getting used

to the work, I actually enjoy it. I like how my muscles respond while lifting the buckets. My body is getting in better shape than any of the exercise programs I've tried. Then there's Steve. I'm attracted to him and he seems to feel the same, if that kiss was any indication." She touched her lips, remembering the sensation. "I'd like to do that again, and maybe more."

She remained silent for a minute. "I guess there's one good thing that came out of all this. I'll get the chance to decide what I really want to do." She looked up; the henhouse door stood slightly ajar. The demon hen was standing in the opening, eyeball glued to her, as if she'd been listening. Alex waited without moving. The hen turned around and went back inside. Alex dashed over to the door and nudged it shut. The latch clicked and she let out her breath.

Alex ambled back over to Anna Belle. "That was a close one. Last thing I'd want to do tonight would be to chase that hen around the barn." Alex rubbed Anna Belle's neck. "You sure are a good listener."

They turned their heads when the cabin door opened. Steve eased over to her. "Are you okay?"

"I'm doing better now after talking to Anna Belle."

He pointed to the much emptier bottle. "You might want to save some for another day. As soon as I've finished the milking, I'll fix dinner. You need to eat something or you'll have a bad hangover tomorrow."

She picked up her tissues and the bottle. "I'll go wash my face. I'm sure it must be a mess."

Steve reached out and stroked her cheek. "Not to me. You're beautiful even when you first wake up and your hair is all over the place."

She shrugged and headed for the cabin.

He watched her stagger toward the cabin, then started his milking. After he'd finished, he patted Anna Belle's side. "Now she's talking to the cow. What next?" He finished up and went in to fix dinner.

After they'd finished the dinner, he asked, "Are you feeling any better now?"

Alex nodded but remained slumped. "Sorry about that. This is the first time I've ever lost a job, and it isn't even my fault."

"Maybe you'll find something better."

"Maybe...I've been wanting to get a different job."

"What are you interested in?"

"After college I was interested in becoming a book editor, or something related."

"You need to meet the other residents. They might be able to help." He reached across the table and took her hand.

Alex nodded. She'd take any help she could get. It was always easier to get another job when you had one, not when you really needed one.

The next day, she entered the henhouse and all the chickens flew down and approached her like they'd been doing ever since she started popping the corn. She reached in the bucket and felt a surge. All the kernels popped at the same time. They flew everywhere, all over the floor, the nesting boxes, all over her head and shoulders, and even on the hens. The hens pounced. Frantic chaos ensued as they tried to get as many pieces as possible. The demon hen paused and eyed her. Alex swiped at the front of her clothes, leaned over and shook her head, and brushed her shoulders off. Anything to get the popcorn off. She could just picture the hen jumping on her and searching for some plunder.

As soon as she'd finished, the hen resumed its search and destroy of the other pieces. Alex breathed a sigh of relief. She checked her clothes one last time and removed a couple of pieces she'd missed.

After they finished with all the chores, Steve approached her and turned her around. He picked something off her back and showed it to her. "Where did you get this?" he asked, holding up a piece of popcorn.

She shrugged and walked back into the cabin. There wasn't any way she could explain it to him. Maybe he'd forget about it or figure she'd brought some popcorn back from Peter's. If he insisted on knowing, that's what she'd tell him—it was from Peter's.

Chapter 11

Most mornings now, Alex had an arm draped across his chest when they woke up. She would try to pretend she hadn't done anything and quickly pull her arm back while he wished for more. He would grin which would make her flush. She was definitely getting better with the chores though. This morning she actually volunteered to help spread the hay around the barn and relocate any unused bales. He wanted to see how she'd cope with the heavy bales. She started by using half of an open one so she had a full bale left to move over to the others. He knew she wouldn't be able to actually lift the bale of hay. It was a struggle for him. Curiosity made him slow down and take a lot more time to clean Anna Belle's stall. What would she do? Would she lose her temper? Immediately ask for help? This would be interesting.

Alex walked over to the bale, placed her arms around it, and tried to lift. Nothing. She took a couple of deep breaths then tried again. This time the bale twitched. After several more tries, she let go and kicked the bale once. She turned around and sat down on the bale.

He lowered his head to be below the top slat of the stall. This way he wasn't clearly visible but could watch her every move.

Alex slowly scanned the barn, occasionally

stopping on one item. She'd shake her head then continue her search. She'd disregarded the obvious pitchfork.

She probably wouldn't know how useful it could be.

She got up, got the empty wheelbarrow and an unused two by four and shovel. She tipped the wheelbarrow down next to the bale, shoved the shovel under the opposite edge, pushed down, then kicked the two by four in the gap. She used the board to get the shovel under the edge of the bale. She practically lay down on the shovel's handle before the bale started to turn. On her first attempt the bale rotated but kicked the wheelbarrow away. On her second try it ended up in the wheelbarrow.

She smiled and started whistling once the bale was in the wheelbarrow. Even with the wheelbarrow, she struggled getting it to the other end of the barn. A couple of times Steve raised up slightly when it looked like she might slip and fall. But she'd regain her balance and start shoving again. Once there, she dumped it next to the other bales and shoved until it ended up right in line. She brushed herself off and headed inside the cabin to get ready to go to Peter's.

Anna Belle stood at her stall's opening watching Alex's every move. Steve moved over to Anna Belle and started to brush her down. He leaned over and whispered in the cow's ear. "That was entertaining. She sure has gotten a lot better at the chores. Maybe she should stay here for a little longer."

Anna Belle turned her head and nudged Steve with her nose.

"I know, I know. No women." He continued to

brush Anna Belle's side and started humming. When he started on the other side, he whispered again. "Shame though. She might be worth trying to figure something out." Anna Belle nudged him again. "Okay, I get the message. I'll keep my distance." Shame though. She was one great looking woman, even bending over a bale of hay. He was comfortable around her, and for the first time he could open up and talk with her. He trusted her. He'd do anything to help her. *And hell, I want her*. He'd been taking more cold showers lately. But it sure would be enjoyable to kiss her again and maybe even—

Anna Belle leaned against him, almost knocking him over. He concentrated on finishing brushing her then went inside for another cold shower.

****

That afternoon they went over to Peter's again for lunch. Alex had packed up her toiletries and a change of clothes. Today she was going to take a long hot shower. She could get clean with a quick rinse, but she missed being able to soak under the hot pounding spray. The moment she got there she took off for the guest bathroom. After she'd turned into a beet, she got out and dressed. Now this was the way to live out here. She looked around the guest bedroom and had to admit that she liked Steve's place. It might be simple, but it fit him. She couldn't picture him living comfortably in a place like this.

She headed downstairs and stopped in the hallway when she heard her name. She took a step back into the stairway, unable to stop listening.

"You know, I'd be more than willing to have Alex stay here," Peter said. "I have a lot more supplies and she'd be more comfortable."

"No," Steve said. "I like having her with me."

Some dishes rattled, covering up part of Peter's comment. "At the end she stayed with him."

"I know, but that can't happen."

"Why not, man? You deserve to have someone."

"You know I can't because…" More plates clattered. "But for now, I enjoy her company."

"Just don't get too involved. I don't want to see her get hurt."

"I know… You spoil these cats rotten."

Why couldn't he be with someone? They started talking about other things so she moved down the hallway. When she entered the kitchen, two tabbies were sitting on the island watching Peter fixing a salad. Every so often he'd toss them a piece of carrot or cheese which they'd catch. She managed to catch a glimpse of a white fluff ball before it took off for the other part of the house. She took a seat next to Steve at the counter. "How many cats do you have?"

"Three," Peter answered. He pointed to the gray tabby, "This is Minerva and the tan one is Albus. You just missed Misty, she's really bashful around strangers."

"Why did you give them those names?"

"I didn't, Caroline did. She's a big fan of the boy wizard."

"Then why Misty?"

"You know, that book about the ponies on the island. She names all the animals after book characters," Peter added.

"I haven't let her in the barn or she'd have all my chickens named," Steve said.

"Did you enjoy the shower?" Peter asked.

"Yes, thanks," Alex said.

"Your hair really looks good." Steve reached over and fingered a strand near her face. "It smells like apples."

"It helps when I can use a hair dryer." Alex blushed but didn't move away from Steve.

"Maybe it would be worth getting a solar panel." He barely brushed her cheek with his finger as he released her hair.

Alex's breath quickened as she watched his eyes soften.

Peter missed the interaction as he finished the salads. "That's what I've been telling you. Your guests could get a reasonable shower if you had one."

Alex looked away and focused on the cats. Steve got up and went around the counter to collect the salads. He carried them over to the table and held out a chair for Alex. She went over and sat down. Steve lingered a hand on her shoulder then sat on her left. Peter sat across from them and chattered on. Steve's leg moved over to touch Alex's leg. She licked her lips and quickly picked up her fork. Alex didn't hear much of what Peter said as she concentrated on the sensation of Steve's body against hers. Steve moved his foot so it crossed hers as he listened to Peter.

After the salads were finished, Peter collected the dishes and fussed with the chili on the stove. As he dipped up the bowls, Alex slipped her left hand on top of Steve's leg. He reached down and placed his hand over hers until Peter approached with the bowls. Then he repositioned his napkin so it covered her hand. Alex gently squeezed her fingers and turned to face him for a moment and he smiled. She tried to engage more in the conversation but was too distracted. After they'd finished the chili, Steve moved his right hand down to his lap then over to Alex's thigh. His warm hand crept upward and her breathing increased. Her body responded with heat and moisture at her core. She could see his nostrils flare as he took a deep breath, as if he could smell her arousal. She wanted to move his hand onto her, but this wasn't the time or place so she jumped up and started clearing the chili bowls.

"Why don't you pick out some ice cream for us," Peter said.

"Where is it?" Alex asked.

"Out in the freezers with the rest of the food."

Alex went out to get some. The first freezer she opened was packed with all kinds of frozen dinners. The second freezer contained the meat, milk, eggs, and other ingredients. She pulled out a tub of chocolate chip and brought it back in. She opened the tub, and Steve reached around her with the scoop.

"Let me," he whispered, his breath teasing the side of her face.

She ducked under his arm and collected the bowls that were already set out. She held one up as Steve transferred the ice cream.

"Chicken," he whispered.

"You bet...I'm not sure—" she whispered back.

"Not sure that you'll enjoy it?"

"It's not that."

"I know it isn't." He paused for her answer.

She held up the second bowl.

"You're stalling."

She nodded, "I'm not sure that we should when we're living together."

"When then, if not now?"

She shrugged and held up the third bowl.

"Stalling again."

She nodded and took the bowls back to the table.

Peter returned carrying a folder and laid it on the table. "Here's the information I have on the solar panels. It'll give you an idea of how much it'll cost."

Peter and Steve leafed through the information and Alex savored her ice cream. Maybe he was right. Why not? She was attracted to him, had been all along. She had been looking for someone normal. Maybe he's the one? She glanced around Peter's house. Would she really want to give up all the comforts and live in a cabin like Steve's? She paused with the spoon half-way to her mouth. If that's where he was, then yes. The comforts weren't all that important. She'd lived most of her life without electric. But could she keep her magic a secret? She took several more spoonfuls. *If it means being happy, you bet.* She set her spoon down in the empty bowl. When she looked over at Steve, he quickly glanced at her and smiled. She'd have to see how it went.

Steve interrupted her thoughts, "We need to get back. A storm looks like it might be moving in."

Alex nodded and carried the bowls out to the kitchen sink.

"I know. Why don't I have a party?" Peter looked at Alex. "You could meet everyone and they might have some ideas on a new job."

"That'd be great," Alex answered.

"I'll get everything set up. Next week we'll have a lunchtime potluck," Peter said. He helped Alex get her coat on and handed her her bag. "Come back whenever

113

you want to get another shower." He smiled at her. "I like having company."

"Especially when it's young women." Steve nudged Peter's shoulder.

"Well, it doesn't hurt. I like women."

"I know you do." Steve looked at Alex. "He wouldn't mind having you stay here so you could get to know him."

"Of course I would," Peter added. "You'd be more than welcome anytime."

"I'll keep that in mind," Alex said, "but I'm fine for now."

Peter touched Alex's arm to get her to stop while Steve headed out. Peter whispered to her, "Watch yourself. Don't get too involved, he's a heart-breaker. I've never known him to date anyone more than a dozen times."

"I'll be careful," Alex quietly said. She headed out to the snowmobile.

"My offer is always open," Peter called from the door. "I put something special in the pack for you."

Steve helped Alex on the snowmobile. "Over my dead body," he mumbled.

"I heard that," Alex said into his ear right before Steve started the engine.

When they got back to the cabin, Alex was hanging up her gear when Steve entered. He moved closer, then closer still. Alex backed up until she was against the wall. He put an arm on each side of her, pinning her there. "You didn't answer my question."

Alex tried to look oblivious, "Which question?"

"The one about us." He moved his body against hers. "About if we should or not."

"Oh...that one."

Steve moved his face within inches of hers, their mouths almost touching. "Think about this." He kissed her, tenderly at first then with his heart and soul. She slid her arms under his coat and encircled him, pulling him closer. He let out a low growl in his throat and kissed her even more intently. His tongue searched and claimed hers. She could feel her magic curling around his, something—like a type of flame—pulling her in even closer, igniting a fire inside her. Her whole body craved for him to take her, claim her. He stopped after a few minutes and leaned his forehead against hers. Her heart pounded as well as his. "I know you want me. Why are you resisting?"

"I need more time," Alex said. "I'm just not sure."

"You'll let me know when you decide?"

"Definitely."

Steve pushed himself away. "Anna Belle's probably waiting to be milked."

Alex nodded. Steve hung up his coat and headed for the barn. Alex leaned against the cold wall for a few minutes until her heart slowed down. She did want him, but she couldn't decide. She felt comfortable with him and trusted him. What else could she want? She wandered over to the fireplace and added more logs. When the fire crackled merrily, she curled up in the chair and wrapped a blanket around herself. She pretended to be engrossed in her book when Steve returned. He didn't say anything but read for a while before going to bed. Alex got as comfortable as she could in the chair. No way was she sleeping in the bed tonight, or she wouldn't be able to resist him. His smell and warmth made her feel like she'd found a home.

And she didn't want to go there until she'd decided to.

Chapter 12

The next morning, Alex unloaded the pack. She placed the canned goods on the shelves in the storage room and pulled out a bag from the bottom, containing those heavenly drops of chocolate wrapped up in silver. She couldn't remember how long it'd been since she'd even had a hot chocolate. The chocolate had taken away some of her cravings for a soft drink. Then she had become obsessed with chocolate. She'd dreamed about sinking her teeth into a luscious candy bar for ages. She wouldn't be picky, any would do, and now she had a bagful to savor. Steve didn't have any type of candy, especially not chocolate. Who could go months without savoring a bit of candy melting in your mouth? It wasn't normal. The longer she spent here, the more accustomed she'd become to the quiet, but she would fare even better with chocolate. She carefully opened the bag and ate three pieces. *Heaven.* She gently placed the bag on a shelf and sighed. By pacing herself, she could last a long time on the bag.

For the next few days, the snowstorms picked up again. Alex stared out the ice-covered glass. If only she could get outside for a few minutes to get a lungful of crisp clean air. Snow had fallen all day, only stopping when night fell. The landscape consisted of dark gray shapes. There was a sliver of light far off down the valley. She didn't think she could see Peter's house

117

from here.

She waited, watching for any movement, any animals, anything, any signs of life. The light started to climb into the sky. It was only the moon.

She watched for several more minutes, enjoying the way the moonlight lit up the scenery. Everything turned golden as a large harvest moon slid up above the trees. The moon would be full within the week. A winter wonderland filled the valley, like something out of a fairy tale. She watched, half expecting a unicorn to wander out of the trees. She was going bonkers. *First it was the crazy hen, now unicorns. Really? Bears, maybe.* She'd been spending too much time inside. She took one last look as the moon shrank when it climbed higher in the night sky and went back to read.

The next morning, she trudged out into the barn to get her chores done. For several days now, she'd been accidentally changing the chicken's corn into popcorn. They loved the stuff. While they chased the white puff balls, she could easily collect all the eggs. Even the demon hen wasn't giving her as much grief lately, but it still stalked her whenever it got the chance. As if on cue, all the hens flew down off their perches and clustered around her feet when she entered the coop. She slid her fingers into the bucket of corn and took a deep breath.

Nothing.

Not even a single pop.

What could be wrong? She should know better by now. When had anything gone as she'd expected? Everything she tried ended up being a comedy of errors. All the hens stood there without uttering a single cluck, turning their heads this way and that on the chance they'd missed something.

She slipped her hand out and tried again. She concentrated. Why couldn't she figure out how to do this? It wasn't exactly a difficult piece of magic. She never did it on purpose, but her magic sometimes erupted without being summoned. The slick kernels slid between her fingers. Still nothing.

"Oh well," she told the hens. "Sorry, girls."

She grabbed a handful and scattered the grain around the floor. All the chickens eyed the kernels but didn't move. They looked up at her again. She tossed more handfuls out. They looked at the kernels again, then wandered away.

"Now I'm disappointing the chickens." She emptied the rest of the bucket and left.

After getting done in the barn, Alex started shoveling the front porch. When she finished, she leaned on the shovel and looked around at the vast white space and shuddered. The absolute silence unnerved her. Not a single car, dog bark, or snow blower to break the quiet. It was unreal, like she'd stepped onto an alien planet devoid of life. *Great.* Now she was thinking about alien planets. It was bad enough that she'd been thinking about unicorns last night. At least she knew that unicorns did exist, but alien planets? Maybe they existed too, after all, there were authors who spent their days dreaming up these possibilities. She'd be content to read about it all, tucked in a comfy blanket in front of a blazing fire. Tomorrow she'd get to talk with her mom again. At least that would vary her day.

The next day it only drizzled a few flakes, so they took off for Peter's. As Alex rode with her arms around

119

Steve, she realized how much more comfortable she felt around him. They were talking more now that they'd fallen into an easy friendship. Maybe there was even more, if his kisses were any indication, but she didn't want to go there yet. She needed time to sort out her feelings. So many changes were happening in her life, but he felt so right. Maybe she should take a chance and find out. He'd been touching her more often and so was she, as if they had a connection they didn't want to sever. And he was always nearby or at least watching. She shifted her hand on his chest and he put his gloved hand over hers as they traversed a flat stretch. She settled a little closer to his back and tightened her arms around his chest. When they reached Peter's, he took her hand to help her off and kept hold of it as they walked to the door. He paused and brushed some snow off her coat and knocked.

Peter opened the door moments later. "Glad to see you again. Hey, why don't you fill up your snowmobile while Alex and I get set up?" Peter said to Steve.

"I should be okay." Steve shuffled.

"Come on, you're feeding her and giving her a place to stay. Let me do this to help out."

"Okay." Steve headed back to the snowmobile.

Peter helped Alex out of her gear, and they headed back to the radio. "I'll be ready in a few moments," Peter said to Alex.

Alex nodded while he contacted his friend. When her mom got on, Alex said, "How is everything?"

"I picked up your last check and cleaned out your desk. That boss of yours isn't too bad of a fellow," her mom answered.

"He's a good man, just couldn't do anything

more."

"Well, your last check was big. It should cover your part of the rent for a good six months. So I don't want you to rush getting back. How's this person you're staying with? Is he a good man?"

Alex looked over to Peter, who was busy sorting through some files. She answered, "Steve's a good man...he's been taking good care of me."

"I recognize that tone. Be careful, I wouldn't want you to break your heart. He might not be the right sort of person for you."

"That doesn't matter and you know that." Alex shifted in her chair.

"You know I've never agreed with this experiment of yours. You shouldn't deny who you really are."

"I know, Mom. You've made your position perfectly clear."

"Okay. I just want you to be happy."

"Even with a normal, everyday sort of man?"

Her mom paused. "Even then. But take your time and be sure."

"I will," Alex answered.

They talked for a few more minutes about the rest of the family. At least everyone there was going on with their lives.

As they closed and said their goodbyes, Alex added, "No birds. I don't want to see a single pigeon. We'll talk later."

Peter thanked his friend and disconnected. "I have to ask about the birds."

"It's a joke between my mom and me," Alex said.

Peter nodded and leaned back in his chair. "So what did you do for work?"

"I used to do technical writing. The company got contracts with other manufacturers to write their manuals for them."

"And now you spend your days taking care of livestock and reading. Do you like to read?"

"I love to read, but I couldn't do as much as I'd like with all the hours I worked." She settled back in the chair. "Guess I have time now."

"I've got an idea. You need to talk with the Gibsons. They work for a book publisher. As long as they have power, they write their own books or help edit others. Maybe they could put in a good word for you."

Was this too much to hope for? "Do you think they might be able to help?" A glimmer of hope lifted some of her worry about finding a new job.

"Can't hurt, they'll be here for the party. As long as we get a clear day so everyone can travel," Peter said.

"Does the snow ever stop out here?"

"Yeah, eventually. The forecast looks like it's starting to break up and we should get more sun."

"I can't wait."

They both got up and walked back out to the kitchen.

Peter nodded. "You're not the only one."

Steve put his magazine down and strolled over to join them. "What's up?"

Peter said, "We were talking about the Gibsons. They might be able to help her get a better job."

Steve reached over the counter and snagged another vegetable. He pointed a celery stick at Peter. "That's a good idea." He moved the celery around to point to Alex. "Have you ever considered editing manuscripts for a job?"

He had to be kidding. Of course she had. Just the thought of becoming an editor was beyond her wildest dream. What a job that would be! How could she approach them? A short story. She'd write a story to ask them to read after the party. She grabbed Steve's arm. "I've got an idea. We need to get back." She rushed to put her coat on.

Steve looked over to Peter. "Something you said must have inspired her. I haven't seen her look this happy since she got stuck here." Except after they'd kissed, she sure smiled then. He snarfed the celery down before she left without him.

Chapter 13

As soon as she got back in the cabin, Alex hurried over to the bookcase where her computer bag was being stored. She started to pull the computer out, paused, then slid it back in. There wouldn't be enough time to get done before the battery died. Instead, she removed a pad of paper and pen. It felt so odd to be using pen and paper. She started jotting down possible story ideas. A man and woman, snow, love, hens, and several other random words. She scratched through half and then pondered the rest. For the rest of the night, she added and subtracted ideas.

The next morning, she still hadn't settled on anything as she headed out to the barn to get the chores done. The demon hen wandered out of the door the moment she'd opened it. It strutted back and forth in front of the door, looking for something to pounce on. Without thinking, Alex waved her hands to shoo the hen back into the henhouse. There was a slight pop and the hen disappeared. *Now what have I done?* Steve looked over from his milking, and Alex pretended she hadn't heard a thing. She carried the bucket over to fill it with corn. Trying to ignore Steve's looks, she entered the henhouse and looked around. The demon hen wandered around with the others as if nothing had happened. "Man, that was lucky," she said. The hens all waited for their popcorn which Alex still couldn't produce. "Sorry girls, only kernels." Convinced that they weren't getting anything special, they hopped back into their nesting boxes.

Alex approached the nicest hen and reached in. The hen ignored her. She tried some of the other nice hens with similar results. Alex worked through the nice birds to the meaner ones. None of them attacked. "At least some good came out of the popcorn. You don't mind me now." Only the demon hen remained. She moved over to its box and looked at the hen. The hen's beady eyes were watching her every move. "Should I trust you, or should I get the oven mitt?" The demon hen continued to eyeball her. Alex reached her hand in and the hen didn't peck. She closed her hand around the egg and eased it out. The hen continued to watch her. Alex held up the egg. "Thank you." The hen gave a single cluck, but still watched her every move. The moment Alex got through the door, she leaned against it and let out a sigh of relief.

She proceeded to fill the water buckets and clean. A faint pop sounded and the demon hen was wandering around in the barn. Alex shooed the hen back into the henhouse and got back to her chores. Moments later she heard another faint pop. She shooed the hen back again. "You"—she pointed her finger at the watching hen— "stay in here." She went back out to the barn and rushed through the rest of her work before the hen decided to make another appearance.

Alex worked the rest of the day on her story and took a break when Steve went out to do Anna Belle's evening milking. She stroked Anna Belle's neck while Steve milked. "I was wondering how Peter can afford all the gadgets and gear he has. Is he really that good?"

Steve looked at Alex then looked back down. "He's that good. The man's a genius when it comes to writing an interesting computer game. His fans anxiously wait for his next game to get released. But he did inherit some money. That money gave him the chance to work on his own. He lived in a cheap broken-down apartment and never went out. Especially when he was working on a project. I got him to invest his money and finally move out here. He does a lot better here; he's not as obsessive. Now he works more normal hours and gets out among the neighbors. You saw how he checks up on everyone. You wouldn't know it but he's a millionaire already." Steve looked up at Alex. "Are you going to be more interested in him now?"

Alex avoided looking at Steve. "No, I was just wondering about him." She picked up the brush and started brushing Anna Belle. "I'm not interested in him."

"Good," Steve whispered.

Alex brushed for a few minutes in silence. "How'd you meet?"

"As a prospector, I spend the summers collecting aquamarines and smoky quartz like my mother did. We met at one of the gem shows where I sell my specimens. He bought some of my crystals and we started talking."

"So why doesn't he have a significant other?"

"He's shy around women, and they aren't attracted to him enough to give him a chance. He's a great guy once you get to know him."

Alex nodded. "I get that. I would have given him a chance; he's a nice guy. If I hadn't met you that is."

Steve stopped milking and stood up. He reached

out for Alex's arms and pulled her closer. The moment she was close enough he kissed her. As he plundered her mouth, she reached out to grab the front of his shirt. She was instantly on fire. They kissed until Anna Belle shifted, breaking them apart. Steve continued to look at Alex, his eyes never leaving hers. "If Anna Belle wasn't between us, I'd do more, a lot more."

Alex nodded and took a step back.

"Have you decided what you want yet?"

"Not yet," Alex whispered. "Everything is so different."

"Different good or different bad?"

"Definitely good." She moved a few inches closer and placed her hands on Anna Belle's back.

Steve clasped both of her hands in his. He brought them up to his mouth and gently kissed the palms. He breathed in deeply then looked at her. "This whole situation might have been the weirdest twist of fate ever. I know we shouldn't get involved but I want to make love to you." He lifted one of her hands up and ever so gently swiped her palm with his tongue.

"I know," she answered. She'd never had a palm licked in her life, except by an animal. It might seem like the weirdest thing in the world to do, but it felt so...so intimate. Her body heated up and tingled all over.

Steve inhaled deeply. "You want me too, admit it." He teased her palm with a slow stroke.

She closed her eyes and moved closer. Her pulse raced as she imagined what it would feel like to have his tongue working on other places of her body. Damn, but she wanted him, all of him. She almost moaned.

"Kiss me." His breath tickled her ear.

Without even realizing it, she had already moved her head close to his. She placed a hand on each side of his face and kissed him with all she had. She entwined her fingers in his hair and deepened the kiss.

His hands found the side of her chest and slowly slid up.

Anna Belle moved so much they broke apart.

They were both breathing hard and focused their eyes on the other.

"I'll wait until you're ready."

Wait? What was he talking about. She wanted to wrap her legs around him, even here in the barn. She wanted to be as close as she possibly could. Why would she want to wait? Oh yeah…that whole normal versus magic thing. For once she regretted her common sense forcing its way into her mind. She hadn't completely decided to live a normal life yet; until then she needed to wait. Alex stepped back, "Yes, we should wait." She strode back into the cabin before she changed her mind. Even after Steve went to bed, Alex continued to work on her story. She had to slow things down. She couldn't risk being near him tonight, not if she wanted to wait.

The next day Alex kept her distance. She took care of the hens and was making good progress on cleaning the barn. A faint pop happened and the demon hen was sitting on her shoulder. Alex screamed, grabbed the hen, and tossed it away. The hen remained stock still for a minute then shook. All of its feathers were standing straight out. Alex eased over to it and reached out a hand. The hen didn't move, so Alex used a finger to stroke the feathers down. The second her finger moved away the feathers popped straight out again. "Oh no," she groaned. She sat down on the nearest bale and the hen jumped up into her lap. Alex started stroking the feathers down. "I'm so sorry. I'd never want to do this on purpose. I'm surprised you don't hate me for this."

Just at that moment Steve walked back out into the barn.

Alex placed both hands around the bird and turned to try and hide the poor creature.

Steve stopped and looked. "What the hell happened"—he pointed to the hen—"to its feathers?"

He'd seen the hen so there wasn't any use in trying to hide it any more. She let the hen go and it jumped up to her shoulder. The hen's talons gently squeezed Alex's shoulder. "I...I...don't know. I looked up and the hen looked like this. Must be static electricity. I'm sure they'll eventually flatten out again."

Yeah right, I am so full of it. I can only hope the feathers will flatten again. Otherwise there's going to be one strange-looking chicken.

Steve walked over and reached out and stroked the hen. The feathers popped straight out again the moment his finger released them. He tried a couple of times, but nothing changed. The hen continued to sit on Alex's shoulder, head up high. "Isn't this the hen you refer to as the demon hen? Why is it perched on your shoulder?"

"I guess she likes me now." Alex petted the hen and it extended its head even higher.

Steve shook his head. "I thought you and the hens didn't get along?"

Alex held her hands straight up in the air and rotated them. "No more oven mitt. I guess we needed some time to get used to each other." Actually, it was the popcorn that won them over, but there wasn't any way she could tell him that.

"What is going to happen next?" He shook his head and got busy milking.

The whole time Alex worked, the hen remained on her shoulder. Several times, the hen would lean forward to get a better look at what Alex was doing. Before Alex went back into the cabin, she gently lifted the hen down and placed her back in the henhouse. She'd no sooner shut the cabin door when there was a pop and the hen was on her shoulder again.

Alex lifted the hen down and held her with both of her hands. She looked the bird in the eye. "I guess I'll have to start calling you Houdini Hen from now on. I sure don't know how this happened. I've never heard of any spell like this." She turned the bird to look at each side. "Maybe it's you. No, that can't be. There's no such thing as a magical hen." The hen clucked a couple of times. "You're enjoying this, aren't you?" Alex shook her head. "You can't keep doing this. This popping up out of nowhere. Steve will notice."

Alex eased the door to the barn open and poked her head in. Steve was still busy milking. She snuck across the barn with the hen. When she'd placed the hen back in the coop she whispered, "You have to stay here. I'll let you ride on my shoulder whenever I'm doing chores. Okay?" The hen just looked at her, so she shut the door. Alex slipped back into the cabin and breathed a sigh of relief. "What will that hen come up with next?"

Mandy looked at Alex and thumped her tail.

Chapter 14

Sunlight streamed in the windows for the day of the party. Alex had helped Steve prepare some deviled eggs the night before. They rushed through the chores, only doing the minimum so they could leave earlier. Alex pulled out her nicest shirt and sweater. She took extra time putting her make-up on and doing her hair. Steve was ready in his usual amount of time. How could men get ready so fast? Alex pulled a pair of sweatpants on over her jeans so they wouldn't get wet. They loaded the snowmobile with the eggs and some milk and headed to Peter's.

As they drew nearer to Peter's house, Alex could see some type of shape made out of a large mound of snow in front of his door. When they got closer, it became more distinct. A long tail appeared and disappeared in the snow leading up to his house. A large fanged head rose up in front of the walkway and shone in the sunlight. A long heavy body stretched out behind the head with plates on its back. Then the scales along the body came into focus.

"A dragon. He's made a dragon out of the snow," she shouted even though the snowmobile drowned her out.

Steve parked the snowmobile with the others outside the snow sculpture. To enter the house, you had to walk through the dragon's gaping jaws. "Now this is something else. How did he do this in so short a time?" she said as she ran a hand over the sculpture.

"He's got way too much time on his hands and likes to go all out for a party." Steve handed her the food, stowed their helmets, and they headed toward the dragon's jaws.

Alex reached up to touch one of the fangs jutting down. "It feels like it might snap the moment we enter and swallow us like helpless prey."

Steve took her hand and gently pulled her into the gaping jaws. "I can't wait to see what he's done inside. He usually carries the theme on. Maybe we'll be knights saving a princess or something gory like entering the dragon's stomach."

She shuddered at the thought of being in a stomach. The idea of knights and princesses would be so much more appealing.

Peter greeted them and took their coats after they'd put the food on the kitchen counter. A row of dishes was already spread out. There was the traditional green bean casserole, tuna casserole, several other veggies, some finger food, and a cake with blood red icing. At the end was a bowl of ice cubes with several different beverages. All the ice cubes were different colors, making them look like large raw jewels or crystals. Peter came back after depositing the coats, carrying crowns cut out of gold paper. He placed one on each of their heads. "Welcome to the feast, Lord Davis and Lady Klein. We will be observing the rules of the gentry." He bowed to them. "Welcome to the castle of His Highness."

Alex giggled and Steve nudged her. "He means it. The rules of the party," Steve said.

"So we have to say lord and lady all night?" Alex managed to contain her fit of giggles by concentrating on fixing a drink.

Steve nodded and started fixing one for himself. "And don't forget His Highness."

Peter took her under his wing and introduced her to the other valley residents. He introduced the gay couple, Daniel and Henri. They had a large greenhouse attached to their home where they grew fresh produce which they shared with the others. They were always laughing and telling jokes, the life of the party. They didn't have to work after inheriting some money, so they spent their time with their vegetables and orchids.

Alex choked on her drink when Peter introduced her to Victoria Vickens and William Dickens. They always went by their pen names. He was a bronze sculptor while she was an oil painter. They were retired but still sold their work for some extra money for summer vacations. Being a sculptor, he could repair metal and she helped decorate their houses.

Peter finally steered her over to Emily and Vincent Gibson. The children, Thomas and Caroline, begged Peter to let them play a computer game. He took their hands and led them back to a computer to get them set up. "Peter, er His Highness, was telling us that you lost your job and were looking for something better," Vincent said.

Alex told them what she'd been doing at work and her college education where she'd majored in English combined with some business.

"He mentioned that you might be interested in doing some editing. I can put you in touch with our editor. They're always on the lookout for good people.

I'll see what I can do."

"That would be fantastic!" Alex answered. "Peter mentioned that you both also wrote."

"I've written a few children's books." Emily touched Vincent's arm. "Vincent helped me get published with his company."

"What about you?" Alex asked Vincent.

"I've written a few action novels, but I really enjoy working with writers getting their manuscripts ready," Vincent said.

Emily leaned closer to Alex. "He's written twelve so far and is working on number thirteen." She patted his arm. "You're too modest."

"I'll see what I can do. After all, no harm no foul," Vincent said.

Steve joined the group. "I see you've met the Gibsons."

Alex said, "Mr. Gibson—"

"Vincent please."

"Vincent was telling me what he did," Alex said.

Emily giggled. "I'm sorry, Steve. I can't get used to seeing you without that face full of wild whiskers. Especially in the winter. I don't think you've ever shortened your beard in the winter before."

Steve stroked his chin. "I thought I'd make a better appearance for Alex."

Emily winked at Alex. "He did this for you?"

"How long are you usually trapped in the valley like this?" Alex asked, trying to deflect attention from her warm cheeks.

Alex had asked this of the others and the consensus was that they didn't feel trapped. They all said that they enjoyed the solitude and peace. The general agreement was from between two to three months before they could venture out.

"How do you go that long without any outside contact? You must have families you talk to?" Alex asked.

"Oh, we have contact. We all have at least one solar panel for electric so we can e-mail and visit with our families. Only Steve here doesn't have a panel," Emily said.

"I was going to try and get a panel this summer if I find enough worthwhile crystals," Steve said. "I like to consider all options carefully as to if I really need them or not."

Peter called them all to the feast. After eating, Caroline cornered Alex.

"I saw a unicorn the last few nights," Caroline said while tugging on one of the ears of her stuffed cat.

"A real honest-to-God unicorn?" Alex asked.

Caroline looked around to see if anyone was paying any attention. "Yup. He was all white with a long horn, just like you see in all the books."

Alex knelt down so they wouldn't be overheard. "Cross your heart and hope to die?"

Caroline nodded. "But no one believes me. They think I imagined it."

"Why?"

"Cause I'm always reading about unicorns, dragons, princesses, princes, elves, fairies, and witches." She looked up at Alex. "Why do so many of the witches get a bad deal? Why can't they all be pretty like Glinda?"

"Maybe they are. Did you ever consider that? Maybe they look just like you and me," Alex whispered.

"That'd be so cool. If only I was a witch, like the boy wizard."

"You like those wizarding books?"

"They're my favorites. Do you like them?"

Alex nodded. "I know, since no one else believes us, why don't we make a pact?"

"What kind?"

"We swear that we'll only talk about this, you know, the unicorns and all, with each other."

"A pinkie swear?"

Alex held out her little finger and Caroline hooked hers around it. "I swear," Alex said.

"I swear," Caroline answered back.

"So where did you see this unicorn?"

Caroline looked around again to see if anyone was paying attention. "I saw him at the edge of the trees across the valley. But each night he was a little closer to here. If he goes much farther, I won't be able to see him."

"I'll keep an eye out for you. If he keeps on moving down the valley I might be able to see him."

Caroline's face brightened up. "You'll tell me if you do?"

Alex held up three fingers then crossed her chest with them. "Cross your heart and hope to die?"

Caroline's brother dashed over and pulled her away to play another computer game. Steve moved over and held out a hand to help her up.

"You two were having some chat," he said.

"Girl talk, that's all."

"I think you have another fan there. If it wasn't for all this snow, she'd be riding her bike down to see you

136

every day."

They visited a little longer. Sunset was fast approaching, so everyone got ready to leave. Alex and Steve thanked Peter for all his help and the great party. They headed out to leave. The sun lit up the snow that covered the mountain's ridges and crevasses as it sank behind the top edge. As they rode back, Alex rested her head on Steve's shoulder, arms snug around his waist. His warmth was a delightful contrast to the crisp air.

In some ways it seemed like only yesterday when she fought the snow driving in here, but a month had already passed. In other ways it felt like it had been a lifetime ago. So much had happened since she'd entered the valley.

Fingers of deep shadows already stretched across the valley. They bounced over a ridge, and Alex squirmed around enough to look back at Peter's house. All his windows were still ablaze with light, casting yellow streaks across the now dark blue snow. She could barely see another snowmobile heading off down the valley. The shape became a bouncing ball of light as it got farther and farther away. The moon wouldn't rise for another hour, so the landscape quickly darkened as they got close to the cabin.

Thank goodness Steve knew where he was going. His cabin was a black shadow among the folds of dark blue snow. She shivered as she remembered when the cabin's light had gone out and she could only locate the cabin by looking for a dark shadow. One thing certain, she'd make sure she'd never be in that predicament again. Mandy's faint barks grew stronger as they approached the cabin.

Chapter 15

Now that they were getting some sunny days, Peter started stopping by for lunch. At first they played cards, but Peter always won. Alex couldn't figure it out until Steve whispered to her that Peter could remember every card that had been played. From then on, they played board games where everyone had a fair chance. At night, she would look out the window, but there wasn't any sign of the unicorn.

One night they got another heavy snow. The next morning Alex went out to shovel the porch off after she'd finished her chores. She'd just finished and was leaning on the shovel to enjoy the view from the yard. Mandy was bounding across the snow drifts enjoying the freedom.

An ominous creaking sound echoed around the area. She looked around trying to figure out the source of the sound.

Nothing obvious.

The creak sounded again. A clump of snow fell from the porch. She looked up as another creak sounded. The snow on the roof moved. *Shit. I'm right under it.* She tried to get her muscles to move but they refused to respond. *Too late.* The snow headed straight toward her. The mounds slid down the tin roof, getting closer and closer. She took a flying leap to try and get a little farther away. It didn't work. Of course not. She'd never been good at sports.

The snow knocked her to the ground. She'd managed to maintain a pocket of air around her face with her arms, but she couldn't move. "Damn," she muttered. "I never had a chance. I swear this storm is out to get me. One way or another."

She took a moment to wiggle her legs, get a little bit of space around her body, to get some air. She couldn't move at all. She had to do something. Anything. Anything that might let her hang on long enough.

Steve must have heard the avalanche. He'll find me. He has to.

The cold started seeping into her limbs.

No one is coming. "Help," she uttered. It became harder to get a breath.

What she wouldn't give for a fresh breath of air. She didn't want to end up under a pile of snow. She wanted to get married and have some children.

She had to relax. Anything to give her a few more seconds, seconds that might matter.

When you think about dying, you come up with so many possibilities. Getting lost in a jungle, being attacked by a tiger, car accident, getting involved in a bar-room shoot-out, or getting shot walking down the street. She never envisioned being buried under snow off a roof.

The small air pocket around her face looked smaller and smaller as the seconds passed. The feeling of helplessness had to be the worst. If she had an arm free, she could at least try to dig. Being trapped like this, she could only wait while her air ran out.

Life's too short. There were too many things she

wanted to do yet. Find a job she enjoyed, find a man to share her life with, even something as simple as going to Hawaii.

Relax.

She had to slow her heart-rate down to give her a few more seconds.

If only Mandy would find her. She kept thinking, *Lassie, go find Timmy,* in the hopes that maybe Mandy could pick up her thoughts. You never know what dogs were capable of.

But no. No one was coming. She was beyond feeling light-headed.

She thought one last time, *I don't want to die.*

Everything faded to black.

****

Steve finished his chores and was headed around the barn to help Alex finish shoveling. Mandy was barking up a storm and frantically digging at a mound of snow. Steve glanced around but didn't see any sign of Alex. She wouldn't have gone in without clearing the pile in front of the porch. Then he noticed the foot sticking out from under the mound.

He ran for all he was worth, dropping the shovel as he got close.

Mandy barked only every few seconds now as she concentrated on her digging.

Both of Alex's feet extended out from under the snow. He grabbed them and pulled as hard as he could, but she didn't budge.

He patted the snow next to Alex's body, "Here girl, dig here." He patted the snow again.

Mandy left the top of the mound and moved to where he'd indicated.

Steve grabbed Alex's feet again, planted his feet and pulled, and pulled. He could feel a slight shift, then another. He strained even harder and Alex started to move an inch at a time. "Hurry girl! Get it!"

Mandy continued to concentrate on the space she'd created, sending snow flying out behind her.

Steve took a deep breath and heaved. Alex started moving. He repositioned his feet and used his weight to help pull. Alex's torso finally cleared the mound, then her head. Steve gave one final pull and her arms came out. He dropped down to his knees and flipped her over. He yanked off a glove and searched her neck for a pulse. It was there. Faint, but there. "Good girl, Mandy, let's get inside."

He lifted Alex and dashed up the steps and into the house. Mandy dashed in after him and he kicked the door shut. He laid her on the floor, his hands trembled as he felt her wrist again to check on her pulse. It beat stronger now, but her skin felt so cold. He pulled all her wet clothes off, carried her into the bathroom, and laid her in the tub. Then he turned the warm water on. As the tub filled, he yanked off his coat and shirt, and crawled in behind her. His legs shook but he scooped the water over her cold skin, and gently rubbed her to get her circulation going again. She jerked, hitting him in the face. He wrapped his arms around her to keep her from hurting herself.

"Alex," he said. "It's okay. You're safe."

Alex jerked one more time.

"You're safe."

She relaxed her muscles.

"Open your eyes. It's okay. You aren't under the snow."

She stirred. "No snow," she whispered.

"No snow, you're inside now."

"No snow," she said and went limp in his arms.

He pulled her up against his chest and continued to rub her limbs and torso. Her body was so cold. The incoming water was starting to cool so he leaned forward to turn the tap off.

"Feels good."

"Are you starting to feel warmer?"

Alex nodded.

"Good, you'll be warmer in a few minutes."

Alex reached out and laid a hand on his twitching leg. She rubbed the jeans material between her fingers. "You have clothes on. In the tub."

"I didn't want to take the time to take them off."

"Why?"

"Do you remember what happened?"

Alex shuddered. "Oh yeah, the snow. Hold me."

Steve wrapped his arms around her and leaned his chin on her shoulder. They sat like that for a couple of minutes.

"Thanks for saving me. It seems like you're always saving me." Alex rested her hands on his forearms. "The way I'm going you might have to again."

"I'll save you any time you need me to." The water was starting to cool down. "I'd better get you dried off before you get cold again." He helped her up, dried her off, then went and got a blanket to wrap around her. "Go on out to the table, and I'll make you a cup of tea." He peeled off his wet clothes and wrapped a towel around his hips. He bustled around the kitchen getting the tea made.

"How did you find me?" Alex finally asked.

"Mandy. If it hadn't been for Mandy I wouldn't have found you in time." Steve handed her a hot cup of tea. "You're lucky she found you and helped dig you out."

Mandy pushed against Alex's leg. Alex ruffled her ears. "Thank you, Lassie. You found Timmy."

"What?"

"It was something I was thinking about." Alex pulled the blanket closer. "Even wrapped up like a cocoon, I still feel cold. The hot tea should help." She shuddered. "For a moment there I thought I'd died." She squirmed and shifted her position. "What made you look for me?"

"Mandy was barking nonstop. She never barks that much." He blew on his tea. "I knew something was wrong. Then I saw a foot and saw Mandy frantically digging. Only your legs were showing." He kept looking at the surface of the tea. "I was afraid I had been too late."

Alex moved around the table and put a hand on his shoulder. "I don't want to talk about it anymore."

Steve stood up and searched her eyes. Then he reached up to touch her cheek. Alex tilted her head against his hand. He kissed her gently and paused, then kissed her again. All of a sudden, he stopped. "I'm sorry. I'm supposed to wait."

"And I wasn't supposed to even be here. Or am I?" She pulled him into a tight embrace and continued kissing him.

After several minutes he shifted back, "Are you sure you want to do this?"

Alex slid the blanket off and let it drop, "I'm sure." She kissed him again, then led him to the bedroom. She tossed the covers back and reached for his towel.

He put a hand over hers. "Are you really sure?"

She pulled the towel loose and tossed it, then climbed in the bed and held out her hand to him. "I've never been more sure of anything in my life."

He took her hand and climbed into bed. After making passionate love their bodies were warm all over. Steve only left to milk Anna Belle and bring them some sandwiches for dinner, then crawled back under the covers. They spent the rest of the evening curled up next to each other reading. Earlier than usual, Alex closed her book. She snuggled up against him and started running her hand slowly over his chest. She moved her hand down to his stomach and started easing it lower when he grabbed her hand.

"All right, I'll quit." He laid his book on the bedside table and extinguished the light. He wanted to fulfill her every desire and then some. He moved over on top of her. "Is this what you want?" He started kissing her neck.

"Yes," she murmured as she encircled him with her arms and legs, pulling him closer.

He pulled away slightly, "We haven't known each other for very long."

"Long enough, now shut up and make love to me."

Later that night, they finally fell asleep after exploring every inch of each other.

Chapter 16

The next morning, he awoke to find her back pressed against his chest, and some new feelings. He was hungry and his hunger wasn't for food. He was hungry for the sensations she had awoken inside of him. While making love to her, he had felt completely content and satisfied. And to say nothing about how wonderful his flame felt entangled with hers. This was something he'd never get tired of experiencing. No other woman made him feel like she did. There was a special energy he sensed when they were joined. He still wanted to feel himself inside her, to please her, and for her to want him as much. These moments were precious, he seldom risked being with someone for fear of not being able to leave.

Without realizing what he had been doing, he had started to gently run his fingers around her chest and ended up massaging her breasts and nipples. Her silken skin made his fingers tingle, especially her nipples. They reacted to his slightest touch, becoming hard and wrinkly. Last night when he had enclosed them with his mouth, a surge of pleasure shot through him. He wanted to protect her and love her, to have her as his own. She let out a pleasurable sigh, rolled over onto her back and slid her hand down. Her fingers sought him out then slowly wrapped around him. He didn't know how such a simple action created so many responses, at least

145

when she was the one closing her fingers.

Her hand started moving up and down. As he swelled, she stopped for a second.

He didn't want her to stop.

She slid his hand down and spread her legs giving him easier access. She trailed her fingers back up taking him back into her hand. Then she started kissing and licking his neck. This was new for her, but he liked it.

He inched his finger in and found her ready for him. He eased his finger out then back in. When he started to speed up he could feel her tighten around him. She groaned and bent her head back. The sight of her reacting to him made him hard. He had to have her, take her, claim her as his. The moment he pulled his hand away, she clasped him tighter to her and wrapped her legs tightly around him. He grabbed a condom and struggled to rip it open. He rolled them over and slipped the condom on. She slid down, welcoming him inside. *Heaven*. He could feel her in a way he'd never experienced before. He struggled to remain in control as he enlarged even more. She slid down, then quickened the pace. He didn't want her to stop. She let out a hungry groan, then cried out as she reached her peak. Unable to hang on any longer, he thrust in hard, as she pulsed around him. The real world spun and he gasped in ecstasy. He wanted the moment to last as long as possible, but she obviously had other plans. She claimed him, body and soul. At first, he thought he might have been reacting to lust, but then he realized this wasn't lust but a feeling of truly wanting her. He wanted to be with her, not just for sex, but to be with her for a long time. Maybe even for the rest of his life. She smiled and sighed then drifted off to sleep again.

He gently caressed her arm wanting to keep touching her.

Never before had he felt this way. Had he fallen in love with her? In another couple of weeks, he would want her to stay and never leave. The idea of marriage and children even started sounding great. All of the women he had become involved with before made him want to run away, especially when the relationship started turning serious. This was one of the reasons he was living among the mountains. Always before he had wanted solitude, but not now. Now he found himself wanting her to stay here with him. He actually enjoyed her company, even when she was going stir-crazy from being trapped inside. If she stayed, he would make sure she never felt cabin fever again. On the snowy days, they could stay inside and make love. Although, he would have to start stocking a lot more condoms. He'd have to ask Peter for some at this rate. Peter kept a good supply of everything else so he probably had a supply of condoms too. His only other option was abstinence, and he considered that as only a last resort. He wanted to spend as much time with her as possible before she left. Time was running out.

The road crews should be digging out the pass shortly. After that they would be able to get through on the snowmobiles and she would leave. She had a life to get back to with her friends and family, and he would be left here. Because of the downed power and phone lines, he wouldn't even get the chance to talk to her until early spring. This was the first time he felt lonely while living here. He was going to miss her smiling face from across the dinner table and miss her fresh scent of roses and apples after a shower. Heck, he even liked the way she smelled after finishing chores, but he especially liked how she smelled while making love with their scents co-mingling. He was going to have to convince her to move in with him.

But who was he kidding? He couldn't put her life in danger. She had to stay away. He'd have to make sure she did before things became any more serious. For today, he'd relax and enjoy life like a man, then the realities of his life could intrude. He'd like nothing better than to have one last go. But after what they just did, he only had a few condoms left. He was going to have to be careful. She'd almost had unprotected sex with him. That couldn't happen again or he'd never be able to let her leave, and then he'd really be in trouble.

He glanced at the bedside clock. Anna Belle was waiting to be milked. He looked at Alex's peaceful expression and decided to let her sleep in. Yesterday had been a bad day for both of them. He slid out of bed making sure he didn't wake her. He only did the necessary chores and let the rest of the tasks wait until tomorrow. He kept thinking about what it would be like to have her living with him. He'd have to make the cabin more comfortable and larger. Currently the design worked well for him, but he would need more storage for two and some solar panels for electricity. She should be able to have a decent hot shower and dryer. She'd probably also need a more reliable phone and Internet connection so she could work from home. But he wasn't being realistic. She wouldn't be staying. He finished quickly so he could bring her breakfast in bed before she woke up.

He paused at the door to watch her sleep before waking her. He leaned over and gave her a gentle kiss.

"It's time to wake up." He handed her a shirt. "Slip this on and sit up. I have a surprise for you." He went out to get the breakfast tray.

Alex looked at the bright light then quickly glanced at the clock. "You let me sleep too late. There are chores to do."

"Not today," he said while bringing the tray in. "We deserve a day off."

Her mouth watered at the sight of the scrambled eggs. She bolted the food down.

"Hungry this morning?"

She nodded as she stuffed her mouth.

"I guess we did work up an appetite last night and this morning."

"This morning? I haven't been awake yet. How could we..." Then something tugged at her thoughts, but that was only a dream. Or was it?

He smiled as he remembered the morning.

Her fork clattered on the almost empty plate. *Oh no.* She hadn't been dreaming. She had actually fondled him and more. She started to blush, "I'm sorry."

"For what?"

"For attacking you."

He smiled even more. "I'm not. I enjoyed your actions tremendously."

She picked up the fork and continued to shovel the eggs in so she wouldn't have to say anything. How embarrassing, she'd molested a man while asleep. When she glanced up he was still watching her and grinning. She kept her eyes on her food until she'd cleared the plate.

The moment she finished, he moved the tray back to the kitchen. She slid down into the covers to try and hide.

"Toss me the shirt," he said when he got back.

Without hesitating she removed the shirt, tossed it to him, and slid farther under the covers. She could hear him undressing. Then she heard a slight tearing sound. "What are you doing?"

He started to slide under the covers, "I thought you might want to refresh your memory. I want you to remember every detail as well as I do."

"Did I really do that?"

"Every little bit. I think you did exactly what you really wanted to." He slid his cool hand across her chest. "Let me show you how wonderful it was." He took her hand and slid it down as he kissed her breasts and nipples. When he moved up to kissing her neck and mouth, he slid his hand down. She played the dream back through her mind and passion overwhelmed her. They re-enacted the morning's events leaving them sated and relaxed. As they cuddled, he whispered in her ear, "Now do you remember?"

"Yes." She sighed. "When did we become so connected?"

"I'm not sure. I think our feelings for each other have been building these last few weeks, but we've been ignoring them."

"Everything is happening so fast," she whispered back.

They both remained quiet as they showered and dressed, each lost to their own thoughts. Steve and Alex both thinking that this relationship couldn't go any farther than it had. They'd just have to settle for the memories of their time together.

Chapter 17

She had to find some kind of distraction. She'd watch for the unicorn Caroline saw. It was probably the girl's imagination, but at least this would give her something to do until Steve fell asleep. He'd been trying to distance himself all day, finding excuses to go to the barn. It was almost as if he was afraid of hurting her, but she couldn't figure out how he could. Still, she should also distance herself before things got out of hand.

Being together for one night could be written off as a reaction to her being trapped under the snow. To keep being intimate would be something else. If he fell asleep before she went to bed, they wouldn't be tempted to make love. Distance herself, that was the ticket. After all she didn't think they had a future. He lived out here, cut off during the winter, while she enjoyed the hustle and bustle of the city. She enjoyed snow, but this was too much with day after day of being stuck inside.

She waited and waited as the clock slowly ticked away. The moon would rise in another hour. The clouds were breaking up and the moon should be visible. She would need that light to search the landscape. As the time approached, she used the excuse that she wanted to brush Anna Belle to relax and work out her muscles. She slipped out into the barn and without even thinking snapped her fingers to light the lantern. She retrieved the stool and placed it near the window. The lantern threw too much reflection on the window so she lowered the wick as much as possible and looked back outside again. The moon rose, casting a glow over the white landscape.

Several minutes passed before she noticed some branches moving in the trees on the far side of the meadow. A unicorn stepped out into the meadow. Its coat shone in the harvest moon's intense light. It really was a unicorn, Caroline wasn't imagining him after all. If anyone else had seen him, they would think they were imagining things. She knew better. She pressed her face up against the cold window to get a better look. Yep, she could make out his horn when it glittered in the moonlight.

A wild unicorn. She'd never seen a wild one before, only the ones at Aspen Glen, a semi-tame herd that wandered around the magic school's protected grounds.

But here? Why would there be one here? She remembered learning that they were attracted to nights with full moons and magic. Could it have been attracted to her? No, her magic wasn't that strong.

Did it come into the valley to avoid the heavy snow? But there were people here. Unicorns avoided people like the plague.

No, the reason had to be magic.

There might be a magical artifact in the valley. If so, she had to find it. Magic that strong couldn't land in the wrong hands. She'd have to find a way to stay here longer. Maybe the snow storms would keep up and she'd be stuck here a while longer.

The perfect excuse, but she still had to get outside alone to look. She couldn't let Steve see her using magic. She watched for a while before the unicorn disappeared back into the trees.

All the next day she took longer than usual to get her chores done. The speckled hen enjoyed spending more time with her. Every day now the hen would ride on Alex's shoulder as she went about her chores. Steve never commented as he was taking longer too. When she tried to read, her thoughts kept returning to the unicorn. Why it was here and what it was looking for? She'd have to go out there and look. Before that, she could watch and figure out if he was staying in one area or wandering aimlessly around. She'd have to watch again tonight. But first, the weather had to clear up a little. With the blowing winds, the snow would be flying everywhere making it impossible to see all the way across the meadow.

The mantel clock ticked away the seconds. The evening inched along, doing nothing for her nerves. There would be another full moon tonight and the winds had abated for the time being. The last time she glanced out the cabin window, the constant snow had eased up to a few flakes. She wanted to look out again, but that would be too obvious. Steve would ask questions. Questions she didn't want to answer.

It was too early anyway. The unicorn wouldn't appear in the meadow until the moon did. Until then he would remain concealed among the snow-laden fir branches. Would he even show up again? Maybe last night was only a fluke? But then Caroline had seen him for several nights.

Without moving her head, she glanced up at the

clock again. Another hour and a half to go. How could she get Steve to go to bed by then? She needed some time to watch the meadow, without him noticing.

The clock ticked on.

She couldn't think of anything. Some type of excuse to go back in the barn without Steve wondering why she was spending so much time there. She could use Anna Belle as an excuse again. Enough times and she'd create a pattern of going to see her, but that wouldn't work for tonight.

She rolled her eyes up to the clock. Only a few minutes had passed. She tried to get involved in the book she was reading. The clock's ticks filled the room. Even the crackling fire seemed quiet in comparison. She looked at the book again and reread the paragraph. She must have read the same paragraph at least five times.

Mandy got up and sat down right in front of her, laying her muzzle on her leg. Alex reached out and scratched behind her ears. Mandy shook her head then lay down.

Alex looked down at Mandy and Mandy looked back. *I swear that dog can read my mind. How did she know what I needed?*

Alex got up. "Go ahead and go to bed. I'm going to go play catch with Mandy for a while. Alex and Mandy went out to the barn. Alex tossed Mandy's ball for a while to kill time. "Sorry girl, but there's something I need to do."

Mandy dropped the ball and started to sniff around the barn.

Alex watched her wandering around. "You must be able to understand me."

Mandy ignored her.

"Oh well, I need to get ready." She lowered the light and carried the stool over to the window. After climbing up, she rubbed the frost off the icy pane. Just in time. The moon was starting to rise. She carefully scanned the trees around the meadow.

Nothing moved.

She watched the area where she had spotted the unicorn last night on the off chance he had settled in. If he was still searching, he would have moved on by now.

She shifted from foot to foot as she watched. She froze. *Was that a small cloud?*

She swiped her hands across the glass again, placed them on the panes, and moved her face closer. *There it is again.* A branch moved, knocking a cloud of snow off. His white face and horn stood out against the black branches. He had stayed in the area; there must be something here. Whether she wanted to or not, she'd have to stay, at least until she found whatever had drawn him here.

Each night she played toss with Mandy and continued her vigil. She'd spotted the unicorn every night. Something was drawing him in. Five days and she hadn't been able to get outside. All it did was snow. She was sick and tired of seeing nothing but white. What she wouldn't give to see green grass. If the unicorn hadn't been wandering around, she'd never have seen him.

As she watched for him, she made a mental note of where he spent his time. So far, he'd concentrated on an unusually thick copse of fir trees. That's where she'd have to search. Getting away from Steve would be problematic.

Then there was the deep snow. She'd have to learn how to use the snowshoes. Her excuse could be that she'd always wanted to try them. Walking to the trees would give her a lot of practice. She hadn't seen another pair of snowshoes anywhere so Steve couldn't go with her, and she'd get the chance to be alone.

Then she could use her wand to search for a magical power source. She'd have to work fast; she couldn't risk Steve seeing anything. Secrecy, that was the wizards' creed. She had to avoid exposing magic to Steve. He wouldn't understand; the powerless never did. She had a plan if only it would stop snowing so she could get outside.

The next day the snow lessened. After finishing her usual chores, Alex headed out to shovel the porch off. She'd worked her way down the steps and removed some of the top layer of where she guessed an approach walk would be. As she worked back closer to the porch a clump of snow fell down on her. She leaned the shovel against the handrail, brushed the snow off, and grabbed the shovel. Another clump of snow fell off the roof covering her shoulder. Again, she set the shovel aside and brushed the snow off.

As she started to reach for the shovel, a movement out of the corner of her eye distracted her. She jerked around. Steve stood off a ways with his hands tucked behind his back.

Alex called out, "What's up?"

"Nothing." He shrugged.

"What are you doing?"

"Just watching."

"I'll be done in a minute. Do you need some help?"

"No, I'm finished."

Alex started to turn back to reach for the shovel when he threw something at the roof. She looked up at a section of snow headed straight for her. It plastered her head and shoulders, working down inside her coat to hit her skin. She spluttered and frantically brushed the snow off her face. She turned. Steve still held a snowball, trying to keep from laughing.

"You did that, didn't you?" She tossed the shovel aside.

Now she could clearly hear him laughing.

"That isn't funny. You covered me with snow. It's cold. It's inside my coat." The more she complained the harder he laughed. He could be so frustrating. She extended her arm and pointed a finger at him. "This is so not funny. Just you wait."

That's when she felt it. Her energy exploded out her finger and hit Steve in the chest. He stood there a moment, stock still, staring at her. In the next second a "puff" broke the silence with an explosion of snow. As soon as the snow cleared, a brown bear stood where Steve had been a moment before.

The bear turned and started to run for the other side of the valley.

"Wait! Don't run away. I can put you right," she yelled at the retreating bear.

The bear plunged through a snowbank, paused, and shook, flinging snow everywhere. Then it resumed running for the far trees.

"I'm sorry," she called out, but the bear was now too far away to hear. "I can turn you back," she mumbled.

Or can I? Now she'd really done it. She didn't

157

know what to do.

She watched for several more minutes but didn't see any sign of the bear. It would be sunset soon. She headed back in the cabin and pulled a kitchen chair up to the front window. She sat and watched until darkness fell, but he still hadn't returned.

Mandy nudged her arm.

"Sorry, girl. Guess I'd better get the chores done." She headed out into the barn and started working.

Anna Belle leaned against her. Alex stroked her back. "I've really done it this time. I changed Steve into a bear. I didn't mean to. It just sort of happened."

Alex got the bucket, filled it, and brought the water bucket back to the stall. "The worst thing is...I don't know how to turn him back. I could go get someone who could, but I'm stuck here. I don't know what to do." She finished and went back inside the cabin. She curled up in a chair, wrapped a blanket around herself, and fell asleep while reading.

The next morning, she still didn't see any sign of Steve until she went out in the barn to get the morning chores done. He was working away and acted as if nothing had happened. The magic must have worn off and he shifted back. Maybe he didn't even remember what happened.

At breakfast she had to find out if he'd been okay. "Where were you last night?" Alex asked.

Steve fussed around setting out pans and dishes before answering. "I spent the night in the barn."

"Why?"

"Anna Belle didn't look quite right. I wanted to be there if she needed anything." He started cracking eggs in the skillet.

"Is she okay?"

He set the dishes and silverware on the table. "Looks so." He went back to the stove to check the eggs. "Hurry up and shower or the eggs will be cold."

He didn't say anything else, so Alex headed in to shower.

Steve watched her leave then whispered to Mandy who was lying close by. "What am I going to do? I can't put her at risk. I'll need to find an excuse to get out of the cabin to think. Peter would take her in. Maybe I'll have to ask him to before it's too late." The water shut off, so he went back to finishing breakfast.

Chapter 18

Steve rushed cleaning up the morning dishes and tried to ignore Alex. He couldn't figure out why he'd become a bear. The animal in him had started stirring ever since making love to Alex. But it wasn't awake enough yet for him to have shifted. As soon as he'd finished, he grabbed the snowshoes and explained that he needed to check on some traps he'd placed out among the trees. But that was an excuse; he wanted to get away from Alex so he could think. He noticed her watching out the cabin's window as he strode across the meadow. He always thought he knew how he'd live his life. Alone. Away from civilization so he couldn't harm another person.

Then Alex crossed his doorstep. She'd changed everything.

Now he wished he could spend the rest of his life with her.

But how could he? He'd be a threat to her whenever he turned into his bear.

He trudged deeper into the woods. The drifts forced him to expend more energy. He could feel the animal within him trying to wake up. It was too early, he should have until spring before he'd shift. Maybe if he got exhausted enough the beast would go back to sleep. He wanted this time with Alex before he had to say goodbye to her. Once spring arrived, his life would become too dangerous for her. It was hard enough keeping his livestock safe.

At least Mandy seemed to sense the danger and stayed inside the cabin at night. Alex wouldn't. She'd want to spend evenings on the cabin's porch, then she'd be in danger. He couldn't take the chance that he might harm her.

No. He had to break it off, get her to return home. When she left, he'd be lost in the darkness of his life. She'd become his light. But all that didn't matter, he had to keep her safe, at all costs. He wandered among the trees for several hours until he felt drained. After returning, he did only the necessary chores, fixed a simple dinner, then crawled into bed.

****

All day while Steve was out, Alex paced. She kept thinking about what she would do when she got back home. The fickle finger of fate offered her a chance she needed to take. She might be able to leave by hopping a ride on the snowmobile, taking a risk with the weather; or she could wait until it had cleared up more. She'd already lost her job and her brother was taking care of her dog Vladimir, so why rush? Maybe she could take this time to figure out what she wanted to do with her life. She liked being involved with writing and books, but never saw herself penning her own. Maybe something involving a magazine or publishing, but what? And she still wanted to find the unicorn. At least when Steve came back, he went to bed early. Tonight, she'd be able to watch from the comfort of the cabin, sitting. Steve had thankfully headed to the opposite end of the trees, away from the area where she'd been seeing the unicorn.

161

The next day during chores, she asked if he would show her how to use the snowshoes so she could stretch her legs. He showed her how to fasten them on and she must have been some entertainment. She tripped and fell with her first steps, but she refused to let him help. After going for a while, she started to get the hang of walking in them.

Alex trudged across the meadow struggling with the unfamiliar snowshoes. After only going a third of the way across she had to stop to catch her breath. Steve made it look so easy, he just plowed on across the meadow. She looked at the firs on the opposite side of the valley. They seemed to be even farther away than when she started.

She leaned over as she tried to breathe the thin air. Each breath burned from the cold.

"This isn't working," she said. She lifted her head and studied the snow-filled meadow. "I'll never make it."

She turned and started retracing her tracks. At least it was a little easier. Part way back she stopped again. *I have to get over there*. The snowmobile would be too noisy. She didn't want to frighten the unicorn. That only left magic.

"Why?" she asked the sky. "I've been doing so well. Twenty-three days and no magic." At least not on purpose. There had been those mishaps though. She turned around and looked at the distant trees again. "I'll just have to do a little spell."

That was the problem.

She'd been relying on magic for too many things. If she ever wanted to live among normal people she'd have to do better. She turned back to the cabin.

"Doesn't matter. I have to find out where the unicorn is and what he's found." She plodded on back.

As soon as she got close to the porch, she saw Steve standing there cradling a mug. "Did you enjoy your walk?"

She forced herself to smile. Of course not, but she couldn't let him know how much of a wimp she was. "I did. I want to go again tomorrow if the weather's like this again." *Yeah right, so freezing cold I can't even feel my ass any more.* But with a little spell she'd be able to stay warm.

Steve handed the mug to her and bent down to unfasten the snowshoes.

She looked into the mug, hot chocolate. She inhaled deeply. "How did you guess?"

"I know you like chocolate."

"In any way, shape, or form. It's a woman thing."

"So I've heard." He smiled, helped her step out of the snowshoes, tapped the snow out, and set them next to the front door. "You want to go out again tomorrow?"

She took a drink and nodded. "It felt good to walk."

"I bet."

"Why?"

"I've never seen anyone walk like you did." He grinned.

"I know. I amused you again." She forced herself to walk normally up the steps and into the cabin. After setting the mug down on the table she hung up her coat. "It was good to get out." She picked up the mug and headed into the barn to get the evening chores done. Last thing she wanted was for him to see how stiff she was. He stayed in the kitchen and kept working on dinner.

The next morning, she could hardly move, but she wasn't going to be defeated by a pair of shoes. She fussed around until the cabin door clicked shut. To make sure he was out of the cabin, she poked her head around the bedroom doorframe and scanned the room. The coast was clear. She rushed to the closet and pulled her suitcase out from under the clothes. After plopping it on the bed and unzipping it, she reached inside the interior pocket and pulled out the bag that held her wand.

She loosened the drawstring and eased the wand out into her hand. Her magic reached out and melded with the wand. The rush of magic invigorated her. Why did she ever think she could live without her magic? It was a part of her very essence. If she became serious with Steve, she'd have to tell him that she was a wizard.

Something scraped across the living room floor. It was probably only Mandy, but she couldn't risk explaining about magic at this time. She slipped the wand in her sweatpants' waistband, put the bag back in the suitcase, and stored the luggage back in the closet. She spread the clothes back out. Once she was satisfied that the closet looked like normal, she headed out into the main room.

She looked around, but Steve was still out in the barn. She quickly slipped her wand into the wand pocket inside her coat. She headed out to the barn to quickly do her chores. After finishing up for the morning and showering, she donned her coat.

"Going out again?" Steve asked, looking up from his book. "What's so interesting?"

She headed to the door. "Nothing." She had to do better or he might follow. "I wanted to cross the meadow."

"That's a long walk."

"I know. I only got a third of the way yesterday."

"What makes you think you'll get any farther?"

"Well. It's easier walking on previous tracks."

He nodded.

"So the first third should be a lot easier. Each day I'll get farther across."

"I could take you over there on the snowmobile."

She had to remain focused. Convince him. "I know it's stupid. It's something I need to try on my own."

He continued to watch her then finally added, "Don't be too long or I'll come looking for you."

She smiled. "You'd do that?"

"Course." He started to get up but she motioned him to stop.

"Just stay comfortable, I want to do this without any help."

"You sure?"

She nodded and opened the door. "I need to prove to myself that I can do this."

"Okay. Holler if you need help getting the snowshoes on."

She waved as she headed out the door. The snowshoe's straps looked like a complicated mess, but she had managed yesterday.

"Oh, well," she whispered. "A little more magic won't make any difference. I've already failed." She pulled out her wand and used it to get the snowshoes on. After stepping away from the porch, she performed a spell to make herself as light as a bird. She figured it would now be a lot easier to walk across the snow.

She glided across the snow. Now this was a lot easier. She had already made it halfway across before she took her first break. Keeping her back to the cabin, she cast a spell to determine if anyone was watching her. Nothing, she was alone. At least now she could get the rest of the way across.

Without magic she would only have gotten a little farther before turning back. If she turned back today, she'd get back too early and he'd ask questions. It was either go on for another hour or she'd have to stop and wait. No way was she simply going to stand in the freezing cold.

She charged on toward the tree line. Today she needed to at least pick up part of the unicorn's trail. After hitting the trees, she studied the ground and moved farther down the valley. After searching for a half hour, she crossed a few faint hoof-prints. Tomorrow she'd have to follow them in under the branches. She was out of time for today.

She studied her surroundings so she could find this spot again. Nothing was immediately obvious except for a large boulder just barely visible. She started to head back when she thought about the snowshoe tracks. Her trail shouldn't be spotted by anyone out for a ride.

A little more magic wouldn't matter. She used a spell to obliterate her tracks part of the way back. There had to be some at least. When she neared the cabin, she removed the spell that made her light and trudged back the last bit.

****

As soon as she approached the cabin, Steve came out on the porch. He helped her remove the snowshoes.

"I missed you," he said. He moved close and maneuvered her back against the front door. "You were gone so long." He placed an arm on each side of her with his hands on the door, pressing her up against the wooden surface. He let his warmth seep into her. "Did you miss me?"

She had barely started to nod when he started kissing her.

He ravished her mouth, letting her rich taste fill his taste buds. Oh, how he enjoyed how she tasted and responded to him. His flame had instantly curled tightly around her energy, never wanting to let go. He moved one hand to stroke her hot face. Their hearts pounded away in the quiet. Then he felt it. The animal stretched, yawned, turned around, and settled back down. He had to stop before the animal awoke.

He broke away from the kiss and placed his hands back beside her. Leaning forward, he touched his forehead to hers. Under his hands, he could feel the gouges in the front door. A finger trailed along one of the deep grooves. The splinters and cracks were obvious through his thick gloves.

He needed to distance himself. But she made him react like no other woman had. The animal in him had never woken up this early before. Being involved with her had to be doing this.

He had to do it. He had to end their relationship to keep her safe.

She'd be leaving in a couple of weeks. That would make it easier. Or would it?

Damn, she was one hot woman.

But that would be taking the easy way out. No. He had to tell her the truth. She deserved to know why he was going to say goodbye. She would fight his decision, but he would remain firm. No backing down. This was too important.

She'd find someone else. Someone who wouldn't put her life in danger. If she stayed here he'd end up hurting her. The animal in him would want to be with her—do anything to be with her.

He traced a gouge in the door again. After all, he'd been responsible for these marks.

"We'd better get inside where it's warm."

She nodded, but he didn't move right away. He opened the door for her and helped her out of her coat once inside. She moved up against his back and wrapped her arms around him.

"How about continuing that kiss in the bedroom?" she asked.

He shouldn't, but oh how he wanted to. He was already hard from her simple kiss. Instinctively, he took a deep breath. Her perspiration from the walk tickled his nose, and her distinctive apples and arousal scents as well. She wanted him.

He flipped around and swept her up in his arms. He carried her to the bedroom where he tossed her onto the bed. He quickly worked at getting her pants off then moved up to nuzzle her neck. "I don't want to disappoint you." He slid away long enough to get a condom on.

"We still have our clothes on," she said.

"Not where it counts." He licked up her neck and shoved himself in.

"You feel so good."

He pulled out and shoved back in with a low growl. He didn't care if it might be a quick one, he needed to feel her wrapped around him.

They spent most of the evening curled up next to each other in bed reading. They only left to milk Anna Belle and eat. After setting the dishes in the sink, they returned to the bed so they could continue to caress each other and make love again before falling asleep.

Steve woke when his animal stretched, moved around, then curled back up. It was only four a.m., but he had to move away from her. He slipped out of the bed, grabbed some work clothes and headed out of the bedroom. Mandy shuffled out and whined. "Stay girl," he whispered as he threw his clothes on. He dashed out to the barn and started working. Shifting hay bales, hauling full water buckets, raking straw—anything to exhaust himself. He had to keep the animal asleep.

****

Alex stretched and touched the cold sheets next to her. The bed was empty. She flipped over and grabbed her glasses to see the clock. "Why didn't you wake me up?" she called out.

No answer.

Alex flipped the covers back, slid her legs over the edge, and ran into Mandy. The dog was plastered against the bed. "What's wrong girl?"

Mandy whimpered.

Alex rubbed her chest and gave her a last pat. "Shame you can't talk to me." She dressed and shuffled out to the living room. Empty. No Steve, no breakfast, so she headed out to the barn. "What's up? You didn't wait for me to help?"

He glanced up, "Go ahead and take your shower. I'll get this." He went back to work.

Alex shrugged and headed in to shower. At least

this way she'd get an earlier start on her hike. Would the hen ride around on Steve's shoulder if she wasn't there? Or would the bird be mad and peck her tomorrow? Today when she started out, she headed directly to where she'd been yesterday. She took a moment and pulled in a couple of deep breaths. The trees looked dark and forbidding. *I'm being silly. I can protect myself.* She pulled her wand out and held it in front of her. If anything attacked, she'd be ready.

She took a hesitant step in. Then another.

The trees lessened some as she got a little farther in. She continued to follow the tracks into the trees. The hoof trails crisscrossed back-and-forth the farther in she went. "This is hopeless," she mumbled. She sat down on a nearby granite rock to catch her breath. Within seconds her butt felt like a block of ice. She took a last look around the fir grove. "I'll be back," she called out. Only silence answered her and nothing moved among the branches. She trudged back the way she'd come. She'd have to come back after a new snowfall. At least with the way the weather had been, she shouldn't have to wait long.

Chapter 19

The next day, Alex hurried through her chores with the hen completely ignoring her. Once finished, she headed back to the area where she'd seen all the trails. The fresh snow last night had filled in all the old tracks. Nothing but smooth snow covered the ground. She wandered deeper into the trees letting a feeling inside her guide her steps. After a couple of minutes, the strange sensation increased. It was almost the way she felt when she met another wizard, different—but still magic.

The unicorn had to be close. She'd never sensed magic this strong, not even when she was at magic school. It had to be because of the lack of other people; people always seemed to create an energy all their own. Her senses hummed the farther in she went. Then she spotted a trail of only one set of hooves coming toward and going away from her. Finally, a trail she could follow.

She knew she needed to be heading back, but she couldn't pass up this chance. The trail wound deeper and deeper into the firs. The boulders got larger the farther she went. She had to be getting close to the side of the mountain.

More trails joined with the one she was following, all leading in the same general direction. Her steps became a little easier with the trampled snow, but exhaustion had settled in. Her legs ached and her breathing had been labored for several minutes now. The unicorn had to be close. She could feel the magic pulling her. After taking a pause to catch her breath, she continued on.

The trees became scattered among the boulders. A narrow trail wound around the large hunks of rock. After rounding a large boulder, a rock face loomed close. The trails all led to a dark narrow slit in the rock face. As soon as she'd gotten a stone's throw away from the crevice, she heard the pounding of hooves.

She stopped and took a couple of steps back.

The unicorn charged forward and stopped just outside. He snorted and huffed. His front hoof dug into the dirt and snow repeatedly, flinging it back.

Alex held up her hands and took several more steps back.

The unicorn tilted his head down and snorted, creating a cloud of steam.

"Whoa," Alex said. "I don't want to hurt you. I'll leave." She stepped carefully backward. The unicorn continued to stand guard, still huffing like a pit bull guarding his bone. She turned around and headed back through the firs.

How could she gain his trust? She trudged back across the meadow. How would you get a pit bull to accept you?

Treats. That was what she had to do. Bribe him. Tomorrow she'd bring a bucket of oats. He should like that. Alex hurried back as fast as she could, not lifting the spell on her until she was near the porch. She clomped in and went over to the fire to warm up.

Steve was sitting in his chair reading. "Did you

enjoy your walk?"

"Immensely. I think I'll go again tomorrow and maybe the day after."

"If you want exercise, I know of a way to do that here."

Alex refused to turn and face him, knowing from the heat in her cheeks that she had to be blushing. "I enjoy being out in the fresh air after being trapped inside for so many days."

Steve set his book down on the table. He moved close and rubbed his hands up and down her arms. He whispered into her ear, "If you want to slow things down, just tell me. You don't have to go out hiking every day to avoid me."

She turned around and wrapped her arms around him. "That's not it."

He lifted a strand of hair off her face.

"I enjoy being outside. Seeing all the snow, trees, and mountains. I don't get to see this in Denver."

"No, I guess you don't." He worked the edge of her ear between his lips.

"At the rate we're going, you're going to run out of condoms."

He pulled back and looked at her. "True. Next time I see Peter, I'll see if he has any I can have."

"I thought you said he didn't date much. Why would he have any?"

"A man can hope, can't he?" He kissed her neck. "I can warm you up better than this fire can." He started kissing her neck again.

"You only have two left."

He took her hand and headed to the bedroom. "Then I think we should pay Peter a visit tomorrow."

She had to bribe the unicorn tomorrow. "Why don't you go while I'm out taking my hike. I'd be too embarrassed to be around when you ask him."

"Sounds like a plan." He started undressing her. "We'll use one now and save the other in case it snows tomorrow."

That evening, they made a nest in front of the fire so they could snuggle while eating dinner and reading. Mandy insisted on lying against them on the blanket.

The next morning, Alex rushed through breakfast and chores so she could get an earlier start. The moment Steve turned his shower water on, Alex rushed over to the front door. She slipped her wand out of her coat and tucked it into her waistband. Without wasting a moment, she dashed out to the barn, Mandy close on her heels.

Mandy ran over and brought a ball back.

"Not right now, girl," Alex said to the excited dog. "I only have a couple of minutes." She looked around the barn and found a spare bucket tucked in next to the hay bales. Alex grabbed the bucket and took it over to the barrel of oats. She popped the lid off and poured scoop after scoop of oats into the bucket.

Anna Belle strolled out of her pen the moment the lid popped open. Alex carried the half-full bucket to the middle of the barn and set it down.

Mandy dropped her ball in the bucket.

Alex pulled it out and brushed the oats off the fuzzy ball. She tossed it away and Mandy bounded after it.

Anna Belle eyed the bucket and started to move toward it.

Alex spotted Anna Belle heading toward her, so

she snatched the bucket up. "These aren't for you," she said to the cow.

Anna Belle was determined.

"Okay, okay," Alex said. She circled around the cow and took the bucket to her pen. Anna Belle stayed close. Alex tipped some of the oats into Anna Belle's bucket and rushed back to the middle of the barn again. This time she didn't waste a second and whipped her wand out. "*Decresco*," she said and touched her wand to the bucket. She continued to touch the bucket as it shrank. Once it was down to the size of a ball she lifted her wand. She snatched the miniature bucket up before Mandy got the idea that it was a new play-toy. Alex tucked her wand back into her waistband and carried the tiny bucket to the cabin. She cracked the door to the cabin open and heard the water still running.

Mandy pushed through the door carrying her ball.

Steve would be finished in only a minute or so. She rushed into the cabin and pulled the brown bag she'd found earlier out of her coat. She slipped the bucket in and folded the bag over several times.

The water turned off.

Alex put the bag in her coat pocket, pulled her wand out of her pants, and put it back in her coat. She could hear Steve getting dressed, so she ran into the bedroom and started snatching some clothes. He would expect her to be ready to get her bath as soon as he'd finished.

"Why does Mandy have her ball in here?"

Alex headed out of the bedroom, trying not to rush. "I guess I missed it." Alex set her clothes down on the table, took the ball from Mandy, and walked out to the barn to drop the ball.

175

The moment she got back to the cabin, Steve said, "I could have done that."

"That's okay." She picked up her clothes. "It'll remind me to be more careful the next time." She went into the bathroom and pulled the sheet closed before he could ask another question. Or notice that Mandy didn't have her ball when they'd first come in. "Poor Anna Belle," Alex mumbled. With giving the unicorn some of the oats she'd have to give Anna Belle less or she'd run out too soon.

As soon as she was showered and dressed she said, "I think I'll pack a lunch and head out earlier today. I want to get a little farther."

"Are you sure? You were gone for several hours yesterday."

Alex nodded as she pulled out some food for lunch. "I'll get ready so I can get back sooner. You can take a long visit with Peter. I'm determined to make it all the way across today, so I'll be gone for several hours again." She headed into the bedroom and put a sweater on over her shirt. Steve was starting to wash the dishes when she came out. "I'll be back a little earlier today," Alex said. She put her hat on and started tucking loose hair in.

Steve walked over to her. "Are you sure you won't get too tired?" He took her coat off the hook and helped her into it.

"The sun is out and it isn't snowing. I want to enjoy this." Alex said as she fastened her coat.

"Keep a watch out for clouds. If you see anything moving in, head back."

"I know, the weather can change in minutes."

Steve removed the bar and set it against the wall.

"Be careful."

Alex headed out and removed the snowshoes out of the box next to the door. "Don't let all the heat out."

He shut the door.

Alex looked back and didn't see him watching out the window. She quickly slipped her wand out. She used it to get the snowshoes on and to make herself lighter. After putting the wand back in her coat, she slipped her gloves on and took off across the meadow. Today, she knew exactly where to go. She headed straight for the rock and through the trees for the unicorn's cave. When she got close, she slowed down and started to hum a simple melody. She passed through the last group of trees. The unicorn guarded the entrance.

He shuffled and pawed the ground.

Alex continued to hum and slowly pulled the bag out of her coat pocket. She unfolded the top and carefully pulled the miniature bucket out. She placed it on the ground in front of her.

The unicorn paused.

Alex slowly pulled her wand out, making sure to keep it pointed away from the unicorn.

The unicorn snorted and lowered his head. The tip of his horn pointed at her.

"*Amplifico*," she said and touched the bucket. Once it was full size, she laid her wand down and dumped the oats out.

The unicorn sniffed and raised his head.

Alex picked up her wand.

The unicorn pawed the ground but didn't lower his head.

She used her wand and shrunk the bucket back

down. Once she'd finished, she put her wand and the tiny bucket back in her coat. "Hope you enjoy the oats. I'll try and bring you some more tomorrow." She took a couple of steps back.

The unicorn sniffed some more and took a step closer.

Alex waved, turned, and headed off. She hummed again so the unicorn could hear her leaving.

The next day the unicorn stood there as she put the oats a little closer. He wouldn't let her enter the cave yet, but he wasn't making any aggressive movements. She did this again the following day. The day after that, she approached and he wasn't standing outside. What if he'd been hurt?

She paused a minute then entered the gaping black hole. *What am I doing?* Her instincts screamed. Wild animals could be hiding inside, waiting for some unsuspecting prey to wander into their lair. She shook her head. No. The unicorn was inside; he wouldn't let anything attack her. His magic called out to her. Normally she would use her wand to provide some light, but unicorns hate wands. They would allow wizards and young children to approach, only if they showed the proper respect.

She unfastened the snowshoes, propped them up against the rock face, and took a step in. Nothing happened. She took another hesitant step, then another. She took one glove off and reached out to touch the wall, running her fingers along the rough granite surface. The solid rock made her feel a little safer.

After another step, she touched fur. She dashed back to the opening and took a moment to slow her breathing. Once her heart had slowed a bit, she crept back in. This time when she felt the fur, she stopped and pulled the hairs off the protruding rock. She rubbed the coarse brown hairs between her fingers and noticed the musky scent of animal.

For a second, the scent reminded her of Steve, but that was stupid. It was only some bits of fur that some bear must have rubbed off as it moved through the crack. Of course some animal would use this cave as a home; these mountains didn't provide many holes large enough for a big animal.

"There is no reason to fear the darkness," Alex kept telling herself as she edged farther into the dark crevice. Her left hand's fingers trailed across the cold stone wall guiding her in. She kept trying to see but gave up for a moment and closed her eyes. There wasn't anything to see anyway. She shuffled her feet across the dirt floor, feeling for any change. The last thing she wanted was to step off a ledge or trip over a rock. With her luck, she'd trip over a rock and lose contact with the wall. Who knew how large the space was? Was it still a narrow passage or had it widened out into a large cavern? If she lost contact with the wall, she could wander around aimlessly and lose all sense of direction.

She patted her coat front with her right hand. Her wand was still there. If worst came to worst, she could use it as a light and find the way out again. It was a shame unicorns were so distrustful of wizards, or she'd already be using it. She kicked a small rock and on instinct she opened her eyes. A faint glow outlined the edge of a wall. The closer she got, the more shapes she could make out. The passage turned to the right. Alex paused and took a deep breath. The unicorn was in here, his glow providing the light.

"I'm not going to hurt you," she whispered. She didn't want to startle him. If he bolted, he'd run into her. The passage was too narrow for the both of them. She edged around the corner and with a couple more steps the crevice opened up to a sizable area.

The snow-white unicorn remained nestled against the farthest end of a slight ledge that ran along the left side. His coat cast a pale glow throughout the space. She paused when he snorted and shook his head.

Chapter 20

She'd found a wild unicorn here in the mountains.

She thought back to her lessons on approaching a unicorn. She bowed and waited. He snorted and bobbed his head, the signal that he'd allow her approach. She tried to approach slowly and held out the back of her open hand for him to sniff.

He snuffled her hand a moment then placed his muzzle under her palm.

She stroked his silky nose then moved over to the ledge to sit down. "So what brings you out here? I know it's not me."

He snorted, stood up, and pawed near a boulder.

Alex got up and moved over to the rock. The unicorn nodded his head again and again as he stepped back.

The rock he'd been lying against was smooth and in the general shape of an egg, a three-foot egg. Alex picked up some nearby leaves and used them to brush off the layers of detritus, thick dirt, and leaves. It must have been collecting junk for hundreds of years. She could feel the rock's hard surface. She let go of the leaves and continued to wipe the surface with her gloves.

The unicorn stepped closer and hung his head over her shoulder.

The light wasn't strong enough to see much of

anything. Using the unicorn's glow, she looked around the cave's space. An old-fashioned mining lamp sat on the shelf inside the entrance. She walked over to it and the unicorn followed her across the room, managing to keep his muzzle slightly above her shoulder. A box of wooden matches lay next to the lamp. She gently shook the lamp, sighing when some liquid sloshed around. She picked up the matches, carefully removed one, and struck it against the box. The unicorn huffed, blowing the match out.

She pushed against the unicorn's chest. "You need to take a step back."

He moved back a foot, shook his head, and pawed the ground.

She opened the lamp's glass door and struck another match, hurrying to light the wick before the unicorn blew it out again. Light flared around the space, sparkling off the quartz crystals in the rock walls. A pile of stones glittered over by the end of the ledge. She went over to look, picking up several of the stones to admire.

The unicorn nudged her in the back almost knocking her over.

"All right, already," she said and placed the stones back into the pile.

The unicorn nudged her again.

She moved back to the two large stones and set the lantern down on the end of the shelf closest to the stones. Using her gloved hand, she cleaned the majority of the dirt off the two rocks. The lantern's light reflected in the surface of the rocks. Alex picked up the lantern and moved it closer. The outside surface showed pieces of crystalline structures like a polished geode, except these crystals were over an inch long. The light danced along the facets and bounced off the walls.

She expected to see edges and points, but the rocks were as smooth as ice.

Alex took her other glove off and ran her fingers across the smooth surfaces. The closest rock was the midnight blue of deep ocean water whereas the second one was blood red. Both contained flecks of gold here and there among the spaces between the crystals.

The unicorn pawed the dirt, breaking the silence.

She stopped moving. *These rocks aren't cold. Could something be alive inside? Trapped inside the crystallized shell? Maybe even calling out that it can't get out?* But she couldn't hear them. Maybe the unicorn could and that was why it was hanging around. Just waiting for whatever waited inside to break free or hatch.

"Now that is a scary thought," she said to the unicorn.

The unicorn shook its mane.

"What could hatch from an egg this large?"

The unicorn watched her.

"A dinosaur?" she asked.

The unicorn shook his head.

"But as large or larger than a dinosaur?"

A nod.

"What could be as large as a dinosaur?" She reached out and caressed the surfaces.

No response.

She could feel an energy emanating from the stones. "Magical?"

A nod and foot paw.

Alex sat down next to the eggs and rested her hand on the midnight blue one. She thought about all the magical creatures she'd learned about in magic school. "Nothing I've studied lays an egg this large. It must be a creature that hasn't been around for ages."

A nod and whinny.

"What hasn't been around? A creature from folklore. Comes from an egg." She drummed her fingers, then traced a crystal's outline.

"What likes crystals and gold?" She looked at the egg's surface. "Gold," she murmured and thought for several minutes.

She snatched her hand away from the egg and sprang up. She looked directly at the unicorn. "A dragon?" she asked and watched the unicorn nod its head. She jumped back a step. "Shit. I thought there weren't any left."

The unicorn hung his head low.

"Don't tell me. This is the last pair." Alex put her hands on her hips and took a step closer to the unicorn.

He gave a slight nod.

She placed a hand on his neck and stroked his warm flesh. "I know it's not your fault. You just happened to find them."

The unicorn pressed his face against her chest.

"But why now? They have probably been here for hundreds of years."

The unicorn shoved her chest.

She took a step back. "Me? Why me?"

He nodded again.

She had to think. She wandered over to the ledge and flopped down. The wand inside her coat poked her in the chest. She took it out and laid it on the ledge next to her. The wood clattered in the quiet cave.

The unicorn looked over at the wand.

"I'm sorry. It was poking me." She picked the wand up and started to place it back inside her coat.

The unicorn moved to her and touched the wand with his nose.

"My wand?"

He nodded several times.

"I found the eggs because of my wand?"

He nodded and shook his head.

"Now that's just plain confusing. Which is it?"

He touched the wand and then her.

"I found them because I have a wand?"

He stepped back and pawed the ground a couple of times.

Then it dawned on her. She jumped up. "Because I'm a wizard!"

He nodded vigorously.

She walked back over to the eggs. "I must be the first wizard to have been in here." She looked back at the unicorn. "I would never have found them if you hadn't been here to lead me to them."

He sauntered over to her and looked at the eggs.

Alex looked down at the eggs and laid a hand on his neck. "What am I going to do? Principal Vale would know. He has to be the smartest wizard I've ever known. But it'll be several weeks before he can get out here to look at them." She pulled her hand back and looked directly at the unicorn. "Can you stay here and protect them until then?"

He nodded his head several times.

"It will be a while."

He nodded again.

"I'll see if I can somehow get a bale of hay and some oats out here. I'm sure you're having a hard time finding enough grass with all this snow."

He pawed the ground.

"Oh, I forgot." She pulled the miniature bucket of oats out, enlarged it, dumped the oats, shrank the bucket, and put it back in her pocket. "I'll make sure no one else knows where you are. But I'll have to use magic to get the food here; it's too heavy for me."

He nodded.

"I'd better cover these up again." She started scooping up the loose dirt and throwing it back over the eggs. It took a lot of work to get the eggs hidden again.

She brushed off her hands and clothes, then knocked the dirt out of her gloves. "All done." She placed the lantern back where she found it. "How am I going to see in the dark once I blow this out?"

The unicorn walked over to the entrance.

"Thanks. I'll follow you." She opened the lantern's door and extinguished the light. At first, she couldn't see anything in the darkness, then the unicorn's glow became more obvious. She followed him through the crevice and reached the cave's opening. Night had fallen.

"Shit! I'm so late. Steve has to be worried by now." At least there was an almost full moon, so she could see shapes. Following her trail back would be another story. She pulled out her wand and spoke the spell for it to generate a weak light.

The unicorn backed up into the opening.

Alex looked back at him. "I'll get some food here one way or another. See you later."

The full moon lit up the landscape, but the trees

cast deep shadows that stretched across her path. She used her wand to quickly get the snowshoes on and headed back along her earlier trail. Her wand's faint light helped her stay on course and not veer off. She was probably halfway back when the wind started to pick up. The snow-laden branches started dumping their load, obliterating some of her steps. She hurried as fast as she could before the path became lost. Then she had to stop. No more tracks. She took a few steps in each direction but couldn't find any tracks. "Now what?" she whispered to the creaking trees. The wind snuck in among the branches, blowing clumps of snow into her face.

She needed help, maybe the unicorn. She tried to whistle, but nothing came out. After cupping her hands around her face and blowing into them, her face warmed up. This time when she whistled, a clear note sounded. Within seconds, a branch behind her moved and the unicorn stepped into view. He must have been following her all along. She extinguished her wand and stuck it back in her coat.

"Thanks." She walked to him and patted his neck. "I always seem to be owing you."

He bobbed his head and shuffled his feet.

"Could you show me the way to the meadow?"

He started moving off at an angle to the way she had been going. His glow was enough to follow, but it didn't show all the rocks and bushes. She ran into a couple of rocks and several bushes before she reached the open meadow. Her shins ached, but she ignored the discomfort and concentrated on her steps.

The unicorn stopped at the edge of the trees.

"Thanks for helping me." She rubbed his neck in

appreciation. "I'll bring as many oats as I can manage. I owe you big time."

He pawed the snow then disappeared back into the trees.

A faint light could be seen from the cabin. She performed the spell to make her lighter and stepped out onto the meadow. Within a few minutes she could hear the rumble of an engine. She hurried on as the sound got louder, and then she saw the headlight. The snowmobile started to veer off. There was nothing left to do but use magic. She pulled out her wand and used it to amplify her voice. When she yelled and started waving her arms, the snowmobile turned back toward her. Within minutes it had reached her.

Steve pulled up next to her and hopped off. He quickly removed the snowshoes, put her on the back, and tore back to the cabin. He put the snowmobile in the shed, grabbed her arm, and pulled her to the cabin. He set the tranquilizer gun down, removed her gloves, and began checking her fingers.

"I'm okay." She pulled her hand back. She took off her coat and hung it up.

Steve stood near the door with his legs planted wide and his lips pressed tightly together.

Alex reached over to touch his arm. "Thanks for coming."

"What the hell were you doing?" His voice was deep and menacing.

"I lost track of time and ventured too far. I would have been back soon."

"Do you know how worried I was?"

"I'm sorry."

"You could have been hurt. I never would have

found you."

"I didn't mean to be gone that long."

"Did you enter the trees?"

Alex nodded. It would be too easy for him to find her tracks away from the trees unless the wind blew them away. She couldn't risk him seeing the hoof prints and looking farther.

"You could have been attacked," he said with a tight voice. "I brought the gun just in case."

Attacked by the unicorn, not likely. "By what?" she asked, trying to feign ignorance.

"By a bear or mountain lions. The tranquilizers wouldn't work well on an animal as large as a bear." He took the gun and put it back under the bed.

She hadn't considered mountain lions. Could the unicorn fend off an attack? He had a horn and magic on his side, but would that be enough against a mountain lion? "Bears should be hibernating, but I didn't think about a mountain lion."

"That's just it. You didn't think. If anything happened to you, I'd never forgive myself. You don't know how to take care of yourself out here."

She put her hands on her hips. "I'm not completely helpless."

He snorted, but at least his posture relaxed some.

Alex walked over to the kitchen sink to get a glass of water. Anything to stall for time. She needed to think about what she said before she accidentally let something slip. She could defend herself with her wand and magic, but he didn't know that. He couldn't know that. She had to keep the secret or she'd really get in trouble with magical security. She was tired of always keeping secrets from her friends. She took a long drink.

He had become more than just a friend. More than anything, she wanted to tell him the truth. She couldn't get involved without him knowing she was a wizard. She set the glass down and gripped the edge of the sink. That was the problem, she was already involved.

Steve finally took off his coat and hung it next to the door. He walked over and gently clasped her arms.

She remained still.

"What's wrong? I'm only trying to keep you safe." He moved in close, pressing his chest against her back.

Why couldn't she have simply met another wizard? It would have made her life so much easier. Here she was falling for a nonmagical and she couldn't stop herself. *Damn the secrets, she'd have to tell him. But not tonight.* She turned around and put her arms around him. "Sorry I worried you," she whispered and kissed him hard.

Steve returned the kiss. Without another word he led her to the bedroom. He quickly removed his clothes while she removed hers. Still not speaking, he started kissing her again while he let his hands roam all over her as if he was examining her for injuries.

Alex leaned her head back as he started kissing her neck, savoring every moment. She planned to take whatever moments she could get, because once he found out what she was, their relationship would probably be over. He continued moving lower and she lost all rational thought, lost to the overwhelming feelings coursing through her body. Tomorrow would be another day. Besides, there was no need to tell him until she had a way to leave. He might kick her out once he learned her secret. She couldn't deal with being stuck in the valley if he wasn't next to her. She wanted

Steve. *All of him. Right now.*

Chapter 21

She woke up with her body entwined in his. They'd spent the whole night making love. She wanted to spend every night with him, but how? Could she live out here with him and be happy? He wouldn't be happy in a large city like Denver. A big city would kill his spirit. She listened to his quiet breathing. He reminded her of a cuddly bear. He might try to act all rough and tough, but she knew better. There wasn't a violent bone in his body; he'd never harm her. He might not ever admit to being in love with her though. She knew he was in love by the way he touched her. He cared. But she couldn't figure out why he wouldn't admit it. There had to be a reason. Tonight, she'd tell him she was in love with him. Tonight, she'd tell him she was a wizard, put her cards on the table and see what happened. She'd see if he cared enough to trust her.

He started sliding his tongue along her neck.

Man, how he could use his tongue. Even on only her neck, she instantly turned on fire. When he lapped at her core she came unglued. She caressed his chest, wanting to savor him one more time before the morning intruded. She nudged his head lower.

When he'd settled his head between her legs, he looked up at her and grinned. Then he unglued her, several times.

While they did the morning chores, he kept finding

ways to bump into her. Each time he did, he would take her into his arms and give her a passionate kiss. The chores might have taken twice as long to get done, but she enjoyed every moment. He even showered with her, spending longer than normal as he lingered by slowly rubbing the soap all over her body. Of course, she returned the favor.

But sometime later, while he prepared breakfast, he seemed to distance himself. He didn't say a word while they ate or while he cleaned up. With her being out after dark, she couldn't take another hike to see the unicorn. The poor animal would have to wait until later for some more oats. She tried to read but couldn't concentrate on the words. Her thoughts kept dwelling on how she would tell him about magic. Everything she thought of sounded hokey or flip. They spent the rest of the day in silence until after dinner was over, when he set the dishes in the sink and sat back down at the table. He reached across and took her hand in his.

"We need to talk."

"Okay." She had to tell him. Get everything out in the open.

"I need to tell you a story," Steve said. "Then maybe you'll understand why I can't have a lasting relationship with anyone."

"I'm not just anyone. We belong together," Alex answered. "Why—"

"Just let me tell you this, then you can ask any questions."

"But—"

He held a finger up to her lips, "Me first."

Alex shut up and decided to listen to his story before telling him hers.

He paused a couple of minutes, then started with his tale.

****

About thirty years ago a man, Paul, found himself lost in the mountains. He wandered through the woods for days, looking for some shelter. Berries had been his source of nourishment, at least giving him enough energy to keep going on. On the fourth day, he fell down a rock face, twisting his ankle. He could hobble along with the aid of a thick stick, but he needed to find some type of shelter where he could give his ankle a chance to recover. He wandered into a meadow without even realizing. An old stone building stood on the far side of a stream-fed pond. As he worked his way around the pond, he could see more details of the structure.

The ancient stones were completely covered with lime green lichen, but the sod roof was ablaze with wildflowers. It looked like the pictures of old buildings in Scandinavia. At least he'd have shelter now. He paused in the doorway to let his eyes adjust to the dark interior. A shiny ax stood next to the door and a stack of wood sat near the fireplace.

He called out.

No one answered.

The silence was only broken by the birds and wind outside. He settled down at the table and propped his foot up. Crystals, in various stages of cleaning, were arranged on one area of the table. There were pale blue and gray stones of various sizes. He picked up one of the gray stones; it had to be smoky quartz. He set the stone back down with the others.

A careful search of the building yielded a stash of

cheese and bread. Now this would be good with the berries he'd passed near the pond. He spent a week alone in the building without seeing anyone.

He had left home on a month-long sales trip, so no one would miss him for at least another week. This was the first time he'd really been alone with his thoughts. He spent time thinking about his fiancé, wondering if he really loved her. Two weeks away from her and he didn't miss her. Was this the way love was supposed to be? If he loved her, wouldn't he feel some type of longing for her?

Nothing.

Just when he thought he was the only person out here, an enchanting woman walked through the door. Her pine green clothes set off her chocolate hair.

The moment she recovered from her surprise she asked, "What are you doing here?"

"I got lost. This was the only shelter I could find."

"You need to get out." She held the door open.

He used the stick to prop himself up. "I'm sorry for my intrusion. I twisted an ankle. I'm only staying until it gets better." He hobbled a step closer. "Could you help me find my way back?"

She watched him for a moment. "Okay. I'll take you to a path tomorrow. It's too late tonight." With this, she closed the door and placed her basket of bread and cheese on the table.

"I'm sorry, but I've eaten some of your supplies. I can pay you back."

"It's okay. I can get more." She bustled around, getting the food set out.

After dinner, she finally spoke. "You need to stay inside at night. There's a bear wandering around the area."

She insisted that he use the bedroom so that his leg would be rested.

He'd almost fallen asleep when he heard a large animal lumbering around outside. He looked out the window and saw a brown bear. The bear looked up and he could swear it had the saddest look he'd ever seen. The animal wandered off and he went back to bed.

The next morning, he looked up at the woman while eating his breakfast. He recognized the same sad look in her eyes.

The same hair color as the bear's fur.

The same gray eyes.

He bolted and moved back from the table.

He knew she was the bear.

****

"Well, to make a long story short…" Steve said.

Alex nodded.

"She wouldn't let him leave for fear he'd tell someone about her. Over the summer, he realized his fiancé didn't really love him, she just didn't want to be alone. She didn't feel the same—not the way he felt about the bear woman. He fell in love with the woman from the woods, but he still needed to break off his engagement. He left for a week to tie up any loose ends. When he came back, he kissed the bear woman and carried her inside. She would shift between sunset and civil twilight so they spent the late summer days together. He experienced the love and passion he'd been searching for. She finally agreed to marry him when she found out she was pregnant."

Steve paused. He quietly said, "With me."

Alex sat there a moment, saying nothing. The

clock's ticking and the fire crackling were the only sounds that disturbed the silence. Then she broke out laughing, tears rolling down her face as she clutched her sides.

"This isn't funny." He jumped out of his chair, hands flat on the table, as he towered over her.

She could see the bear as he stood there. It took her a couple of minutes to control her laughter. She reached out and placed a hand on his. "You're a wizard. Of all the people to meet," she managed to say before laughing again.

He yanked his hand away from hers and stood up straight.

Just like a bear would posture. "Magic," she finally managed to get out before another fit of laughter hit her.

"What do you mean?" Steve asked.

She finally managed to stop laughing. "You know—wands, wizards, spells. That kind of stuff," Alex answered, wiping away the tears.

"But that's just in books."

"It is. But there is a world of magic hidden from the nonmagical."

Steve shook his head.

"I can prove it. Wait here." Alex went to her coat and pulled her wand out of the pocket.

Steve was still standing straight and tall when she turned back to face him.

She held up her wand vertically so she wouldn't accidentally perform a spell and waved it so Steve could see it. "What I was laughing about was that I'd been worrying all day about how to explain that I'm a wizard. Maybe not the most gifted." She snapped her fingers and the lantern on the table went out. She snapped again and the lantern re-lit. Then she lifted her wand tip and the lantern rose. When she lowered the tip, the lantern floated back down on the table. "But still a wizard."

Steve stared at the lamp, eyes wide, shaking his head. "Not…possible," he stammered.

She waved the wand again. "I can do magic. Just like you can do magic."

"I can't do any magic," he said in a soft voice.

"You turn into a bear. That's doing magic," she said calmly. "Maybe a different kind, but still magic."

Alex walked back to the table and sat back down. "You probably didn't even know." She placed her wand on the table. "A lot of wizards don't."

He shook his head and sat back down, facing her. He picked up her wand with his right hand. When he ran his left hand's fingertips along the cherry grain, some red sparks shot out the tip of the wand. He froze.

"Only a wizard can get a wand to spark. It takes magic to do that."

"I didn't know." He handled the wand as if it was delicate glass, placing it back on the table.

She watched in silence as he reached out with a finger to caress the wand again. He was drawn to it, to the bear hair that made up the magical core. Now she was certain. *This shape-shifter bear is my other half.*

"And you say I have magic?" Steve asked.

"If you didn't you wouldn't be able to change into a bear."

"But that's just genetic."

"Magic is usually genetic. How did you think you could shift?"

"I thought it was a version of a werewolf."

"Despite what the movies say, werewolves have magic. They don't just get it by being bitten." Alex placed one of her hands on his.

"But this is the way it's always been. My mother changed and I do too. I close the shutters and bolt the doors on the inside so my bear can't enter the cabin during the night."

"And you'll keep changing until you learn how to control it."

"That's impossible." He leaned forward in the chair.

"With specific potions you could control it."

"Not roam around all night?"

"No, just sleep."

"Would I still change?"

Alex paused. "I don't know." She twirled her wand in the fingers of her free hand. "But I know someone who probably would."

****

He had to think. What would it be like to not change? It had become so much a part of who he was. Would he even want to stop? He looked at Alex. If he could do this, would she be safe to be around him? He wouldn't have to worry about her being in danger. He reached out and she handed her wand to him.

He inched his fingers across the satiny surface. A warm tingly sensation answered his touch. He could swear he could catch a faint trace of apples. *Her scent.* Why would touching a piece of wood make him visualize her so vividly? He thought about her so often, but this was something else. It felt like he was touching her. He passed his fingers over the surface again and handed it back to her.

He finally asked, "Can you get in touch with this person?"

"Once I get back to Denver."

"Then what?"

"Then he'll come out to talk to you."

"Who is this person?"

"Principal Vale. He's in charge of a wizarding school, Aspen Glen, that's here in the mountains of Colorado."

"There's actually a school for magic?"

Alex nodded. "I went there."

"I'm an adult."

"They have summer classes for adults. I don't know that much about them."

"How long are you talking?"

"Six years," Alex answered.

He stood up and started pacing. Six years of school. Could he even sit through a single class? He'd been home schooled ever since he started changing. "I hated school," he muttered.

"This is different."

"I swore I'd never set a foot in a school again."

"You'd be learning magic."

"I don't know."

"At least talk to Principal Vale before you make a final decision."

"I'll hear what he has to say, once the roads clear."

Alex picked up the book she'd been reading. "I'll give you some time to think." She took her wand and book to the bedroom.

Steve watched her go. Mandy leaned against his leg. "I don't know." Mandy put a paw on his thigh. "It is worth considering. Maybe I could have a semi-normal life." He ruffled the fur on Mandy's chest. "I hated school. Why would I want to go for six years?" He thought for a few minutes. "It might be worth doing...for Alex."

Chapter 22

Alex woke up alone with her glasses still on and her book on the floor. Steve must have spent the night mulling over the new information. She looked over at the clock, it was already seven thirty. Steve hadn't woken her, so she'd missed chores. A faint clatter came from the kitchen. Alex still had on her clothes from last night, so she hopped out of bed and headed out of the bedroom. She paused at the door.

"Should I come out or do you need some more time alone?" she asked.

"Come on and get some breakfast." He waved her in with the spatula.

"Did you decide anything?"

He started dishing up the eggs. "Not yet. I want to hear more about this magical world of yours."

That was a good sign. At least he hadn't completely rejected the idea. "What do you want to know?"

"Everything." He set the plates on the table. "But let's eat first, then you can tell me."

Alex dashed into the bathroom, then quickly took her place at the table. "What do you want to know?" she asked between bites of egg.

"After breakfast."

"You're going to make me wait?"

"Patience."

"But—"

"Eat first."

She sat there looking at his determined face. He wasn't going to talk until they'd finished the meal. She started shoveling in mouthfuls of egg. Within minutes she'd cleaned her plate, but Steve was only two-thirds done. She jumped up, took her plate to the sink, and watched him take one slow bite after another. She grabbed his almost clean plate and put it in the sink. "Breakfast is over. Let's talk."

He sat there for a moment, still holding his empty fork. "Okay, okay. I knew you couldn't resist." He dropped his fork off at the sink and sauntered over to his chair in front of the fire.

She sat down in the other chair but fidgeted the whole time.

"You need to practice patience." He took his time settling into his chair.

She waved her hand. "Who needs patience. I want to know what you've decided." After all, her future was at stake.

"I haven't decided anything, but I'm interested in learning more."

At least that was a step in the right direction. Alex shifted to the edge of the chair. "The most important thing to remember is that magic has to remain secret."

"Why? Is someone going to come get me if I tell?"

She nodded.

"No way."

"Way." She shifted even closer to the edge of the seat. "Magical security will come."

"So what can they do?"

"They could erase your memory and whoever's

memory you tell."

"Is that the worst?"

She shook her head. "You need to understand...some spells aren't exactly precise. They would remove any discussions about magic and maybe more."

"How much more?"

"Maybe a little bit or a lot. The least would be removing any memories about me."

"Why you?"

"They don't know how much I might have told you or when I told you. So, they'd erase all your memories of me. It would be as if we'd never met."

"They wouldn't do that." He leaned forward.

She nodded. "You wouldn't remember me or anything that has happened since before I showed up on your doorstep."

He reached over and took her hand. "I'd never let them do that."

"You'd never know it happened. They'd show up and do what they had to." She looked down at the floor.

"I couldn't stop it from happening?"

She shook her head and kept staring at the floor.

"They're that good?"

"They're the best there is, that's why they hold such an important job. Even so, they could still make a mistake and wipe too much."

He reached over and squeezed her hand. "So, what do I need to do to keep them at bay?"

She looked directly at him. "Follow the rules."

"And the number one rule is to not tell anyone else about magic."

"Yes."

He released her hand and leaned back in the chair. He placed his elbows on the arms of the chair, forming a triangle with his fingers in front of his face. "What else?"

"There's a few irritations, like having to pay magical taxes as well as federal taxes. But we have our own health care since our treatments incorporate magic. We have magic schools that children can go to so they can learn how to use their magic."

"This was the school you were talking about?"

She looked at him, but he was still contemplating his fingers. "Yes. We do have some great advantages though. We can travel between places in minutes."

He looked over at her. "So why didn't you?"

She looked away to the fire. "I'd been trying to see if I could get by for a month without using any magic."

"How did that turn out?"

"I'd been doing well until a few days ago."

He thought for a moment. "When you started going out for walks?"

She nodded.

"Why?"

"You won't believe me."

"Like I'd never believe in magic? What else wouldn't I believe?"

She looked over at him and hesitated. "I've been looking for the wild unicorn."

He snorted, dropped his hands, and studied her face. "Did you find one?"

"That's why I was so late last night."

He jumped up. "You were out there searching for a mythological creature?"

She looked back at the fire. "Yes." She turned to

look at him. "And I found him."

"Where in the world did you find him?"

"In a cave on the other side of the meadow."

He quickly sat back down and remained silent for a moment. "Did you see anything else in this cave?"

"Just a pile of crystals."

He looked down to the floor. "You were in my cave. That's where I go in the summer when I'm a bear."

That explained the fur on the wall and the lantern. The fur reminded her of Steve because it was his. "So you know how to get there?"

"All too well. Why?"

"I promised the unicorn I'd bring him some hay and oats. He helped me get back to the meadow or I would have gotten lost."

"Why can't he move on to an area where there's more food?"

"He's guarding something."

Steve leaned over toward her. "And pray tell me...What would a unicorn guard?"

"Dragon eggs." She continued to watch him. "I'll take you there tomorrow so you can see for yourself."

"I've been in that cave so many times I know it by heart. Where are these supposed eggs?"

"At the end of the shelf."

"There's only rocks there."

"Those aren't rocks. They're probably the reason you picked that cave to go to."

He started to shake his head.

"Magic calls out to magic. That's how I found the cave."

"So you're telling me that you can sense another

wizard? Why didn't you sense my magic?"

"I can tell when another wizard is close, but your form of magic is different. I think we felt it when I cut your hair. And when we touch now." Of course, she wouldn't admit that she was attracted to him from the start. Maybe his magic was why. Maybe that even explained why sex with him was so intense. No. Making love to him was intense because she really cared about him. Probably even loved him. But first she needed to help him deal with the magical world so they could be together.

A snowmobile's engine interrupted their conversation. "Peter is probably checking up on you again." Steve got up and went to the front door. Peter entered the cabin stomping the last bits of snow off his boots. Steve took his coat. "Any news or calls?"

"Yeah. I checked the pass, and it looks like we can get through." Peter looked at Alex. "I guess that means you'll be leaving."

"I have to take care of some things at home." Alex looked at Steve.

"It's been a lot more fun with you here. Anything I can do to convince you to stay?" Peter asked.

"I've got an apartment to get back to, and a job to find so I can make the rent," Alex said.

Peter scuffed his foot. "I'll pay your rent if you stay."

"I can't let you do that."

"I can afford it."

"That's not the point. It wouldn't be right."

Steve put his arm around Alex's shoulder. "When can we make arrangements for her?"

"I'll set things up for next Friday," Peter answered.

Alex asked, "So how do we do this?"

"I'll contact your parents and have them meet us at the hotel by the highway," Peter said.

"What about my car?"

"After the road crews get through, we'll dig it out and meet you at the hotel," Steve said.

Peter shuffled his feet. "Wish you could stay. Well, I'd better go and let the others know."

Steve helped Peter back into his coat. As Peter headed out, Steve said to Alex, "I'll be back in a minute. I need to ask him for a few supplies."

She had to figure out what she'd do. A big part of her wanted to stay here with Steve in the cabin, but she knew she must go home. Her parents were worried, and she needed to contact Principal Vale. She couldn't impose on Steve any longer. He hadn't asked her to stay, and she wouldn't be comfortable living with him unless they were married. Hopefully, they'd stay in touch over the rest of the winter. She didn't want to lose him. Good men were hard to come by, and she believed he was one of the best.

Steve came back in and shivered. "I still want to learn more about this school."

Alex rubbed his arms, "Principal Vale could tell you more than I can."

Steve wrapped his arms around her. "How did you like going there?"

"I was only a kid when I went. As an adult, you should enjoy it more. All the history, English, and math bored me."

Steve kissed her. "What about the magic classes?"

"I enjoyed those."

"Fall in love with anyone?" he asked as he kissed

her neck with his cold lips.

"No one special or I wouldn't be here today."

"Good for me," he whispered in her ear as he nibbled on her earlobe. "We'd better take advantage of the few days left."

They only made it over to the rug in front of the fire before getting all their clothes off. The rest of the afternoon they spent in front of the crackling fire like a pair of newlyweds.

Chapter 23

Up until now, time seemed to stretch on. Her days had fallen into a relaxed routine with morning chores, mid-day reading, before dinner chores, evenings in front of the fire, and the occasional night making love. With a set date for leaving, it seemed like there wasn't enough time.

She had less than a week left. While here, all she had thought about was when she'd get to leave and go home. Now, the thought of leaving made her panic. When had she grown so used to the cabin and chores? The stupid hens? And Steve? She'd miss seeing his face every day. They'd become comfortable around each other. She'd never been this comfortable around a man before. What had changed? She had. She had the time to really get to know him instead of ending the relationship before she ever really became close. But then there had never been anyone she'd wanted to get close to before.

She'd be leaving until late spring, when she wouldn't get trapped again by snow. Although, thinking about being stranded again brought a smile. But with her luck, she might get stuck with a toothless old codger, not in this valley with Steve. No. She'd have to wait for spring, a time when she'd have weekends available to come visit. Until then, she needed a job to pay her bills. If she didn't find work soon she could lose everything.

Peter stopped by the next day. He handed a paper lunch bag to Steve and hung up his coat. "Everything's arranged. Your parents will meet us at the hotel around noon."

"That's it then. I'm really leaving," Alex said.

Steve moved over to her and wrapped his arms around her, placing her back against his chest.

"Unless I can convince you to stay," Peter added.

Alex waited, but Steve remained quiet. He wasn't going to invite her to stay after all. He was still too hung up on his shifting to give them a chance. "No," she whispered, "I have to get back." At least this would give Steve an easy out.

Peter stared at Steve and shook his head. He pointed to the bag Steve had placed on the table. "Such a waste. Damn it. You're passing on something great, and you're too dense to see it."

"It's out of my control," Steve answered.

Peter grabbed his coat and marched out the door. Alex and Steve followed him out onto the porch.

Alex could hear Peter mutter all the way to his snowmobile. "Stupid man. I wouldn't let her get away. He'll never find someone if he keeps this up." Peter fired up the motor and roared off.

Alex headed back inside and peeked in the paper bag. She pulled out the box of condoms and waved them at Steve. "More? You needed more than what you'd gotten before?"

Steve nodded and snatched the box out of her hand. "I'm almost out. I didn't get very many the last time. I wanted to make these last few days memorable." He set the box back down on the table and pulled Alex into an

211

embrace. "Want to take one for a test drive?" He waggled his eyebrows.

She broke away from him and strode over to a back window.

He followed her and gently placed a hand on her shoulder. "I can't make any decisions until I learn more about my shifting. I can't put you in any danger."

Alex turned to face him. "I know. I want you to believe that you'd never harm me."

"That's just it. I don't know if I would. Until then, I have to let you leave. I can feel the bear awakening early. Being with you is having an effect on him."

Alex ran a hand down Steve's arm. "Talk to Principal Vale and go to school. It'll change everything." She gently squeezed his forearm, "Until then, let's see if we can use the whole box."

Steve raised his eyebrows. "Really?"

Alex clutched the front of his shirt and pulled him in for a kiss.

The next day Alex showed Steve where to head with the snowmobile. They parked it inside the line of trees and Steve led her through the trees to the cave opening. Alex had him stop several yards away from the cave opening and softly whistled. No sooner had she made a sound and the unicorn's nose was barely visible. She bowed and waited.

He snorted, shook his head, and pawed at the ground.

Alex looked at Steve. "Back up some more, bow, and stay still." She looked back at the unicorn while she maintained her bow. "This man is going to help. He can bring you the hay and oats when I'm gone." She stayed still and waited.

The unicorn eased out of the cave and bobbed his head at Alex. He pawed the ground in Steve's direction.

"Holy shit! It really is a unicorn."

"I told you so."

"Now what?" Steve asked.

"Unicorns don't like men as well. He should be familiar with your scent since he's been living in your bear cave, so that should help. Stay still and keep bowing until he gets a chance to sniff you." Alex slowly straightened.

The unicorn edged over to Steve, extending his head to get a noseful without having to get too close. After taking a deep breath, he bobbed his head.

"Now you can straighten up," Alex edged closer to the unicorn. "He can understand what wizards say."

"Now what?"

"Let him get a chance to get used to you." She spoke to the unicorn and nodded her head toward Steve. "This is Steve. He is the bear that you've been smelling in the cave. He wants to see the eggs."

The unicorn snorted and turned back toward the cave.

"We need to follow him or else we won't be able to see the way in." Alex followed the unicorn.

"I know the way by heart. After all, I spend my summer nights here," he said as he followed her in. After going in a couple of feet, he whispered, "Is the unicorn actually glowing?"

Alex nudged him.

Once in, Steve walked over to the ledge and lit the lantern.

Alex brushed some of the dirt away to expose the surface of the eggs.

Steve walked over, knelt down next to the eggs, and ran his hand over the surface. "What is this? I feel something strange, like a humming. It reminds me of you."

"You're sensing the magic."

"I never knew." He kept rubbing his hands over the eggs. "They're stunning. I've never seen anything like them."

"You probably never will. They're really rare."

The unicorn approached them and snorted on the back of Steve's neck, causing him to jump.

Alex brushed a hand down the unicorn's back. "It's okay. He's going to help us until I get a chance to contact a wizard that's trustworthy. I'll have to leave for a while, but Steve will make sure you get some hay and oats."

"Thanks for volunteering me." He stood up and looked at Alex. "I never would have believed this existed if it hadn't been for you."

Alex started covering the eggs back up with dirt. "It's a lot to take in. It even surprised me, and I know about magic."

The unicorn shoved Steve's arm.

Steve unconsciously reached out to run his hand down along the unicorn's neck. He looked into the unicorn's eyes. "I never would have believed you could even be possible."

The unicorn bobbed his head.

"I'll make sure you have plenty to eat, but I'll have to bring it in on my snowmobile. Hope you don't mind."

"We'd better show him the snowmobile so he doesn't freak out," Alex added. She walked over to the pile of crystals and picked one up. "What are these?"

"Those are the aquamarines I collect all summer. I keep them in here for protection until I'm going to a show."

Alex placed the stone back down on the pile. "We'd better go so you have enough time to bring some hay back."

Steve blew out the lantern and they all headed back out of the cave.

Alex looked at the unicorn, "We want to show you the snowmobile. It's really noisy, but it's the only way Steve can bring you a bale of hay. I could do it with magic, but I won't be here."

The unicorn bobbed his head and started along their trail with Alex and Steve bringing up the rear.

At first the unicorn didn't want to approach the machine, but curiosity won out. After sniffing it thoroughly, he headed back into the trees. After dropping Alex back at the cabin, Steve took a bale of hay and some oats back.

That evening as they finished dinner Steve asked, "Is magic the reason I feel so on fire when we touch?"

Alex thought a moment before answering. "Not necessarily. I've had wizard boyfriends before, but this feels different."

"I didn't completely believe you until today."

Alex got up and walked around the table. Steve stood and pulled her into his arms.

Alex kissed him before saying, "This is just special."

Steve picked her up and carried her into the bedroom. "You're special," he whispered before kissing her all over.

****

With each passing day, they became more restless. They took every opportunity to enjoy each other before their time ran out. Every morning, every evening, and even a couple of times during the day were spent making love. A shower was never taken alone, and even when they were reading, they curled up together on the floor in front of the fireplace. They never missed a moment to remain in contact with each other.

Alex made sure to take some oats out to the unicorn every few days and Steve promised to make sure he had enough hay so he wouldn't go hungry. Would the unicorn stay until the eggs were taken away to safety? Or would he leave now that she had found the eggs?

The day before Alex left, Peter threw another party for her. Again, everyone brought a dish to make it potluck. Alex helped Steve fix some deviled eggs, his specialty since he owned chickens. She packed them and eggs for the others in straw so they'd arrive safely. Once the packs had been loaded on the snowmobile, Alex stopped and took a slow look around the valley.

"What's up?" Steve asked as he stopped next to her.

"I think I'm actually going to miss this." She swept her arm across the area. "I never thought the snow would ever stop and now I wish it hadn't."

"It grows on you."

Alex nodded.

Steve helped her onto the snowmobile, and they took off to Peter's. The dragon snow sculpture was a lot smaller, but now the sides glistened with ice. Alex shuddered when they walked into the gaping jaws. She had to wonder if Peter had any idea about the two dragon eggs nestled in the cave or if he just liked the idea of dragons. After all, he did write computer games for a living. She could see him writing one where the valiant prince had to rescue the helpless damsel from the wrath of a menacing dragon. Someday, she ought to find out what type of games he did come up with.

Steve took the eggs while she went to talk to some of the other guests. As soon as Caroline spotted Alex, she dashed over.

Alex asked, "Have you seen anything else?"

"Nah," Caroline mumbled as she shuffled her feet. "I did see the unicorn a couple more times. Mom doesn't believe." Caroline looked directly at Alex. "You believe me though. Don't you?"

Alex knelt down on one knee and placed a hand on Caroline's shoulder. "I believe you. I'm afraid no one else will though, so let's keep this to ourselves."

"Like a secret?"

Alex nodded. "A secret just between us." She motioned to her and Caroline. Alex looked over to Steve, and Caroline followed her gaze. "Mr. Davis might listen to you if I'm not here."

"Where're you going?"

"I'm going home tomorrow." Alex watched Caroline's face.

"Denver, isn't it?" Caroline looked back to Alex.

Alex nodded.

"You coming back?"

"I don't know. Would you want me to?"

Caroline's face brightened. "Yeah."

"Then I'll just have to come back in the spring or summer when the roads are better. Maybe Mr.

Robertson will have another party."

"That'd be fun. Then you could come to my house and we could play a game or something."

"I'll do that." Alex looked back over to Steve. "Until then, you could tell Mr. Davis if you see the unicorn again or anything else interesting."

"He'd believe me?" Caroline quickly glanced at Steve.

"He'll believe you."

"Okay."

Alex stood up. "Would you show me where you last saw the unicorn?"

"Okay." Caroline took Alex's hand and led her over to a back window. She pointed to the trees on the far side. "Usually I see him strolling among the trees. He's really hard to see unless the moon's out."

Alex relaxed. Caroline had pointed out an area away from where the cave was. Obviously, she'd spotted him before he'd located the eggs. "Have you seen him recently?"

"No. Not for over a week now, but I keep watching."

Emily and Vincent, Caroline's parents, walked over to join them.

Emily said, "Is she telling you about the unicorn again?"

Emily spoke to Caroline, "What did we talk about?"

"It's okay," Alex said. "We were talking about the moon highlighting the trees." She smiled at Caroline.

"Yeah," Caroline answered.

Emily put her hands on her daughter's shoulders. "She loves to read anything about magic. Witches, unicorns, fairies—anything even remotely related."

Alex looked at Emily. "I enjoy those books too."

Emily pulled out a piece of paper from her pants pocket. "I mentioned you to my editor, and she said to give her a call as soon as you get back to town. She might have something that you might be interested in considering."

Alex took the paper and unfolded the note, checking the name inside. "I'll do that." She refolded the note and put it in her pocket. "I don't know how I'll ever thank you."

Emily blushed a little. "It was nothing. You took the time to listen to our Caroline. She doesn't get the chance to play with other kids much with us living here."

Caroline looked up at her mom. "Ms. Klein said she'd come back this summer and play with me."

"We can't expect you to do that." Emily looked at Caroline. "She might not want to risk coming back here again."

"No. I was already planning on coming back." Alex glanced at Steve. "I've actually had a good time while I was here, even with all the snow."

"We don't usually get this much. You hit a bad set of storms."

Vincent touched Caroline's shoulder, "We'd better go visit with the others before we have to take off." He steered his wife and daughter off.

Alex looked back out the window. She knew she'd be back again at least one more time to bring Principal Vale to meet with Steve. If Steve wanted her to stop by after that, still remained to be seen. At least these last few days made her believe he might.

Steve came up and rubbed a hand down her arm. "A penny for your thoughts," he whispered.

"Just enjoying the view one more time."

He moved closer. "It's something else in the spring with all the wildflowers in bloom. Then there's the summer when the meadow grass is deep and lush. In the fall, the aspens pepper the firs with yellow and red."

Alex put her arm around Steve's waist. "So what's your favorite season?"

"I never could decide before." He placed his arm around her shoulders. "Now it'll be the winter. I'll always think about you whenever I see the snow."

Peter interrupted their thoughts. "Come on you two. You can't keep her all to yourself. It's a party for her after all." He pulled Alex away.

She enjoyed getting to visit with everyone one more time. No way around it—she wanted to come back. The party only lasted a couple of hours so everyone could get back home while the sun was still out. Alex arranged with Peter when they'd call so she could stay in touch. At least with Peter's radio, she could still get through to Steve and Peter, even if the phone lines were down.

After Alex and Steve got back, Alex went out on the front porch to watch the sun set behind the mountains. She sipped a hot chocolate as she watched. Steve joined her.

"I forgot to mention, Caroline saw the unicorn. She told me about seeing him at the other party. Her parents don't believe her, but I told her that you would," Alex said, cradling the warm mug between her hands.

"Thanks." Steve wrapped his arms around her and snuggled up against her back. "Now she'll be pestering me continuously. What did you say?"

"I told her I believed her and you would too. I suggested that she and I keep it a secret between the two of us."

"I was beginning to wonder." He laid his head against hers. "What are you doing out here in the cold?"

"Watching the sunset."

"Could you picture yourself living out here in such a remote place now?"

Alex took a deep breath. Was he going to finally say something? "Actually. I never thought I'd ever enjoy being away from a big city, but I love it here. It's so peaceful."

"Even with all the work?"

"Even then. Why?"

"Just wondering." He let go of her and headed back inside without saying another word.

"He's still afraid to take a chance," she whispered to the empty porch. "All I can do is keep trying." She took several more sips before she went back inside.

They spent her last night making love. She wanted to remember every moment in as much detail as possible, especially every plane and angle of his body.

Chapter 24

Alex finally dragged out her suitcase and started packing her clothes and toiletries. Mandy kept trying to pull the clothes out as fast as Alex could put them in. Steve stretched out on the bed and held Mandy's collar so she couldn't interfere. Alex held up one of Steve's dirty flannel shirts. "Would you mind if I took this with me?"

Steve had been watching her every move. "You could take one of the clean ones. Why the dirty one?"

"It smells like you and it's my favorite."

Steve looked down at Mandy. "Women." He looked back to Alex. "Go ahead." He reached in her suitcase and held up a black silk and lace nightgown she'd worn the last few nights. "As long as I can keep this."

She started to take it out of his hand, but he pulled it out of her reach. "That's just a nightgown."

"Maybe to you, but not to me. Whenever I see you putting it on, I know you want sex, and it isn't just me tempting you."

Alex blushed. "Did I really do that?"

He nodded. "And you've put it on every night since Peter told us we could get through the pass." He got up and carried the gown over to her. "Put it on once more." He held it out to her.

She looked at him, "Do we have time?"

"We have all the time we want." He flung the gown across his shoulder and pulled her sweater off. Without hesitating, he went to work on the clasp on her bra. The moment her breasts were free he wrapped a hand around one while he took possession of the other with his mouth.

She had barely undone a couple of buttons on his shirt. She gasped and tried to hurry with the others, but her fingers kept fumbling.

He broke away and yanked his shirt off over his head. He took her breast back in his mouth and slid his hands down to unfasten her jeans.

She ran her hands over his chest then around to his back. When he slid her jeans and underwear down, she unfastened his.

He pulled away and quickly stepped out of his pants and briefs. He retrieved the gown and slipped it on her. As he kissed her neck, he inched his hands up her legs, sliding the edge of the gown up. He eased a finger inside her. She was already wet and clamped down on his finger the moment it entered. He slipped his finger out, then back in, and she gasped. He backed her up to the bed and shoved her suitcase onto the floor. Mandy jumped down and took off for the other room.

Alex wrapped her fingers around him and slowly slid them up and down.

He broke away and quickly reached for a condom that was lying on the bedside table.

She took it, ripped it open, and slid it on him.

He paused and looked deeply into her eyes as he positioned himself between her legs. "I love you," he whispered.

She ran her fingers across his forehead, pushing a

strand of his hair back. "I love you."

He pushed himself in as he watched her eyes. "I wish you could stay." He started moving faster.

"Me too," she managed to say before giving herself over to her increasing desire.

They climaxed and he held her for only a couple of minutes. He got up, quickly pulled the condom off, and got dressed again. He pulled her up and slipped the nightgown off. After folding it carefully, he placed it in the drawer of the bedside table.

She gathered her clothes and started to head for the bathroom when he stopped her.

"Don't shower. I want to think about you this way when we have to part."

She paused a moment then started dressing.

Steve placed her suitcase back on the bed and started folding up her clothes, placing them in. "Peter should be here any minute, we'd better hurry."

"Do I look okay?" she asked after pulling her sweater back on.

Steve ran his fingers through her hair. "Never better." He gave her a quick kiss and went out to the living room.

Alex took one last look around and didn't see anything else. She wedged her toiletries in and zipped the case. She wrestled the case out into the living room and placed it with her purse and computer. "Do you see anything else?"

Steve took a look around the room. "Do you want to borrow the book you were reading?"

She shook her head, "I'll check out a copy after I get home." What was she doing? Talking about a book instead of saying goodbye? How could she say goodbye to him?

They could hear a snowmobile approaching.

Alex walked over to Mandy and gave her a hug. "You take good care of him."

Mandy barked.

"Sometimes I swear she understands me."

Steve placed a hand on her shoulder. "I know what you mean." He draped her purse across her chest.

Peter knocked.

The men tied Alex's suitcase onto Peter's snowmobile. Peter slipped the computer across his shoulder and climbed on. Steve helped Alex on behind him and they took off. Alex clutched Steve, holding on tightly as they made their way up the driveway. They had to squeeze past the mound of snow that was her car and pulled out onto the road. The snowmobiles tilted as they clung to the snowy slope that had once been level. The mountains loomed up and narrowed as they got closer to the pass. Alex squeezed her eyes shut not wanting to see their precarious position. After what seemed like forever, they broke through to a level area. Alex squinted open one eye and saw the narrow opening behind them. They'd made it through. She opened both eyes and could see the highway looming ahead in the bright sunlight. From this side it looked like another world. The snowmobiles stopped before reaching the bottom of the ramp.

Steve helped her off and went to help Peter untie her suitcase. Cars and trucks zoomed by on the highway and the hotel glinted in the bright sunlight. It was hard to imagine that she had once been sitting right there trying to decide which way to go. If she'd gone left, she would have reached the hotel. But she'd turned right and ended up in the valley with Steve.

Her wrong choice turned out to be the best thing to happen to her. She didn't regret a moment. The world had continued to go on without her and she didn't mind.

Steve took her hand and pulled her suitcase as they walked over to the hotel.

Alex spotted her parents' car moments before they came rushing out of the hotel's front doors. Her parents grabbed her the moment they got close. "Mom. Dad. You need to let me breathe," Alex struggled to say.

They let go, but her mom kept fussing. First, she straightened Alex's coat then she pushed back Alex's hair.

Alex pulled away and motioned to Peter. "This is Peter Robertson. He's the one who was able to contact you. Peter, these are my parents, Joy and Thomas."

Her father and mother clasped his hand and gave it a hearty shake.

Alex motioned to Steve. "This is Steven Davis. He rescued me from the snow and gave me a place to stay."

Dad clasped his hand and shook hard. Her mother flung her arms around Steve. "I'm so glad you took care of my baby."

Alex shook her head while Steve gave her a pleading look. Peter giggled and tried to stop.

Alex's father, Thomas, stepped up and pulled on one of his wife's arms. "That's enough, Mother. He doesn't know us."

Her mom, Joy, broke away and straightened Steve's coat. "I don't how to thank you for taking care of our little girl."

Steve mumbled, "It was a pleasure."

Thomas eyed Steve.

Joy interrupted. "Have you eaten? Why don't we all go in the hotel and get a quick bite before you have to leave."

Peter answered, "It would be a pleasure, but I insist on treating." He took Joy's arm and escorted her toward the hotel doors. Thomas followed, with Steve and Alex bringing up the rear.

Steve whispered, "What's he up to?"

Alex whispered back, "Probably going to embarrass the hell out of you."

"He wouldn't dare."

Alex giggled and squeezed Steve's free hand.

Peter carried the conversation over lunch, while Steve and Alex remained quiet. Alex picked at her food, leaving most of it on the plate. Peter and Joy argued over the bill and they got ready to leave.

She only had minutes left. What could she say? Do? Anything to let him know how she felt.

Her parents and Peter took her suitcase to the car giving Alex a chance to say goodbye.

Steve slipped a rock into her hand holding her fingers around the stone. "Whenever you look at this, remember your time here with me. I hope we get a chance to get together really soon. We can meet here at the hotel." He released her hands and slid his arms inside her coat to clasp her to him. He gave her a long passionate kiss, then he dashed off toward the snowmobiles where Peter was waiting.

Alex couldn't blame him for leaving so quickly. The last thing she wanted was a drawn-out goodbye. Uncurling her fingers, she looked at a snow-white piece of quartz. The rock would definitely remind her of her time spent with him.

She wanted to run as fast as she could and catch him. But then what? Stay here? No. She had to get a job. She needed money and he'd never hinted at wanting her to stay with him forever. Forever? Now that was a new thought for her. She'd never developed the forever kind of feelings for any other man. Was he the one she was meant to be with? Maybe she would find out more in the spring when she would be able to travel more freely. Everyone always said that time would tell. Even so, she was going to miss him.

Horribly.

She watched Steve and Peter climb back on their snowmobiles and take off back through the pass. When she finally turned, her parents stood by their car watching her. She climbed in the back seat.

Her mom finally spoke, "You came through that slit?" She pointed to where the snowmobiles had disappeared into the pass.

"Yeah."

"You shouldn't have risked it."

"And what? Stay another month before the road crews are able to dig a way through?" Alex shut the car door and didn't pay any more attention to what her Mom babbled on about. Her parents kept trying to keep her engaged, but she could only contemplate how she was getting farther and farther away with each passing minute. The car rumbled on past one mountain peak then another as the tears trickled down her cheeks. It seemed to take forever before they crested the last pass and started the descent into Denver.

Alex kept her mind focused on getting a new job. She pulled out Emily's note and looked at the name again. If only this lead would work out. Her money would only last another month or two before she would be in trouble. Her brother, Joseph, had found a job and was helping with more of the rent now. She wondered how Vladimir, her chocolate lab had been faring without her. At least he liked Joe because Joe always took the time to play tug and fetch. Mandy's smiling face popped into her mind. Alex would miss her and Anna Belle. She'd even miss the demon hen. The hen had formed some sort of truce over the last few weeks. Most of all she'd miss Steve. Miss seeing him every day whether it was across the dinner table, doing chores, or even sitting in front of the fire reading. No more. If she concentrated and worked hard, maybe she could find a new job and talk to Principal Vale before seeing Steve again. He needed some answers so he could adjust to his new life and move on, hopefully with her beside him. She wiped her tears away as they headed into the city.

It took some arguing until her parents agreed to drop her off at her apartment. Alex didn't want to go into a lot of details yet. She had plenty of time for her parents to grill her about Steve. Right now, she wanted to concentrate on moving on with her life.

When she entered her apartment, Joe and Vladimir were out. Her parents kept fussing until she agreed to let them take her out to dinner later. When she finally closed the door, the apartment was silent. Only it wasn't really. She could hear the cars going down the neighborhood streets, doors slamming, kids yelling, and dogs barking. It was so different from the valley, where it was actually silent except for the wind and the crackling of the fire. She looked around the apartment. When had she acquired so much stuff? Maybe it was time to clean out some of the clutter.

She lugged her suitcase into her bedroom and tossed it on the bed. Then she pulled her laptop out and plugged it in to charge. In the past, the computer would be the first thing she'd check. Now she wasn't interested. She didn't really care what her college friends were doing. The only person she wanted to hear from was Steve, and he would be the least likely to e-mail her. She flipped the top open and looked for any e-mails from Peter. He'd sent something over an hour ago to let her know that they made it back safe and sound. She sent him a short note that she was back home and asked if he'd check on Steve for her. That done, she sent a note off to Principal Vale requesting a private meeting as soon as possible. The apartment door opened and dog toenails clattered across the oak floors.

"Hey, big sis, you in there?" Joe knocked on her doorframe then entered her bedroom. Vladimir was bouncing on the bed trying to lick every inch of Alex's face. "How you doing?" Joe sat down on her bed and looked at her.

"I don't know. Don't tell Mom or Dad any of this."

Joe did the cross-your-heart gesture. "This is just between us. Give."

"I'm not sure what to do." Alex got up and wandered around the room.

Joe watched her progress. "If you could do whatever you wanted, what would you do?"

Alex sat back down on the bed and scratched Vladimir's ears. She pondered the question for a minute. "I'd have stayed there with Steve."

"How do you feel about him?"

"I'm pretty sure I love him, but how could I?

We've only known each other such a short time."

"Doesn't matter. When you meet the right person, you know."

Alex fingered the nearest bed post's knobs. "I guess so, but this is so complicated."

"There's never anything easy about love. It's the demon that haunts us all, and it's finally found my big sister."

Alex really looked at Joe. When had he gotten so insightful? She got up and paced the room some more. After a few minutes she settled into her desk chair. "So what should I do? It's not like I could move in with him. He didn't ask, and Mom would have a cow."

"Mom can spit fairy dust. Don't let her control your life any more. Do what you want."

Alex fingered the cording on the chair's arm. "He doesn't even have a phone, so I can't call him to talk about this."

"That's a problem without using magic." This time Joe got up and paced. He finally stopped in front of her, "Would you really want to live in such a secluded place?"

Alex looked at Joe. "More than I'd ever have thought."

"Then we'll have to see what we can do." He patted her shoulder and left the room.

When had her little brother grown up into a young man? She watched her brother leave with her dog following. Great, even Vladimir was deserting her.

Monday, she called the number Emily had given her and set up an appointment for an interview in the following week. Later in the morning, Principal Vale messaged her back to see if Wednesday would be a good day to meet. She called him back and set up an appointment at ten for Wednesday. By lunch time she felt bored so she caught a bus to the library and checked out a stack of books. She missed being able to hop in her car and take off but getting her car back would be a good excuse to go see Steve again.

Chapter 25

Several sunny, clear days arrived which helped Alex remain hopeful. If this kept up, the pass would clear and she could get her car. And see Steve again. He called on Sunday, but he seemed reserved. Of course, that could be because he was at Peter's. She wished she could see him face to face to find out what he was feeling. Had his bear already awakened? He had felt it coming awake while she was still there. She had turned his life upside down. To find out he was a wizard and fall in love over a month's time would be overwhelming. He had to be contemplating his life and what his future would bring. She was facing a new job and that alone was bothering her. She couldn't sleep but paced the apartment or read until the wee hours of the morning. Would she be able to function well next week for the job interview? It had been years since she had to interview. Could she do it or would she fumble and get nervous, making a fool of herself? She breathed deeply. She had to get control and not worry or else she would be nervous. She kept repeating to herself, "She's just a person like me. Relax."

Alex got Joe to drop her off at the wizarding mall Wednesday morning. Next week she'd have to rent a car. The location for the interview wasn't on a bus route. She didn't want to have to walk several miles and arrive all sweaty. Maybe she could rent one for the day?

Her budget would take too big of a hit if she did a whole week. After all, other people used the buses all the time, and it worked for them. She'd have to buck up and learn how to plan the bus routes.

She stood outside The Dirty Dog for several minutes thinking. The Dirty Dog was a restaurant which contained the entrance to the wizard mall. She hadn't realized how much she'd missed coming here. Why had she ever wanted to give this up? She'd been a fool to ignore the gift. Not anymore. She was going to embrace the magic and try to do something with it. She didn't know what, but maybe Principal Vale could give her some suggestions. She yanked the outside door open and strode down the entry hall. For the first time in her life, she proudly signed the entry board and opened the door. She took one of the booths along the edge and watched the other wizards. The candles on the tables were red so someone in here wasn't a wizard, otherwise they'd be white.

At first, she thought about ordering something fancy for breakfast, but then she saw scrambled eggs on the menu. She missed having some every morning. She dug in when they came. After savoring a hot tea, she went to the back and signed the board which would give her access to the rest of the mall. For the first time she really looked around. Several hummingbirds and butterflies buzzed her head as she wandered around the mall. At a quarter till ten, she headed back to the traveling booths and took one to Aspen Glen, the wizarding school where Principal Vale was. Why did she ever consider not using magic would be a good idea? She could travel in minutes by the booths instead of making long drives. Of course, driving to Aspen

Glen wasn't even an option. The school kept its location a highly guarded secret.

She donned her traveling cloak and stepped into the booth. After signing the board and depositing a token she was transported to the booth at Aspen Glen. Exiting the booth and small building, she reached the gates. The school's gray stone buildings stood like proud sentinels as several students dashed here and there in the distance. The snow-covered grounds brought back a flood of cherished memories. *Would Steve enjoy it here? Would he even come*? Maybe she should mention Caroline to Vale. Caroline would love it here.

Alex signed the entry board and waited for the gate to open. The gate clicked, creaking when Alex pulled it open. After entering, the gate shut with a resounding click. Alex headed to the admin building. She took a seat in the hard wooden chairs where she'd spent many times waiting to find out if she was in trouble for some prank she'd pulled when she attended school here. Pranks had been her way of standing out among the more talented wizards. Even old Mrs. Pratt was still here, glaring down her button nose at the troublemakers. Mrs. Pratt was definitely looking older, but she still wasn't someone Alex would want to have upset with her.

Alex had to clear her throat so she could get something out. "I'm Alex Klein. I'm here to see Principal Vale."

"Of course you are, dearie. He'll be with you in a minute." She glared at Alex for another minute. "Not into any trouble, are you?"

"No, ma'am."

Mrs. Pratt turned her attention back to the job she'd been doing when Alex came in.

Principal Vale exited his office in his usual flurry, robes billowing behind as he approached Alex.

"Ms. Klein, you have something that we need to discuss?" He shook her hand.

All those years at Aspen Glen, she'd admired him, always feeling worse for disappointing him than about the prank that had gotten her into trouble. He still carried an air of authority and power that she was immediately drawn to. She guessed it was his magic that pulled her in. He had to be the most powerful wizard she'd ever met. She choked out a weak, "Yes."

He took her elbow and escorted her to his office, holding the door open as she entered.

Always the gentleman. No wonder all the girls at school were impressed, so few men showed such respect to women these days. He held out one of the office chairs as she sat, then he sat in the neighboring chair so he could be close, like a friend.

He moved his chair a little closer and spoke in a quiet voice. "What did you need to tell me? You said it was an urgent matter that only I could help you with."

Alex looked down at the floor and took a deep breath. She whispered, "I found a magical object."

"Did you bring the object with you?"

She shook her head. "They're too big."

Vale got up and poured her a glass of water from the pitcher on his credenza. He handed it to her then took his seat again. "Maybe you should start at the beginning."

Alex took a sip and twisted the glass in her hand.

He reached over and touched her arm. "Relax. We

are simply wizards discussing something interesting. You do not need to fear me or be nervous."

"It's not that…exactly." She looked into his eyes and set the glass on the edge of his desk. "This place brings back so many memories."

"Not all bad, I hope."

"Oh no. I have a lot of good memories of my time spent here. Some of my best memories are from here."

"Then just relax. We have as much time as you need." He settled back in his chair, resting his forearms on the chair arms.

Alex took another deep breath. "A little over a month ago, I was driving back from Grand Junction when I got caught in a blizzard. I ended up taking refuge in a cabin where I met Steven Davis. He let me stay and gave me food while the storm lasted for days. One of his neighbors stopped by and later planned a party for the people living there. The daughter of one of the couples kept talking about seeing a unicorn wandering around under the full moon. I spent the next few nights watching and I also saw him."

"A wild unicorn?"

She nodded. "I remember studying about how rare they are. When the storms finally broke, I went out to find him. I remembered learning that they are drawn to magic. I knew he wasn't drawn to me so I wanted to find out what pulled him into the valley. It took me a couple of days, but I found him in a cave. He had located two rocks that must have been there for ages."

"Describe them for me."

"They are about three feet long and egg shaped. After I brushed all the dirt away, I could get a good look. Both have a crystalline structure for the shell but are as smooth as glass. One is as blue as the deep ocean, and the other is blood red. At first, I couldn't figure out what they were. I kept asking the unicorn questions. I ran my bare hands across the surface and could feel a strong magic coming from them. I knew they had to be some magical creature, but I couldn't figure out what would come from an egg that size." She stopped a moment to catch her breath.

Vale remained silent.

"After another round of questions, I figured out the answer with the unicorn's help." She sat up straight, "They're dragon eggs."

"Dragon eggs? They have been extremely rare for centuries."

"I know, but the unicorn was insistent. I figured he would know with his magic being greater than mine and all."

Vale got up and paced for a few minutes while Alex remained silent. He spoke more to himself than to her. "A pair of dragon eggs. I seem to recall a prophecy about a pair of eggs. I will have to find out more." He sat back down in the chair. "Can you show me where they are?"

Alex nodded. "There's a slight problem with that though. The pass I came through to enter the mountain valley is blocked. I only got out by making a hair-raising ride on the back of a snowmobile. We'll have to wait until the pass has been opened before I can take you there."

"Okay then. We will have to wait. Are the eggs protected?"

"I covered them with dirt again and the unicorn is staying in the cave watching over them."

"Do you think he will be a problem if we try to move them?"

"He seemed friendly enough, but you can never tell. He is a wild animal." Alex took a sip of the water. "That's not all."

Vale waited for her to continue.

"The man I stayed with, Steven Davis, promised to bring the unicorn some food."

Vale leaned forward. "The unicorn allowed a man to approach him?"

"That's not the problem. The problem is that Steve is a natural shape-shifter. He shifts into a bear."

Vale touched her arm, "You did not put yourself in any danger, did you?"

Alex shook her head. "The bear's hibernating right now, although I'm not sure for how much longer. Steve was worried that he could feel the bear waking up."

Vale pulled his hand back. "A natural shape-shifter."

"So they really exist?"

Vale nodded. "But they are also extremely rare. The only identified ones have been in the far north. Imagine finding one right here."

Alex leaned forward and touched Vale's arm. "He's really worried about putting anyone in danger. I told him about Aspen Glen. Can you help him?"

"I believe we could, but are you sure he can do any magic?"

Alex leaned back in her chair. "When he touched my wand, some red sparks shot out. That means he's a wizard, doesn't it?"

"Yes, it does. Tell me a little about his family."

"He said the change is automatic when the bear

isn't hibernating. His mom was one and his dad was normal."

"That is interesting."

"The eggs are in the cave where Steve spends his time as a bear."

"I guess he was pulled in by their magic without realizing anything."

"He could also feel the eggs' energy when he touched them."

"He never knew they were there?"

Alex shook her head. "I guess not."

Vale got up and went around his desk. He sat down in his desk chair, opened the black notebook that was on top of his desk, and started making some notes.

"I also wanted to let you know about Caroline Gibson. She's a young girl that spotted the unicorn. I don't know if she has any magic, but she's certainly fascinated by magic and everything magical."

"I guess I will have to look into her while I am out there. What is her name again?"

"Caroline Gibson." Alex got up and approached Vale's desk. "Do you mind if I ask you a personal favor?"

Vale closed his notebook, set his pen down, and looked at Alex. "After all you have done, you can ask, and I will see."

Alex pulled the guest chair closer and sat back down. "When I was here I wasn't serious about my magic. With what's happened, I've found a new calling." She ran a finger along the edge of his desk, then asked, "When I was here, the Book of Prophecy responded with a vague answer of writing. I took some time to re-evaluate my life, and I was interested if the

Book can give me any better information now. Could you look?"

"Give me a few minutes of privacy, and I will look."

Alex stood. "I'll wait outside." She opened the door and walked back out to the reception area to wait.

"Anything I can help you with?" Mrs. Pratt asked.

"No, thank you. Principal Vale asked me to wait here for a few minutes." Alex started pacing around the small area.

Mrs. Pratt kept watching her. "Take a seat, or you'll wear out the threads in that old carpet."

Alex stopped then sat in a nearby chair. Within moments Principal Vale opened his door and motioned Alex in. Alex sat back down in the guest chair while Vale took his seat behind his desk.

"I checked the book, and I have an answer for you."

Alex moved forward on her chair.

"The book now recommends that you should write stories for children and adults. The stories should be about people discovering that they have magic. When the readers check out the author website we will be able to look at their responses and judge if they should be considered as possible candidates for attending school. Hopefully this will help us find more wizards than we currently have."

"It actually said all that?"

Vale nodded. "It did. The writing was minuscule so all the information could be included in the small space. I have never seen such a specific answer. Does that help?"

Alex nodded, "I've contacted a publishing

company about getting a job there, but I'm not as sure about becoming an author."

"You have time. Try to start writing in your spare time for now, then maybe more if you are still interested."

"Thanks for looking. I really appreciate it."

"Are you keeping in touch with Mr. Davis?"

"I'm trying to, but it's hard. His cabin is on the basic side. He has to go to a neighbor, his best friend, to make a radio call. Right now, the phone lines are out."

"Let me know when we can make a trip out there. I want to talk with Mr. Davis and see the eggs. Until then, I will find out as much as I can about dragons."

They both stood and shook hands. Vale showed her out of his office and walked her back to the gate. After unlocking the gate, he said, "I always appreciate it when a former student contacts me. My door is always open."

"I'm glad you could help. I'll let you know when we can get out there."

Vale nodded and shut the gate. Alex headed back to the traveling booths and back to Denver. She ate a quick lunch before calling a cab to take her back to her apartment.

That afternoon she got a call from the publisher she'd contacted. "This is Tami Fisher. I talked with Ms. Gibson, and you came highly recommended. I have three assignments I want you to do before we speak next week. As soon as you finish each task I want you to send it in, and I'll send you the next task at noon the next day. Based on your input we can see if you'll be a good fit."

"Okay," Alex answered. "What's the first task?"

"I want you to write a short segment that advertises a movie, maybe something like *The Wizard of Oz*. This should be like what you find on the back cover or the inside flap of a book. Something that will entice the customer to want to read the book."

"Okay," Alex said.

"Do you have any questions?"

"No, it seems clear enough."

"Good then. I'll be looking forward to see what you send. If you have any other questions, send an e-mail. My assistant watches my inbox all the time."

Alex hung up and powered up her computer. The "as soon as you finish" meant they were interested in finding out how long she took to get the task done. The sooner she finished the more impressive it would be, as long as she did a good job. By late that night, she'd sent in her piece.

The next day she got a request to write ten pages about anything she wanted to write about, fiction or nonfiction. She wrote a bit about Caroline seeing the unicorn and had it in by the next day. The following day Tami sent the first three chapters of a book asking her to read it and make any comments or suggestions. By the next day, Alex had sent back her response. She received only one more e-mail confirming her appointment to meet with Tami.

Alex rented a car the day of her appointment and arrived at the building where Tami had her offices. The location was a two-story brick building that had probably been someone's home at one time. The assistant showed her in to the conference room.

Tami strode in and shook Alex's hand. "I'm so glad we could meet."

"I expected your offices would be in some big office building," Alex said.

"Most of my clients, and half of my staff, work from their homes. We give them the choice to do what works best for them. We only meet here when we need to discuss things face to face." Tami motioned Alex to a chair at the end of the conference table and took the seat next to her. "I liked what you sent in. What are you interested in?"

"I'm looking for something that will be more creative than my last job."

"You have a gift for writing. Ever consider writing a book?"

"I might later on, but right now I need something that will pay my rent."

Tami opened the manila folder she'd brought in. "I liked your suggestions on the three chapters. Are you interested in working as an editor?"

"This would be something I could do from anywhere?"

Tami nodded. "All you'd need is a good Internet connection. Then you would have to come here when needed to go over the project's status with the rest of the team."

"That would be great."

Tami and Alex talked for over an hour going over the details of the job and the company's policies. Two hours later, Alex walked out with a job which she could possibly do from the valley. She'd have to borrow Peter's Internet connection to send things in, but it could work. As long as she could convince Steve that he could control his bear. On the way home, she bought a bottle of champagne and a couple of steaks to celebrate with Joe.

The weather continued to warm up. Three weeks after she'd left, Steve set a date for meeting at the hotel so she could get her car. Joe drove her out but left as soon as they saw her car and Steve waiting inside. Alex checked in and got a room for the night.

Alex asked, "How are the roads?" They headed into the restaurant and selected a table away from any of the other customers.

"Still snow-packed. The plows came through but there's still a layer of snow and ice."

Alex looked up from the menu she'd been perusing. "How'd you get my car here then?"

"I towed it behind my truck. I put my chains on so I got pretty good traction." Steve reached across and took her hand. "Let's grab a quick lunch, then we can go up to the room and you can tell me what you found out."

They talked about Mandy, Anna Belle, and Peter until their food arrived. After wolfing down their sandwiches, they headed up to the room. Steve paced. "What did you find out?"

"I talked with Principal Vale, and he believes he can help."

"How?"

"As soon as I can drive in, I'll set up a meeting with you and him. He can tell you more than I can, and you can ask questions. He also wants to see the eggs."

Steve nodded. "I've started a list of questions I need to ask."

"Is the unicorn still there?"

"Yeah, he's enjoying the hay. As soon as I get close, he comes out to meet me. I've been driving up to the cave now and he doesn't seem to mind."

Alex reached out to Steve. He took her hand and sat down on the bed next to her. She asked, "How are you doing?"

"Other than missing you?"

Alex nodded.

"Okay, I guess. Nothing changes much."

"Only when someone stumbles onto your front porch?"

He pulled her into his arms and gently brushed his fingertips down her cheek. "The luckiest moment of my life."

"I missed you."

He started undoing the buttons on her denim blouse. "This fits you a lot better than my flannel shirts do."

"But I enjoy your flannel shirts, especially when you're in them."

"Shut up and kiss me already." He pulled her down onto the bed with him.

They spent the next few hours making love or wrapped around each other. They left the room when sunset approached.

Alex asked, "When will I see you again?" once they were outside.

Steve pulled her coat tightly shut as they stood next to her car. "I guess when you can come with Principal Vale."

"That won't give us any time to be alone."

"No. We'll have to see how this goes first." He gave her a long passionate kiss and headed back to his truck.

He definitely didn't believe in long goodbyes. Alex

watched his truck disappear into the pass before she headed back in for some dinner. As much as she enjoyed their time together, it was over too quickly. She headed back to Denver the next morning.

At least in Denver the grass was finally starting to send up some green blades, and she could see tiny leaves forming on the crabapple trees. Spring was finally starting. Now she'd be able to get to Steve's. But then there were also the April snows to worry about. As much as she would like to, she couldn't risk getting stuck there again.

Her new job was keeping her busy. She had a stack of manuscripts to review, and she had to have electricity to power her computer to do this. She could work at Peter's with all his solar panels, but Steve didn't have any. No matter how much she hinted about getting some, he seemed wary. After spending most of his life with only limited electric, this would be a major change she'd be bringing about. Would he start feeling overwhelmed by all the changes? She couldn't blame him if he did. All she could do was try and convince him how much better his life would be.

Chapter 26

Alex kept calling Steve now that the phone lines were back in service. Each time they talked, he seemed to become more distant. At first it was little things, then he started finding excuses to end the conversation. At least the snow had ended for the most part. Steve mentioned how they had gotten a few more storms that only dropped a couple of inches. He said the road in was getting better, but it still had some icy spots. Since Alex didn't have chains for her car, she had to wait.

Her new job was a vast improvement over her last one. She was finally enjoying what she did. Tami would send her a manuscript and Alex would work with the author polishing the story. Alex even tried writing. At first, she only wrote a few small bits that gradually increased in size. Three weeks after she'd picked up her car, Steve let her know that the road in was clear enough for her to drive in safely. She would finally get a chance to see how Steve was doing. Did his distance mean his bear was indeed waking up early, or was he not interested in having a relationship with her? How she missed seeing him every day.

Alex arranged to pick up Principal Vale at The Dirty Dog and take him to see Steve. At first, she didn't recognize Vale dressed in a dark gray suit. He looked so different from the way she'd always seen him wearing robes. He presented a striking image with his crisp suit. He stood outside the door holding his hands loosely behind his back. As soon as she pulled to the curb, he opened the passenger door, tossed his coat in the back seat, and settled into the front passenger seat.

He gave her a wink and an easy nod. "This is going to be interesting. I cannot wait to meet Mr. Davis." He closed the door and Alex pulled away. She headed to the nearby highway. "Is the unicorn still there?"

"Steve said he was. He mentioned that the unicorn comes out to meet him when he brings the hay. He can even drive the snowmobile close to the cave now."

Vale touched his fingertips together forming a steeple as he peered out the front window. "It appears that our unicorn is becoming tame. That puts an interesting twist on things."

"How?" Alex asked as she pulled onto the highway.

"We will probably need to bring the unicorn with the eggs. I imagine he will want to continue guarding them, or he would have left by now."

"Why would he leave?"

"He did his job by locating them and making sure someone is aware that they exist."

Alex thought for several minutes about the unicorn. "But he's decided to stay."

"Indeed."

"He would actually keep watch over them? It isn't as if an animal could eat them, they're hard rocks."

"No, but an unscrupulous wizard might try to use them for nefarious purposes."

"Someone would do that?"

"I am afraid so. Not all wizards are noble, some have evil in their heart just like everyone else. Magic does not make one good or evil, it is simply a gift a few of us possess."

Alex could see the mountains looming ahead as she started her ascent. "I never gave it much thought."

"Why would you? You have not had to deal with someone who leans to the dark side of magic."

"Have you?"

"Only on occasion. I have been lucky. I am sure our security force has dealt with several."

Alex nodded. For the first time she understood the implications. She'd never considered the matter before, just lived in her happy cocoon.

"I understand that you have secured a new job."

"How did you find out?"

"The Book. When I looked in it the day of your visit the writing was faint. Now it is as plain as day. I take it you have started writing something?"

"A little. Nothing of any significance."

"You have taken the first step on to a new path. It will take time."

Alex giggled. "You sound like a wise old sage."

"And that surprises you? I nurture new wizards, what would you expect?"

"A wise sage."

"Do not let my age fool you. I am still only one man."

Alex took a quick glance at him. He was watching her and grinning.

He broke out in a booming laugh.

"You're teasing me."

"Of course. Everyone expects me to be some master who knows everything. I try to live up to their expectations."

"Did you learn anything more about shape-shifting? Do you think you can help Steve?"

"I believe so. As long as he wants to learn about magic."

"Why wouldn't he?"

"You would be surprised, not everyone does. I encounter many who continue to deny the existence of magic, especially in themselves."

"Why?"

"Many reasons, although religious beliefs seem to be the most prominent. They refuse to believe that magic and God can co-exist."

This was an area Alex had never considered much. She'd gone to church with some of her roommates in college but had never settled into any specific religion. She believed in striving to lead a moral life but always steered away from any one church. If they discovered she had magic, she hated to think about what they might do. She paid more attention to the road as it wound in among the mountains.

Vale leaned back putting his hands behind his head. "The mountains still manage to amaze me."

"I'd think you'd be used to them by now. You live right in among them."

"Maybe, but you get a different perspective when you are actually winding around them. The school grounds are in a high meadow, so you forget how tall the mountains actually are."

"I love taking this road for that very reason."

"Is that why you chose to drive to Grand Junction?"

"Um…" Alex could feel her face heating up. "No."

He pulled his arms back down, "I do not want to

pry, but why would you drive instead of taking the traveling booth?"

"I was being stupid."

"How so?"

"I was trying to see if I could go thirty days without using any magic."

He remained silent and waited for her to continue.

"It was dumb. I'd become disappointed with trying to find a wizard boyfriend, so I decided to see if I could find someone in the normal world."

Vale remained silent.

"So I decided to try and live only in the normal world."

"Did you have any luck with that?"

"Thankfully no. I had gone twenty-three days before using magic on purpose. I might not have except for going to Grand Junction to visit some college friends. Then I got snowbound."

"I bet you had a lot of mishaps during those days, especially the longer it was."

"As a matter of fact, I did." Alex worried her lip. "Why?"

"When you ignore your magic, especially over a long period, it wants to find its own way of getting out. What happened?"

"I popped a lot of corn, I gave a hen some interesting quirks, and I changed Steve into a bear...Or did I?"

"Probably not directly, not with your level of power. You were just the final push to force his change." Vale laughed. "To think you ended up with another wizard," he managed to get out. "And a rare shape-shifter at that."

Alex nodded. "I didn't know he was."

Vale stopped laughing. "Couldn't you sense him?"

"I may have noticed at first, then the situation distracted me. There were some signs when we got more involved. But I never thought about it again until he told me about him being a shifter."

"Now that is interesting." Vale nodded slowly.

"My powers aren't that strong. Maybe you'll feel something that I don't."

"Maybe."

"What else could it be?"

"Think back to the first moment you met him."

Alex thought about waking up in his bed, his touching her hands and feet checking for frostbite, and when they shook hands.

"Did you feel anything the first time you touched?"

Alex concentrated on the memory, then answered, "I don't remember."

"Where you attracted to him when you looked at him?"

Alex nodded.

"But you did not sense anything?"

She shook her head.

"Interesting." He sat in silence for several minutes. "What is your wand core?"

"Bear hair."

"Do you have any idea where the hair came from?"

"No."

"I will have to check with Glenda. It might be possible that the hair in your wand is from Mr. Davis or his mother."

"How would that affect my sensing him?"

"You may have been touching a part of him ever

since you got your wand. I have only heard of a couple of cases where the wand owner falls in love with the being who donated the wand's core."

"As if they were destined to be together," Alex whispered.

"I take it you feel this way about Mr. Davis?"

Alex gave a slight nod.

"I assumed so the moment you first told me about him. Your face lit up as you talked about him."

"It did?"

"Yes, it did." He reached over and gave her arm one pat. "There is a person out in this wide world we are meant to be with and you have found yours."

"What about you? I know you've never married."

"I have met the woman for me, but I cannot seem to convince her that my intentions are serious."

"Sorry."

He patted her arm again. "I will succeed eventually."

They chatted on about what was happening in the wizarding world. When Alex pulled off and headed into the pass, Vale whistled. He leaned forward and looked at the mountains towering over them.

"This is where you ended up?"

Alex nodded.

"This is almost as secluded as Aspen Glen."

Alex took in the scenery. Snow clung only to the deep crevices on the rock face, highlighting the jagged boulders. The meadow already had wildflowers poking through in a few spots. It didn't look like the same place. If it wasn't for the highway signs, she wouldn't even know this was the right valley. She smiled when she spotted Anna Belle grazing in a pen attached to the barn. She might just be a cow, but she felt like family to Alex. She eased into Steve's driveway and headed up to the cabin. It was all so different. Getting caught in the snow seemed so long ago, but yet just like yesterday. Her life had changed so much since that fateful day.

The moment Alex pulled up, Mandy bounded out the front door and Steve stepped out onto the front porch. Alex exited the car and greeted Mandy, while Vale put his suit coat on and approached Steve.

"I am Principal Vale from the wizarding school, Aspen Glen." He clasped Steve's hand between his. "You're not sensing him must be because of your wand core," he said to Alex.

"I'm Steven Davis." Steve looked over at Alex with a question mirrored on his face then turned back to Vale. "Alex has told me a little about you and the school."

"We can discuss all that later. First, I would like to meet the unicorn. I know it gets dark early in the mountains."

Steve motioned to the two snowmobiles parked by the side of the cabin. "Do you know how to operate one?"

"I do." Vale walked over to one of the machines. "I prefer a horse drawn sleigh though, much quieter and I get excellent fertilizer for my roses."

Steve stifled a laugh. He looked at Alex. "Then you can ride with me." He put Mandy back in the cabin, climbed on a snowmobile, and helped Alex on behind him. He whispered to her, "Hold on tight."

She wrapped her arms around his waist and kissed him on the back of the neck.

"After you," Vale said.

They took off for the cave, dodging several areas where the snow had already melted.

As Steve had explained, the unicorn was waiting at the entrance when they pulled up and shut the machines down.

Vale approached the unicorn and bowed deeply. "It is an honor."

The unicorn snorted and bobbed his head.

They followed the unicorn into the cave and Steve lit the lantern.

Vale immediately headed for the eggs and wiped the dirt off with his gloves. Once the surface was clean he removed his gloves, stuffing them back in his coat pocket, and ran his hands across the surface. After a minute of silence, he gave a soft whistle. "This is beyond my wildest dreams." He turned and nodded to the unicorn. "Thank you for finding them." Then he looked at Alex. "And thank you for investigating. This is an amazing find. Everyone wondered if there were any hidden."

"Are they dragon eggs?" Steve asked.

Vale nodded and started covering them with dirt again. "A pair, we are very fortunate."

Alex moved closer. "So why haven't they hatched?"

Vale stood up and headed back to the entrance. "A specific wizard has to touch the egg before it will hatch."

"Who'll be the wizard?"

"No one knows. The dragon picks the wizard and will bond with them when the egg is touched. A male dragon is said to pick a female wizard and a female dragon will pick a man. As long as the wizard lives, they will remain bonded. Once this happens, the wizards will also be bonded for life. They will never be able to bond with anyone else. At least that is what the stories say."

"What if the man and woman don't know each other or worse yet, hate each other?" Alex asked.

"Too bad for them. The dragon's magic will force them to mate and become a part of each other."

Alex giggled. "I could see that. Glad it isn't me."

"How do you know?" Steve asked.

"Because all three of us have now touched them and nothing has happened."

"Oh yeah," Steve said.

"So with your choice of a spouse removed, why would a wizard ever want to risk touching an egg?" Alex asked.

"Imagine the prestige and power that would come from being selected by a dragon. As well as twice the usual life-span," Vale said.

"Twice?" Alex glanced over and saw Vale nod his head.

"You could do a lot with that many years. As wizards, we already have a hundred plus years."

Of course, more years could mean more stupid mistakes or wrong turns you could make. So far, she hadn't done much with her life.

Vale exited the cave. "We had better get back." He looked at Steve. "Mr. Davis here probably has a hundred questions for me."

Steve nodded and got on his snowmobile. After they got back, they all entered the cabin. Alex made a pit stop, got a glass of water, and took Mandy out onto the front porch.

Chapter 27

After Alex left the room, Vale said, "I would like to see how much power you have, if you do not mind."

"What do you need me to do?" Steve asked.

"Open your shirt so I can lay my hand over your heart."

Steve unbuttoned his shirt and held it open for him.

Vale placed his palm directly over Steve's heart and closed his eyes. After a half a minute he said, "Thank you, you can button up again."

"What happened?"

"Nothing happened, it is one way to check a wizard's power levels."

"How?" Steve placed his own palm over his heart.

"Close your eyes and reach out with your senses. You should be able to feel something other than the beating of your heart."

Steve did as recommended, concentrated, then started to nod.

"Do you feel an energy pulsing?"

Steve nodded.

"That's your magic coursing through your body. A powerful wizard has a strong flow where a weak or injured wizard has only a faint trace."

"Do you mind if I try this on you?"

"Be my guest." Vale unbuttoned his shirt and held it open.

Steve reached in and barely touched Vale's chest when he could feel it. The strong pounding was as clear as day. He pulled his hand away. "Thanks, I wanted to understand it better."

"Shall we have a seat?" Vale nodded toward the table as he buttoned his shirt. Steve and Vale took a seat at the table facing each other. Steve brushed his hand across a sheet of paper that had all his questions.

"May I?" Vale asked and held a hand out for the piece of paper, while he pulled his glasses out and put them on.

Steve handed it to him and waited while he read.

Vale handed the sheet back to Steve and removed his glasses. "Most of your questions will be answered by attending school, especially those on how the magic works. Most of our first-year adult students know nothing about magic until they receive their invitation to attend Aspen Glen."

"Am I some type of...warlock or something?"

"We prefer to use the term wizard. Witch and warlock remind everyone of the witch trials, so everyone is only a wizard."

"What if I don't want to come?"

"I cannot stress enough how important it is that you come." Vale put his glasses back in his front suit coat pocket.

"Why?" Steve asked. "I've gone this long without knowing anything about all this."

"Yes, but do you want to continue living the way you have. Alone. Always afraid you might accidentally hurt someone. Never allowing a woman to get close for fear of harming her. By attending Aspen Glen, you will learn how to control your shifting."

"Do you think it's possible I might be able to not shift?"

"I believe so. But I have to let you know that I have not encountered your type of shifting before so there are no guarantees." He held up a hand to stop Steve from asking a question. "It is not that black and white; there are many possible variations. You may be able to not change, only change during a full moon, always change, or some combination. At the very least you will be able to sleep through the night instead of prowling around. Were-animals have to change at the full moon. Most shape-shifters only change for the three peak days to absorb power from the moon's influence or when they want to for other reasons."

"I could sleep through the night and be awake during the day?"

Vale nodded.

He had never been able to dream of such a possibility. Ever since puberty he spent his nights wandering. Only during winter did he get a break, when his bear hibernated.

Vale broke into his thoughts. "You have a destiny if you want it. Learn magic and find out what your possibilities are. A whole world awaits. Just take a chance."

"I don't know," Steve answered, but concentrated on inspecting his fingers.

"Come for one summer and then you can decide if you want to continue."

"I could quit?" Steve looked up.

"Yes, but you will still need to abide by our magical laws. If you do not finish, then security will have to explain our rules."

"Alex mentioned security might come." Steve jumped up from the chair and started to pace.

"We have our own security and medical. You will have to follow the rules so you might as well enjoy the benefits." Vale watched Steve pace.

"What if I want to forget all this happened?"

"You can't. Once a wizard has been identified, they are part of our world." Vale paused. "Would you really want to have all of your memories about Alex erased? They have to remove everything so nothing will resurface."

"What about Peter and the other valley's residents? They've met her; they've even helped her get a new job." Steve clutched the back of the chair.

"Security would erase all of their memories too, and Alex would have to find work somewhere else. Would you really want that?"

"No." Steve sighed and sat back down. "So I have to come."

"I would highly recommend that it is in your best interest to come. You are not the only person to debate about coming to school or not. Think about what is available to you in our world. I cannot imagine that you would want anything else. With the training, you could even marry."

"She would be safe?" If only it was possible. He enjoyed seeing her every day and touching her. She filled his life with a joy he'd never known before. He wanted her to be a part of his life.

"It would be better if she was also a wizard."

Steve smiled.

Vale looked straight into Steve's eyes. "Maybe even a wizard like Ms. Klein."

"How'd you know?"

"I do have some skills." Vale smiled. "But it was not necessary to use anything. I have seen enough women in love to recognize the signs. I can tell by the way she talks about you."

"She talks about me?"

Vale nodded.

"If I attend this school, she'd be safe?" He moved forward in the chair, perching on the edge.

"Probably." Principal Vale pulled out an envelope and tapped it against his hand. "Inside is a list of supplies you will need. Ms. Klein can take you to the mall to get everything."

"I want to know more about wands, if you don't mind."

"No two wands are the same, just as no two unicorns, crows, phoenixes, or even bears are quite the same. Even wands with unicorn hairs are different because each unicorn and each wood imparts different properties to the wand. There are limitless possibilities, but one unique combination will be the best fit. This wand will perform better for the wizard than any other." Vale pulled out his wand and handed it to Steve.

When Steve held it, only a couple of stars managed to squeeze out. "Why do I get a lot more with Alex's wand?"

"The bear hair in her wand responds to the bear in you. It might even be that the hair in her wand came from you or your mother."

"Could that even be possible?"

"Maybe." Vale nodded toward the wand. "Concentrate and reach out. What do you feel when you touch the wand?"

Steve closed his eyes and ran his left hand fingers over the surface. "I can feel a warmth to the wood…and it tingles."

"That is because you are a wizard. If you were normal you would only feel the wood."

"So how do I find the wand that best suits me?" Steve handed the wand back.

"There is an excellent wand shop in Denver. It is on the list that you will need to get before coming." Vale slipped his wand back in his coat's wand pocket.

"How am I going to afford all of this?"

"If you let us take responsibility for the dragon eggs, all your costs will be covered."

"Why?"

"They are on your property. We cannot remove them unless you give us permission. They are priceless to us. The least we can do is cover your costs of becoming a full wizard."

"Are you sure?"

Vale nodded. "Let the shops know who you are and I will see to it that your expenses are covered."

"What if I have any questions?" he asked, reaching out to take the envelope.

"Ms. Klein can probably answer them, but my phone number is on the letter if you have more questions."

"I've already started shifting. I will be all summer. Will that be a problem?"

"No. I have talked to Nurse Apple. She knows about your condition and believes she has the perfect potion to keep you asleep at night. But she wants you to come a week early so she can get the potion customized to your needs. She wants to keep you in the infirmary until she knows that she has it perfected. Then she will teach you how to brew it yourself so you can keep taking it once you leave school after the summer."

"That'll be a welcome relief." Steve ripped the envelope open and pulled the sheets of parchment out.

"Any other questions for now?"

Steve shook his head as he continued to scan the list. He stopped Vale. "I don't have a computer or cell phone. Will that be a problem?"

"No, we have phones, and several computers at the school that you can use to do your homework on. The librarian can show you how to use them, or maybe Ms. Klein can stop by and teach you?"

Steve shook his head. "I can't let her be around. Not with my bear awake. You won't tell her, will you? You see...her presence stirs him up. I've already accidentally shifted when she was only several feet away. I'll get one of the neighbors to teach me."

"Think of me as you would your doctor; what you say to me stays with only me."

"I've never seen a doctor except to get my childhood shots."

"You have never been sick?"

"Never. My mother never got sick either. It must be related to our shifting."

"I look forward to learning more about your talent." Vale stood up. "I will see you in a few months. Good luck," he said shaking Steve's hand.

Vale went out to the porch. He looked at the sun dipping behind the mountains. "We should leave," he said to Alex.

"I'll say goodbye then." Alex stood up from her chair and started to enter the cabin. Vale grabbed her arm, stopping her.

"No. We need to leave right now."

Alex looked at the door. "It'll only take a moment."

"We don't have a moment left." Vale continued to firmly hold her upper arm and escorted her to the car. The moment she got in, he closed the door and rushed around to the get in the passenger side. "Let's go."

Alex started the car and pulled out onto the road. She'd never heard him use a contraction before; he always took his time when he spoke. It had to be important or he wouldn't have rushed her. Did he have another appointment, and was he running late? She had to concentrate on the twisting road as darkness fell.

She finally broke the silence when she got on the highway. "Why did we have to leave so fast?"

"He would shift into his bear in minutes. I could feel the energy coming from him, and he needed to lock the cabin up. Have you noticed the gouges in the front door?"

Alex nodded.

"He did that."

"How do you know he did that and not another bear?"

"He looked at them when we went inside. He made them. Can you imagine what he would do if you were around. Even if you were behind the barred door, he would probably claw through the wood when his bear wanted to mate with you."

"His bear would want to mate with me? I'm not a bear."

"Neither is he entirely. I can assume that you have been intimate, since you both love each other."

Alex nodded and kept looking out the windshield.

"The bear in him will want to propagate. Nature drives animals to want to multiply. He is no different. Even as a man, I am sure he wants children or he would have completely isolated himself from others. He would not have created his own little community."

Alex thought for a minute. "If we had children, would they be shape-shifters?" Her hands tightened on the steering wheel.

"Probably. He has a lot of magic in him. I would expect his children will also be strong wizards." Vale turned in his seat to face her.

"Even with me not having much?"

"Even then, but you have more magic in you than you ever gave yourself credit for."

"I do? Then why didn't I do better at school?" She quickly glanced over.

"Your powers had not fully developed. It would have been better if you had waited to come when you were an adult."

"Then why didn't I?"

"Your parents did not want you to be left out. They wanted you to attend Aspen Glen like your siblings."

Alex stayed silent for a few minutes. "They were right. I would have resented it if they hadn't let me come as a kid."

"Most children from wizarding families feel that way, so we take them unless they show no abilities or very little. In these cases, it would be harder on them than not going."

"I can see that." She stayed quiet for another minute and loosened her grip. "So, if I went back over the class material, I'd do better?"

"Yes."

"Then maybe I should also come to school this summer and relearn everything?"

"No, you only need to practice. And can you imagine how hard it would be for Mr. Davis and the other students if you were there. Especially since you already know how to do most of the spells."

"I guess." She stayed silent another minute. "You're losing your touch. I've never known you to take so long to convince someone to do something."

"Usually a student is thrilled to find out that magic is real."

"True. Steve hasn't been thrilled."

"At least he knows why he can turn now, thanks to you."

"Do you think he'll continue past the first year?" She glanced over again.

"I hope so."

"He said he hates school."

"Aspen Glen is different."

Alex smiled when she remembered how she'd enjoyed being there. It was only when she went to college that she felt out of place. Why would she ever want to not use magic? Obviously, she wasn't thinking clearly.

"I would hate to lose someone like Mr. Davis. He has a unique talent." Vale shifted back and watched the mountains pass by.

"How?"

"I have never heard of anyone shifting without using a spell or wand—to be a natural. A bear is an unusual shape to take. Most wizards become cats or dogs."

"Could the dragon eggs be the reason he picked this valley to live in?"

"I believe so. I think they have an influence on him. After all, he spends time in that cave when he is a bear." Vale pointed to the next exit. "Why not stop and get a quick bite to eat. I never get fast food at the school. Do not get me wrong, the food there is excellent. I just miss sinking my teeth into a juicy burger."

Alex tapped her fingers on the steering wheel while she exited the highway. Steve would have turned into his bear by now. The moment she turned the car off she grabbed Vale's arm. "The unicorn. Will he be safe in the cave if Steve is a bear?"

He looked at her. "Unicorns have a magic all their own. He will be safe. He probably has a calming effect on all animals, not just people."

As they ate their greasy burgers and fries, Alex looked at a photo on the wall of a bear standing on a rock, looking out over an open meadow. She quickly whispered, "I'm the reason Steve started turning early. Aren't I?"

Vale dipped some fries in his pile of ketchup and inspected them without ever looking at her. He stuffed the fries into his mouth. "These are great, aren't they?"

Another contraction. Vale was letting her know without saying a word. She thought back to her conversations over the last few weeks. Steve had been distancing himself because his bear was awake. He didn't want to endanger her. And she was the reason why. She looked at Vale. He was watching her every expression. Her face probably said everything she was thinking and sometimes she swore he could read her mind.

"You know, it never fails to astound me what happens when two people fall in love. They change in oh so many ways," he said.

It was amazing how he could tell you something without ever telling you—a gift all its own. She whispered, "I caused him to change that one day, and I was standing right there. He could have hurt me without meaning to, and I didn't have my wand with me to protect me. It's no wonder he's been avoiding me."

"He shifted last year and the year before. He will keep shifting until he can manage to control it. That is the nature of a shifter." He reached out and patted her hand. "Have faith that everything will work out." He picked up his burger and took a big bite.

The rest of the way back to Denver, they kept the conversation on other things. When she pulled up to The Dirty Dog, he said, "It has been an honor, Ms. Klein. I will stay in touch so we can figure out when it is the best time to move the eggs to Aspen Glen. I do not know of another location that is as well guarded. Until then..." He waved and entered the building.

As she drove the rest of the way home, the day's events kept running through her mind. At least Steve was willing to try school. She'd have to keep positive that the magic would enable him to not shift. Otherwise, he'd refuse to keep seeing her. He'd do anything within his power to keep her out of danger. She'd have to convince him that this was the right path or else lose him.

Chapter 28

Two weeks after Principal Vale's visit, Alex got a call from Steve. "I can't figure out who can look after my animals if I'm gone all summer. Peter can do the occasional day, but he isn't up to a whole summer."

"I can," Alex answered. "I can come out and spend the summer there."

"What about your new job?"

"I can do it from almost anywhere. With Peter's Internet access, I won't have any problems."

"I don't know. You had a lot of trouble when you were here."

Alex guffawed. "You haven't even begun to see what can be done with magic. I'll come out in ten days and prove it to you."

"You'll have to leave well before sunset."

"No problem. I can stay at the hotel or Peter's."

"Okay, I'll see you in ten days."

Alex hung up and grabbed a piece of paper. It had been years since she'd cleaned a barn with magic. Not since her days at Aspen Glen. She thought about all the chores they'd done when she was there and made a list. Next, she contacted Principal Vale and asked if she could come to the school and get a refresher session from Mr. Sheppard, or whoever taught the Animal Husbandry course now. Of course, it would probably be a crash course since she figured she'd forgotten it all by now. He agreed and arranged for her to come between one and three on the upcoming Tuesday afternoon. That settled, she went over to her parents so she could practice household chores. Her parents had limited electronics so she could practice there. Her apartment had way too many gadgets. She couldn't afford to fry her TV or computers by practicing. With a couple of hours practice, she had honed up on the spells, leaving her parents' house spotless.

By the time she headed to Steve's, she felt confident she could impress him. Her sessions at school went pretty well, except for the small disaster of cooking the horse droppings instead of making them transport to the pile outside. The stench filled the barn for several hours. For some reason, their horses' mess didn't respond to her magic.

While driving to Steve's, she kept reviewing the spells the instructor had gone over. By spending the whole summer there, she would have the spells perfected. So many changes had happened since they'd met. Steve led her to believe that he loved her. Did he still after everything? All she knew for certain was that she loved him. No way was she going to let him slip away without a fight. He was worth it. Alex hadn't quite reached the drive when she stopped and looked toward the cabin.

Mandy was sitting there holding a hose in her jaws. Steve was bent over rinsing his hair under the running water. He thoroughly rinsed his hair, arms, and upper chest. Then he threw his head back and shook, flinging water like a wet dog. Alex sucked in some air and slowly released it. The water glistened in the sunlight, showcasing his broad shoulders and arms. It had been too long since she'd come for a visit. She took another deep breath and drove into the driveway. Steve had shaken out his t-shirt and had slipped it on by the time she pulled up. Mandy bounded out to the car and jumped up on her door the moment she stopped.

"I was just chopping some firewood." Steve pushed Mandy down and opened her door. "How are you?"

"I'm better, now that I'm here," she said.

"I purposely didn't clean for several days to make sure you had enough to work with."

Anna Belle was grazing in the outside pasture. When she walked into the barn, the odor overwhelmed her. *Whatever it takes, I will get this done*. She looked around to see what could be taken care of first to get rid of the stench. She decided to clean up Anna Belle's pies so she could at least move around the barn without stepping in one. *Now I'll show him what a wizard can really do*. With this, she pulled her wand out of her purse and took another look around. She said, "*Levare*," and waved her wand around the barn. All the cow pies lifted up five feet and hung there. "Where do you want them?"

Steve's mouth hung open, but he pointed to the open barn door.

Alex pointed her wand at the open door. "*Evolare*." All the drifting hunks flew out the door and landed in a pile outside. She headed to the hen house. The moment she walked in, the speckled hen squawked loudly, flew at Alex, and pecked her on the arm. Then the hen flew to the far corner and turned her back on Alex. Alex repeated the spells that she'd used in the barn, and all the droppings joined the pile outside. She filled the water and corn for the chickens. The Houdini hen ruffled her feathers but remained in the far corner ignoring Alex. Then Alex performed a spell that collected all the eggs and put them in her basket. The startled hens flew up to the perches and eyed Alex from a safe distance. Alex stepped out of the hen house and handed the basket to Steve. Next, she used her wand to spread some more hay around the barn and moved a bale over to Anna Belle's stall. Brandishing her wand some more, she filled the buckets with water, then the oats, making them empty in the correct place. Satisfied that the barn was done, Alex headed into the cabin.

The sink was full of dirty dishes, books were strewn all over the place, and hair balls floated along the cabinets. *This'll be a piece of cake.* She did spell after spell. The dish cloth washed all the dishes, the towel dried them, and they all went back into the cabinets. The books flew around the room and re-shelved themselves. Hair balls, dust, and trash flew into the trash can that Alex held out. She wiped her hands together and looked at an astonished Steve.

"What in hell?" he asked as he wandered around looking.

"Isn't magic wonderful?" Alex brimmed with glee. She'd shown him.

"It only took you minutes to get everything done!"

Alex nodded.

"You could have done this all along?"

"Except...I didn't know you were a wizard, so I couldn't do magic in front of you." She walked over to the kitchen sink and got a glass of water. "I couldn't have done this if you had a lot of electronics. Magic tends to fry electrical gadgets. It would be disastrous to try this in Peter's house."

Steve walked out to the barn and carefully inspected everything. Alex watched him trying to find anything she'd missed. He went out and brought Anna Belle in. She wandered into her stall, and Steve handed Alex the footstool.

She took the stool. "What's this for?"

"Anna Belle. You need to milk her. She'll be tapering down in June and you won't be milking her in July and August. She isn't due to have her calf until September, but I'll make sure you have the vet's number."

Shit, shit, shit. She forgot to find out how to milk the cow. She thought back to her years at school and remembered how they had to do that by hand. She took the stool and placed it near Anna Belle, like she'd seen Steve do every day. But she couldn't remember what to do next.

Steve whispered into her ear. "You can do this. I know you can, you've done it to me, sort of."

Alex chewed on her lip, trying to remember.

"Take your fingers and wrap them around a teat, like you do me."

Alex reached out and grasped a teat. Steve put his arms around her and reached in. He showed her how to do it. Her heart pounded and her pulse raced with him wrapped around her like this. As she got the milk to come out, he moved away. This made it easier to concentrate on the milking, but she didn't want him to leave. Once she'd gotten enough milk, he picked the bucket up and carried it back into the cabin. Anna Belle shoved Alex as she tried to head back into the cabin. Alex rubbed her neck. "Not right now, I have something I need to do."

She walked into the cabin and shut the door.

Steve left the milk on the counter and started to wander around. "You know, if I could learn to do this, it would be worth going to school. I know you know how to fill the lanterns and brush Anna Belle but—"

Alex had moved close. She pulled him into her arms and started kissing him. As she worked to undo his buttons, she whispered, "Do you still have any of those condoms left?"

Steve nodded and Alex pulled him into the bedroom. She quickly removed their clothes as he pulled the box of condoms out of the bedside table's drawer. She lingered over slipping it on him while she plundered his mouth. He never said a word, but quickly became an active participant. After they'd exhausted themselves they lay entwined on top of the bed.

He kept running his fingers over her, exploring every inch. "I didn't mean for that to happen."

"Any regrets?"

"No…it's just…everything's changing. I don't know if we can ever have anything more."

Alex rolled over on top of him. "We can have a lot more if you want to." She took out another condom and slowly slipped it on his already enlarging member. "At least…I want a lot more." She started kissing him, and they made love again.

The afternoon was already slipping by as they lay on the bed. "We missed lunch," Steve said.

"I had the kind of lunch I wanted." Alex continued to stroke his chest.

"I'd invite you to dinner, but we know I can't."

"I know."

"I need to ask you about something else, but it'll have to wait now. Did you make plans to stay somewhere overnight?"

"I'm staying with Peter. He invited me."

They both got up and started dressing.

"Can you come by about nine?" Steve asked.

"Sure."

Steve helped her into her t-shirt and they headed to the front door. He walked with her onto the front porch. "Make sure you stay inside tonight. I don't want to run the risk of smelling you. I'll see you tomorrow." He turned and went back into the cabin.

Alex walked down to her car. As she pulled out onto the road, she looked at the cabin again and shook her head. She and Peter fixed a steak dinner with all the fixings and talked until bedtime. She stayed up a while and watched out the second-floor window. A large brown bear could be seen wandering around the fir trees in the far distance, but he seemed to be staying in the trees away from Peter's. She sighed. If only she could convince him that everything would work out.

The next day when she pulled in, Steve was waiting on the porch. His eyes had circles under them and he was drinking a large mug of hot tea. "Are you okay?" she asked.

"I didn't get any sleep yesterday. Someone kept me awake all afternoon."

Of course; she'd interrupted. If he prowled all night, he'd have to sleep during the day. "Sorry."

He got up and headed toward his truck. "I need you to help me with something else."

She got in his truck and they headed off down the valley. After passing the other houses, the road turned into a rutted dirt path. He drove on until they reached the edge of a mountain. He got out and walked over to the boulders. "If I'm going to be gone all summer, how am I supposed to get my prospecting done. Without the stones, I won't have enough money to get by." He looked up into the rocks.

Alex walked over and stood next to him. "Are some of the stones on the surface?"

He nodded.

"Show me one of the most valuable."

He pulled an aquamarine crystal out of his pocket.

Alex took it from his hand and looked at it closely. She pulled out her wand and placed it in her hands with the stone. She closed her hands and concentrated on how the stone felt—its inner structure, temperature, and shape. She lifted up her arms and opened her hands. Sweat poured down her face, but she refused to give up. After what felt like an eternity, her hands started filling with one rock after another. When she felt she couldn't go on, she closed her hands and collapsed.

The next thing she knew, Steve was speaking to her. He was using the end of his shirt to wipe her forehead.

"I'll be okay, just give me a moment," she managed to whisper.

He continued to touch her face.

"Do you have any water?" she whispered. She could hear his feet pound and crunch over the rocks as he ran back to the truck.

He helped her sit up and gently tipped the water bottle so she could drink.

After a couple of minutes, she'd recovered a little. She cracked her hands open and held them out to him.

"Is this enough for this year?" She poured the stones into his hand.

He looked down at the rocks and gasped. "How'd you do that?"

"Magic."

"You can call them to you?"

She gave a slight nod. "But this type of magic comes with a cost."

"What do you mean?"

"You'll learn that at school." She sat up more and brushed her dusty hands off on her jeans. "I don't have as much power as some wizards so I can only do this type of magic on special occasions."

"You did that for me?"

She inclined her head. "If it means you'll go to school, I'll help however I can. You've done so much for me. This is my way of repaying some of the debt."

"You don't owe me anything."

"You took me in. You gave me a reason to go back to my magic." She tried to stand but couldn't.

"Wait a second," he said and stuffed the stones in a canvas bag he'd brought back from the truck. He leaned down, picked her up, carried her back to the truck, and settled her in the seat. "Let me get you back to the cabin." He ran around the truck, then started back. When he pulled in next to the cabin, Alex managed to get out. She headed straight to her car and got in. "Are you sure you're okay to drive?" he asked.

Alex nodded. She started the engine and pulled out of his driveway. She could see him still standing in front of the cabin as she pulled onto the road. He didn't know, but she wasn't okay to drive. She got to the hotel, checked in for two nights, then went up to the room and crashed on the bed.

Peter headed out the next morning and noticed Alex's car at the hotel. He pulled in and headed for the front counter. Victoria, their neighbor, was on duty so he stopped and asked, "Did Alex Klein check in? I saw her car out in the lot and wondered."

"Let me check," Victoria said. She checked the computer. "She checked in for two nights."

"She said she had to go home yesterday. I wonder what changed her mind. What's her room number?"

Victoria looked around. "Don't let anyone know, but for you...she's in room 207."

Peter tapped the counter. "Mums the word. I'll see you later." He headed up and knocked on the door, but no one answered. He left and headed back home. As he approached Steve's, he slowed, then pulled into the drive.

Steve met him at the driveway as he pulled in. "What's up?" He leaned on the door.

Peter rolled down his window. "That's what I wanted to know. I thought Alex was heading home yesterday."

"She did."

Peter shook his head. "She's checked in at the hotel. I knocked on her door but no answer."

"She was probably getting something to eat."

"I looked. No sign of her. How was she when she left?"

Steve thought. "I don't know. She said she was fine." But he had to wonder. She had passed out right after doing the magic and mentioned something about paying a price. Steve walked around Peter's fancy SUV and got in. The SUV was the closest thing to an armored troop carrier a civilian could get. "Let's go find out."

Peter looked at Steve. "Is everything okay?"

"I don't know, maybe not. How'd you find out she was there?"

"Her car is in the lot, and Victoria was on duty, so I asked." Peter pulled out and headed back to the hotel. They both walked in but had to wait while another guest was at the desk. As soon as the guest had left they approached.

"We think Alex might not be feeling well and need to check. Can you help us?" Steve whispered.

Victoria looked around. No one was near. "Don't tell anyone."

Peter and Steve zipped their lips.

"I'd never do this for anyone else, but I don't want anything to happen to Alex." She set out the Be Right Back sign and motioned them to the elevator.

They knocked again, but Alex didn't answer. Victoria used the master key card to open the door and they walked in. Alex was stretched out face-down on the bed still in the clothes from the day before. "Thanks Victoria, we'll make sure she's okay," Steve said.

"Let me know if you need anything," she said and left.

"Alex. Alex. It's me, Steve. Talk to me." He shook her shoulder, but she didn't respond.

Peter hovered beside him. "Any idea what's wrong?"

Steve lifted up her wrist and felt her pulse. "No, but I know someone who might. Can I use your phone?"

Peter handed Steve his phone.

Steve pulled out his wallet and removed a card. He dialed. "Mr. Vale please?" He could barely hear over all the static.

"This is Vale. Who's calling?"

"Thank God. It's Steve Davis. I think something has happened to Alex Klein." The phone crackled again. "Can you hear me," he shouted.

"Just barely. Put the phone on speaker and set it down."

Steve handed the phone to Peter. Peter pressed a button and set it down on the nearby nightstand.

"Can you hear me now?" Steve asked.

"Yes. Can you tell me what happened?"

"Peter, a neighbor, saw Alex's car at the hotel and came to see me. We thought we'd better check and found Alex on the bed. She isn't responding, but she has a good pulse."

"Is Peter with you right now?"

"Yes," Steve answered.

"As carefully as you can, tell me what happened."

Steve had to think for a moment, how could he explain without talking about magic? "Alex helped me with one of my jobs yesterday. After she finished, she passed out. When she woke up, she said she was tired but okay. She left as soon as she got back to her car and I guess she came to the hotel. She did mention something about there being a price to pay for what she did."

"Place your hand over her heart, like I did to you. Concentrate hard and tell me if you feel anything. Take your time and pay attention."

Steve rolled Alex over and pulled up her t-shirt. He wiped his hand down his jeans then placed it flat over her heart. He closed his eyes and concentrated. Her heart beat steadily as he tried to feel anything else. Vale made this look so easy. Then he felt it—a tiny flicker. He yanked his hand away. After a moment, he slid his hand under his shirt. He could feel a similar sensation, but a lot stronger in him. He looked over to Peter. "Can you give me a minute?"

Peter nodded and went into the bathroom.

"We're alone. I can feel a little flicker but nothing like what I have. What can I do?"

"She should be okay after a few days of sleeping," Vale answered.

"What happened?"

"My best guess is that she used too much power doing what she did. It will take several days for her to build it back up enough so she can function again."

"Is there any way we could speed up the process?"

"Only one that I know of…But it will require you to do something you might not want to do."

"Anything. I'll do anything to help her. Just tell me what I have to do."

"You have to have unprotected sex with her."

"What?"

"Unprotected sex is the only way for one wizard to share power with another. It will change you. It will create a bond between the two of you. Do you still want to do this?"

"But unprotected? What if she gets pregnant?"

"That is a risk you will have to take. If the worst happens, will you do right by her?"

"Yes. But I don't understand why."

"The act of totally joining is what allows the transfer. If you do not want to do this, I understand. She will recover without this, but it will take longer. It is up to you to decide. If I can help in any other way, please call."

"Okay." Steve turned off the phone and pulled her shirt back down. "Peter," he called. Peter opened the bathroom door. "Help me get her to your house. We can make sure she's okay until she feels better."

Peter pocketed his phone and they checked the room to make sure they didn't leave anything behind. Peter picked up her overnight bag, and Steve carried Alex out. They nodded to Victoria as they left. Steve cradled Alex as they drove back. Steve asked, "Could you take care of her for a few days?"

"Don't you want to do that?"

"You know I can't. She wouldn't be safe alone in my cabin."

"How do I know your bear won't rip into my place trying to get to her? You've told me about what you did to your front door."

"I'll use the shackles so I can't wander around."

"Will you be safe all tied up like that?"

"I can barricade myself in my cave so nothing can attack me."

Peter slowed down at Steve's driveway. "You're sure about this?"

"I'm sure."

Peter drove on down to his house. Steve carried Alex up to the guest room and tucked her into the bed.

As Peter drove Steve home, Steve said, "I'll come by in the morning as soon as I finish taking care of the animals."

"Is she going to be okay?"

"I was told she needs a lot of rest and then she'll be

fine." Steve got out and headed into his cabin. He took care of the animals then barricaded the doors and closed the window shutters. He grabbed the shackles and headed for his cave.

As soon as he approached, the unicorn was waiting at the entrance. Steve carried the shackles in and started putting them on.

The unicorn sniffed the shackles and backed up.

"I need your help for the next few evenings."

The unicorn pawed the ground.

"Can you lie in the passage so I can't possibly get out?"

The unicorn nodded.

"Thanks. Alex is at Peter's, and I don't want to accidentally hurt them."

The unicorn nodded.

The next day Alex stirred. Steve was asleep in a chair and Peter had entered the room.

"How is he?"

"He's had a bad night. He put the shackles on so he couldn't get here."

"Oh no. You should have left me at the hotel."

"You know we couldn't do that." Peter set a tray of food down next to her. "The best thing you can do is eat and sleep so you can leave."

Alex ate whenever Peter came with food and slept the rest of the time. The next day, when Peter woke her for lunch, she looked over at Steve sleeping and noticed the bandages around his wrists.

"What happened to him?"

"He tries to get out of the shackles."

"He shouldn't have to do that for me." A tear trickled down her cheek. "I'll leave tomorrow. I should be rested enough to get home."

After two days of sleeping and eating, she had recovered enough to drive home. Even then, she spent most of the week sleeping. She fell behind on her work but spent every waking hour getting done what she could. She tried calling Steve to find out how he was faring, but he never answered. Would he reconsider and not go to Aspen Glen?

Chapter 29

A week before school started, Steve drove into Denver to the wizarding mall. He parked along the curb and waited until Alex showed up. He kept looking over the sheets of paper Principal Vale had given him as he killed time. *I'm actually going to do this.* He'd seen how fast Alex had gotten the chores done with magic. If he could learn a fraction of what she could do, this would all be worth it. Then there were the stones. She'd gathered in minutes what took him a couple of years of hard work to get. He'd agreed to her spending the summer at his cabin. He'd given her the phone numbers for ordering a refill on the propane tank. Getting the hay in still worried him. Usually he rented a mower to harvest the meadow, instead she'd have to hire someone to come in. She kept insisting that she could take care of it. He had to trust that she could deal with it or call him if she had any problems.

He had to wait ten minutes until the scheduled meeting time. Two minutes before ten Alex stepped out of the door that was under a swaying metal sign that said, The Dirty Dog. He'd wondered if this was the right place as he drove through the neighborhood of deserted brick warehouses. The sign and a few parked cars were the only indications that he'd followed the directions correctly.

Alex led him in the first door through a brick

hallway made from the same brick as the building. The hallway extended to the right along the edge of the building, with another door at the end. Next to this door was a chalkboard with a sign that said, "High Tension Lines Present Inside This Building. Management Is Not Responsible For Any Damage to Electrical Equipment. Please Leave All Electronics and Weapons Outside."

Alex led him through the door into another brick hallway that led back to the left. At the end of this hallway were various-sized lockers with a chalkboard on each one. Steve wondered why they had so many chalkboards and what they were for. The sign on the door at the end of this hallway said, "No Weapons Beyond This Point." He was too busy looking around to notice what Alex wrote on the chalkboard. She opened the door and led him in.

Once inside, Alex flagged down a waitress. "We have an appointment with Ms. Meggin."

The waitress led them through the tables toward the back. The restaurant had dark wood tables in the center and booths hugging the walls off to the left and to the right of the door. Dark wood paneling covered the bottom four feet of the walls and a richly colored mountain scene was painted above this. The scene seemed to blend right into the paneling. The colors lightened as the scenes turned to mountains, and the sky above the mountains continued up the walls onto the ceiling. An oil lamp with a red globe was on each of the tables. A wonderful scent of freshly baked bread and soups permeated the air. There were several tables with customers, so Steve wondered if the hours on the outside door hadn't been correct. There was soft lighting throughout the restaurant cast by the many burning oil lamps hanging from the ceiling. He was reminded of an old-fashioned ale house, one from the nineteenth century.

They were then shown to Ms. Meggin's office. Alex sat down at one of the tables outside the office. "I'll wait here while she gets you registered."

The office was another wood-paneled room with the whole left side covered with bookshelves containing large leather-bound volumes. Ms. Meggin was an older woman who seemed to always be smiling. She rose as he entered her office. After shaking his hand, she motioned for him to take a chair. She added, "Hi, I'm Dana Meggin. Please call me Dana. I'm glad to meet you. Congratulations on being accepted at Aspen Glen. You'll enjoy your upcoming years there. First, I need to see a picture ID to verify who you are." He pulled out an ID and showed it to her. "Good, now I need to get you registered so you can access the buildings."

With this, she opened one of the large volumes that had been lying on her desk. She continued. "You need to sign on the line next to your name. This book is magically connected to the chalkboards located at all of the entrances. To access the buildings, you sign one of the chalkboards, which verifies your signature, and the door will open. To access other malls in the different cities, you sign your name and then print Dirty Dog below. The board will then verify your signature with these books on the shelves. Now to get the bad part over with, I have the math and English tests. If you'll have a seat at one of the tables, you can get these out of the way." With this she led him back out to the tables outside her office. She motioned the waitress over and added, "Please have a complimentary milk, tea, soft drink, water, or coffee while you're working. The tests are only to see if you might need some help in these areas."

Steve mentioned, "All the lamps on the tables had red globes when I came in. Now they're all clear."

"When a nonmagical customer enters the building all of the globes turn red so the other customers know to not do any magic. They, and now you, are not allowed to do magic until the globes turn clear. You'll notice that the kitchen is completely hidden from view. This is to enable the cook to continue working while nonmagical customers are here. We'll go over some more of this after you've finished your tests," answered Dana while placing a test, some extra sheets of paper, and a couple of pencils on his table. "Take your time, and please show all work on the test sheet so the teacher can see how you formulated your answer. If you're not sure about a question, write 'My best guess is' in the space." With this he ordered a drink and sat down to work on the test.

The first page was a math test with ten questions. He could tell that they were checking addition, subtraction, multiplication, division, fractions, a little algebra, with a little geometry thrown in. He struggled through but thought he had done well enough. The second part was to write a page or less on either "What is your favorite hobby and tell me why you like it" or "Tell me about your favorite pet." He wrote a little over a page on the unicorn. He quickly finished and took his answers back to Dana's office.

After he entered, she added, "As a reward for getting through the test, I have a coupon for you for one free meal in the restaurant. The restaurant is open to the magical community from five a.m. to midnight. From five to eight a.m. and between eight p.m. and midnight we only have a partial selection of menu items available. Whereas, between eight a.m. and eight p.m. we have a full selection. On Friday and Saturday evenings from five thirty to seven thirty, the chef offers some specials that are out of this world. We usually have a waiting line during these times. If you need food at another time, some special arrangements can usually be made. We have one staff member here in the restaurant area twenty-four hours a day. They make sure that everything is running efficiently and can handle almost any problem. There are also rooms for rent on the second and third floors and a couple of suites on the fourth. Let me give you a tour of the facilities."

Alex got up and followed them.

With this, Dana showed him to a door with a chalkboard on the back, left wall. "I would like you to try the door to make sure your signature has been accepted. If you are entering with someone else, one person needs to sign and write below *escorting* followed by the other names. Each person needs to personally sign except for the board accessing the garage, where the driver can sign everyone in. This is done as a security measure. If you're in trouble, sign with your left hand, spell your name wrong, or write completely different; and you will all be sent to the security office for questioning."

With this, he signed the board next to the door and entered another hallway. The door they had come through had a Dirty Dog sign attached on the back where the door opposite had a sign Mall. To their left was a set of steps with a handrail on each side and one in the middle. As soon as Steve stepped on the first step, it started moving like an escalator. She explained, "Both sides go in either direction, but we always recommend that you only use the right." She stepped on the other side and it also moved up.

"The second floor has several items of interest." By now they had reached the top. "To the left is the walkway that connects to the parking garage and is where the arrival and departure booths are located." They could see a door at the end with a Parking Garage sign. On the right side were about a dozen doors labeled Departures. The left doors were labeled Arrivals. "These will be explained at the end of this summer. Here, near the steps, is where you are to meet your escort on Saturday morning. Now, let's head down the hallway on the right." After going a few feet past a series of lockers, she said, "The lockers are available for use for several hours. You sign the chalkboard on the locker, and they will stay locked until you sign a second time. If you need to store something for an extended time, check in at the registration desk. Here is the registration desk for the rooms. We operate them the same as any other hotel would. If there isn't anyone at the desk, ring the bell and a waitress will be up to assist you. If you call ahead with an estimated arrival time, we can see to it that there is someone here. If you have any questions, please feel free to ask me or a waitress."

Dana added, "The first level of the garage is usually for people staying two or more days and employees. There is a ten dollar fee for parking long-term, regardless of the number of days. The second level is for short stays. On really busy weekends, we usually make people park in the long-term unless they are only here for less than a day. Once the short-term fills up, you have to park in the long-term area. The entrance is across from where you parked. We'll wait here while you move your car."

Steve headed back down through the restaurant and back through the two hallways. He got in his truck and pulled into the garage entrance. After pulling in, he noticed a chalkboard where a ticket booth would normally be. Once he signed his name the gates parted, allowing him access. He headed to the first-floor area and pulled into one of the long-term slots. He unloaded his duffel bags as a man came out to greet him. The man performed a spell on the truck and it shrank until it was reduced to about five inches long. The man picked up the truck and entered a room next to the spaces. Then he returned with a numbered key and reminded Steve that he'd need to pay ten dollars when he came back. Steve took his bags up the stairs to the second level and noticed the door labeled "Dirty Dog - Please Sign in for Access." He signed again and entered the second-floor hallway and quickly went back to where they were waiting.

Dana handed him a book and supply list. She added, "Go to Blue Columbine first for your school robes. It takes some time for hemming, then go to Glenda's Fine Wands. I would then recommend that you pick up your books at The Dusty Tomes. After you know about a wand, go to the stores as indicated on your list. Don't forget to pick up your robes before leaving. You'll probably want to make several trips back to the car to drop off your supplies. Good luck this summer, and if I can be of any further assistance, please feel free to knock on my office door." With this she shook his hand and headed back into The Dirty Dog.

"I don't understand. She mentioned meeting someone on Saturday, taking my supplies to the car, and something about a wand. Aren't I leaving today?" Steve asked.

"That's probably the spiel she tells all the summer students," Alex said. She helped him get his bags into one of the lockers, and they headed back to the first level. Finally, they entered the mall door. Immediately, a wave of floral-scented air washed over them with underlying scents of damp earth. The mall was impressive. All of the stores were made from the same old red brick that was on the outside. The aisle was flooded with brilliant light from a row of large skylights. The shops all had three levels, with large display windows on the first level. Several shops had also placed larger windows on the second level, some even had bay windows. The shop signs were very distinct from one another. Some were intricate wood carvings with the names painted or gilded. Others had only the shop's name painted on their window.

Every so often there were tables with chairs in the middle of the aisles. Most of these were placed so that they were shaded by a tree planting. The plantings usually consisted of a couple of large trees with many different flowering plants spread among them. Usually fragrances from flowers would bother him. But because of all the wildflowers blooming in the meadow, he'd recently built up a tolerance to the smells. As they walked along, butterflies flitted among the plants. Various types of hummingbirds flew to and fro. The hummingbirds would almost hit Alex, they flew so close, but they gave him a wide berth.

Steve asked, "Which direction is the robe shop?"

"Blue Columbine, for robes, is three quarters of the way down on the right. The bookstore, The Dusty Tomes, is a couple stores back toward The Dirty Dog and Glenda's Fine Wands is in the middle," replied Alex.

They headed off for the Blue Columbine. This shop had a large window on the first floor where several drawings of robes were displayed. A sheer curtain hung over the bottom half of the window. As Steve opened the door an old-fashioned bell rang. A clerk immediately approached them and Steve said, "I need to get my robes for Aspen Glen."

The clerk ushered him to the back, right side where a platform was in front of three mirrors. As he stepped up onto the platform the clerk selected two black robes to try on. The robes had a yoke with two pleats on each side of the back with an embroidered symbol on the left front. The embroidery contained a group of aspen trees complete with their white trunks and the branches had green and yellow leaves. The whole design was very intricate. "I believe that this will be the best fit for you, but I'd like to check the second one to be sure," said the clerk. She was close, but the second one he tried on fit him better in the shoulders. The clerk quickly checked a length then added, "I'll have two robes hemmed up for you. We also embroider your name below the school patch so please print it very clearly on the form. They should be ready to pick up within a half an hour." Steve filled out the order form for the clerk and headed back out to go get his wand.

Chapter 30

About halfway down the mall, they came to Glenda's Fine Wands. Upon entering, they were standing in front of a large counter that stretched across the front of the shop. The air inside the shop crackled with excitement. Behind the counter, rows and rows of shelves extended from the back wall of the shop to the front, reminiscent of the stacks in a library. Each shelf contained hundreds of compartments resembling a post office in the old west. Shelves with compartments also covered both side walls of the shop. All the areas were neatly labeled. He couldn't even begin to imagine how many wands were in all of the different compartments. An elderly woman, with beautiful silvery white hair, approached. She was wearing a royal purple robe, and had her hair pulled back into a French twist, giving her a stately appearance.

She spoke in a confident voice, "Welcome to Glenda's. I've been expecting you."

With this, Steve moved toward the counter.

She clasped Steve's hand between hers. She released his hand immediately. "Sorry about that, you startled me. I've never met a shape-shifter like you before." She clasped his hand again and kept his gaze riveted to her misty blue eyes. Finally, she released his hand and added, "Welcome to a wonderful new world. I'm Glenda. I make the wands that are here. Hopefully we'll be able to find the perfect wand for you. Each wand is handmade from wood and contains a unique magical core. Let's start with some general cores and move on from there." With this she pulled out and handed one of the wands to him. "Give the wand a slight wave." He gave the wand a wave and nothing happened. She tried several more, producing the same results. She jotted down what wands she had tried in the binder that had been lying open on the counter. Then she pulled out another wand for Steve to try. Again nothing. She kept pulling out different wands and nothing appeared. This kept happening time after time after time as the page started filling up with notes. She kept muttering, "I know I'll find the right one, maybe this one." After trying what seemed like a couple dozen different wands, she remarked, "I know I have something that will work."

Steve said, "When I touched Alex's wand some sparks came out."

Glenda looked at Alex, "May I see your wand?"

Alex handed Glenda her wand.

"Oh yes. You have a very unusual core. It came from a special bear that I knew a long time ago," Glenda murmured.

Steve looked down and mumbled, "The bear may have been my mother."

Glenda took Steve's hand again and stared into his eyes. "Yes, yes, I see it now. You might be in luck. I still have a couple of wands left with that fur as a core." She headed off to the very back of the room and returned with five more wands. "Let's see if one of these works."

Four of them produced a few stars, but one of them

shot out a stream of stars. Glenda placed this wand in a box and handed it to him along with a sheet of paper. "Red Fir and Bear, an unusual combination," she said. "But it suits you. The paper contains an additional list of books you'll need, now that we know you'll be able to do the magical lessons. I'm glad I got to meet you. Good luck." Glenda was already making additional notes in the binder by the time Steve reached the door.

The Dusty Tomes was the best bookstore he had ever been in. The store had two check-out desks near the door where a clerk directed them to the second floor for his textbooks. All of the rest of the store was rows of book shelves from floor to ceiling. Through the middle was a break in the rows of books with groupings of big comfy stuffed chairs. There were stairways on both sides near the back leading up to the second floor. Up here were more rows of books, but at the front were large windows that let in a flood of light. In front of the windows additional comfy chairs were huddled together like a bunch of gossiping women. This would be a great place to sit down and browse through the wonderful selection of books.

He finally located the section where the books for school were arranged by year. These included new as well as used copies in various conditions. Some were so heavily marked that the original print was barely legible. He selected many of the used versions. He needed all the help he could get to learn everything. There weren't any used copies of the cookbook so he got a new copy. The cookbook consisted of a whole package of pages along with a three-ring binder which turned out to be the cheapest of them all. He also picked up a marked-up copy of *The Encyclopedia of Potion*

Ingredients. The script was clear and distinct, making it easy to read. This one was the largest and most expensive of all the required texts.

The stairs continued on up to a third level which was arranged like the second floor, except one wall contained a bunch of boxes. The labels on the ends of the bookcases indicated that these covered more advanced studies. He only spent a minute looking through this floor, just to get an indication of what was here. There was so much to learn. Would he be able to? He'd never been very good with schoolwork. He checked out and found Alex thumbing through one of the books.

As they headed back out to the mall, Alex looked at her watch and said, "Your robes should be finished by now. Why don't we pick them up and store them in the locker? This way we'll be able to handle the heavy and awkward packages."

They headed back to the Blue Columbine. This time when they entered, the clerk led them up to the second floor. Whereas, the first level contained only finished garments, this part had row after row of fabric bolts. The clerk introduced them to the owner and went back downstairs.

The owner had them deposit their packages along the side and showed them to the back. "First year students have three sewing projects to complete this term. The first project is a simple bed quilt. I have many kits already made up for your selection. There are three designs to pick from and then you can select a kit."

"So why do I need to learn how to sew?" he asked.

"The school believes that men and women can

benefit from learning how to sew, cook, and do household repairs. These skills are becoming lost arts with everyone letting someone else do them."

"That's for sure," he said. Since he had never sewn anything before, he let Alex pick the design. She selected the one with the fewest seams to match so he could easily finish. Then they looked through the kits. He ended up pulling out one that was very wintry. "This will remind me of you," he whispered to Alex. "So did you learn how to fix stuff and sew?"

"It was fun. I especially liked woodworking," she said.

He squinted at her. "Woodworking, I wouldn't have ever guessed that."

The owner continued, "Your second project is black pants. We already have some kits assembled." He pulled out a package and added it to the other kit. She then said, "Your last project is a simple white shirt. I would really recommend using one of these three cotton fabrics. These are the easiest to use so you'll get good results." He got the white fabric cut. The owner pulled the patterns and notions and also handed him a basic sewing kit.

Finally, he had all his supplies, including a set of sheets, put into a large bag. His robes were already neatly folded in another bag. They took these bags, and the ones with his books, back to the lockers. It took several minutes to get everything inside the empty duffel bags.

Alex commented, "Why don't we grab a bite?"

After eating a quick lunch, they headed to Merlin's Mixes. Here he picked up a cauldron and a kit of basic ingredients. The ingredients were conveniently packaged to fit snugly inside the cauldron. He also had a list of additional ingredients that he added on top of the others.

The last shop on their list was Simply Samantha for office supplies. They picked up notebooks, 3-ring binders, paper, pens, and anything else he needed. The clerk checked Steve's name against his copy of the student roster. "Ah, a new student! Congratulations on being accepted. I see you haven't picked up any lead-lined bags. Don't you need some?"

Steve asked, "Why do I need lead-lined bags?"

"For your electronics. You need a bag for every electronic device you're planning on taking." The clerk grinned at Steve's confused look. "For your computer, phone, and computer flash drives."

Alex told Steve, "You'll want one for a couple of flash drives." She showed him the section where the bags were hung up. She selected a small bag and a couple of simple flash drives and went back to check-out. The clerk cautioned him. "Make sure you get your devices fully inside and the bags tightly sealed. I would also highly recommend placing these items in the middle of your suitcase. You don't want anything damaged on your trip to school."

They found themselves loaded down with bags again. This necessitated another trip to the lockers. They pulled everything out and tightly packed it into as few bags as possible, making sure the flash drives were in his bags and buried in the middle. Then they spent a couple of hours wandering through the mall, killing time before they were supposed to meet Principal Vale at the traveling booths. Occasionally, he would duck into one of the shops to look at something, make a purchase, or to have a general look-see. A few minutes before he met Vale, they unloaded the lockers and hauled everything down to the departure booths. While the hallway was empty, Steve gave Alex a goodbye kiss.

They stopped kissing when a man behind them coughed. Vale said, "Sorry to interrupt, but we have to get going so we have enough time to get you settled and in the infirmary. We do not want you to wander."

"Yes," Steve said. "I don't want that."

Alex looked at Vale, "Take good care of him." She turned red, "Now I sound like my mom. Sorry."

"We know, you worry," Vale said. "I will keep him safe."

"I know…"

"You worry," Vale said. "Say goodbye so we can get going." He opened one of the departure doors and held it open for Steve.

"Take good care of Mandy and Anna Belle," Steve said before taking his bags into the booth.

Alex had already promised to leave the next morning to make sure Mandy and Anna Belle were okay. Peter could watch them for a day, but he didn't fare well doing the chores.

Steve stepped into a small room the size of an over-sized closet.

"Pile all your bags as tightly as possible," Vale said as he closed the door. He wrote on the blackboard mounted on the wall. "Sign your name at the bottom."

Steve signed the board.

"If you will stand on one side of your bags, I will stand on the other and drape my cloak around you. Stand still."

Steve heard another voice saying something and Vale said, "Ready."

Less than a minute passed when Vale unwrapped the cloak and said, "Here we are."

Steve started to move and stumbled a little.

"Oops. Sorry. I forgot to mention that it helps to close your eyes." Vale opened the door and stepped out into a different hallway.

"I don't understand."

"I feel this is one of our greatest benefits. Traveling booths, they take you to far-off places in minutes." Vale grabbed two of the bags. "Make sure you get everything."

Steve grabbed the rest of his bags and headed out of the building. A long, tall, stone wall stretched off into the distance. He followed Vale over to the ornate, wrought iron gate.

"Sign in please."

Steve signed below Vale and the gate opened. They stepped through.

Vale swept his arm across the area. "Welcome to Aspen Glen."

Steve looked around at the gray stone buildings located in a flat valley, surrounded by hills and then on up into the mountains.

Vale headed down the path that angled to the right. "This large building on the left is the cafeteria and the first one on the right is the men's dormitory. Once Ms. Apple deems it safe, you will move into a room there with three others, or I would suggest you take one of the empty rooms so you can lock the door. Do you have any electronics in your bags?"

"Only a couple of flash drives that Alex suggested

I would need."

"Anything on them?"

"No."

"They should be okay then."

Vale pointed out the buildings as they walked past them. They walked past the regular school building, a barn on the right, as well as some greenhouses on the left. They headed to the right, down a covered walkway through a grove of firs.

Vale added, "We are headed to the magic school where the infirmary is. Ms. Apple, our nurse, will take you on a tour and go over more of the details. Right now, school is still in session so make sure you are back in the infirmary well before sunset; as soon as dinner is over would be better. Our math teacher has agreed to help you get familiar with the computers between ten to noon and three to five, until you get a handle on how to use them."

They headed into another stone building and took the stairs up to the second floor. Vale deposited Steve's bags on a far bed and said, "Welcome to Aspen Glen." With this he turned and left.

A woman called out, "I'll be with you in a moment."

Steve set the rest of his bags down and sat on the bed. So this would be his home over the summer. Not too bad. He just hoped he could learn how to control his bear.

A woman walked out of the room in the back and held out her hand. "I have wonderful news. I've been talking with some of the other healers and potion masters, and I believe I have the perfect potion for you."

Chapter 31

Alex looked around her apartment one more time to see if she'd packed everything she might want for the summer. She looked over everything again. She had several reams of paper, red pens, flash drives, and a bag of her books. Steve's collection had some big gaps, no romances or steam-punk. She'd been wanting to read some steam-punk, but she'd never gotten a chance. The cabin would provide the perfect atmosphere.

On a more practical level, she packed some bug spray, several packs of sodas, chocolate bars, bags of chips, and some comfy clothes. She checked to make sure she had packed her engagement calendar. A lot of the days were already filled with the extra jobs she had to make sure got done. All the summer tasks had to be completed before the weather changed in the fall. This time she'd be able to drive out if she needed anything or ran out of necessities. She loaded the car and drove into the mountains. The drive was so much more enjoyable than when she'd come through in the snow. A cool breeze drifted in the cracked windows. She'd forgotten how much cooler the mountains were compared to Denver. At least she'd remembered to toss in a sweater.

Had Steve made any changes? Would the Houdini hen still be as friendly, or would it be in stalk and attack mode again? She'd picked up some balls and toys for

Mandy as well as a fancy brush for Anna Belle. Anna Belle should be spending more time outside. She also got a brush for the unicorn. She didn't know if he'd allow her to brush him down, but Steve had told her that he was really friendly now. It would be enjoyable wandering through the thick firs and smelling the wildflowers. This time she'd make sure she always carried her wand. She didn't want to meet any mountain lions or skunks unarmed. With the wand she'd be able to discourage any wild animals that became too interested, or else she might have to shoot them. That might be what the rest of the residents would do, but she at least had another option.

She checked in with Peter then headed back to the cabin. Mandy almost knocked her over when she opened the door. "It's good to see you, girl," she said to the happy dog. Alex let Mandy run between the car and cabin as she unloaded everything. It took more trips than she'd expected with all the items she'd brought. After unloading the car, she opened all the cabin windows while she unpacked and settled in. By now it was time to get the evening chores finished so she could turn in early. She opened the door to the barn and Anna Belle lifted her head. Anna Belle immediately headed for her. Alex said, "I'm glad to see you too. I bet you're really going to miss Steve. At least I'll be here with you. But I guess you're used to being the only cow." Tonight, she took the time to do the simple chores without magic. It felt good to use her muscles again.

Mandy woke her up the next morning by trying to lick her face.

"Okay, okay, I'm awake," Alex said. "I guess you want me to get going." She ruffled Mandy's ears and slipped on some clothes. Alex walked into the barn and looked around. She missed seeing Steve here. He was a part of this life, a life she wanted to become a part of too. Alex had said good morning to Anna Belle when the Houdini hen popped onto her shoulder. Alex lifted the bird onto a bale of hay. "Let me look at you." The hen stood there, head extended upward, as if posing. "I see your feathers finally decided to lie down again." The hen clucked and reappeared back on Alex's shoulder. Alex turned her head toward the hen, "Just do not do that if someone else is around. Do you hear me?"

The hen shifted and placed a foot on Alex's exposed shoulder. That's when a faint voice whispered in her mind, "*I won't.*"

Alex put the bird back down on the bale. "Did you do that?" She pointed a finger at the bird.

The bird vanished and popped back on her shoulder. "*I have to be closer, you dolt. Didn't anyone ever explain familiars to you? Didn't you learn anything? And what's up with not using your magic this winter? What kind of stupid wizard are you?*" the voice said in her head. "*And that bit with my feathers...I don't know if I want to forgive you for that.*"

"I'm sorry," Alex said. "I never meant to have that happen."

"*I should say. It was downright rude of you. The other hens made my life unbearable. I was the laughing stock of the coop.*"

"Wait a minute." Alex paused. "Me make your life miserable? What about all that stalking and attacking you did? You almost made it impossible for me to collect the eggs. And why didn't you make yourself known to me then? Why wait until now?"

The hen shifted her feet a couple of times. "*I wanted to see if you were worthy.*" She stomped a foot. "*Don't you know anything about familiars?*"

"Not really...you see I've never had one before. But why didn't you let me know before I left? What if I didn't come back?"

The hen shuffled her feet then settled down. "*You did leave, and I didn't know if you would come back. At least not until I saw you falling in love with the bear.*"

"You knew about him all along?"

"*Of course I did, all the animals did. We can sense another animal. We aren't stupid you know.*" The hen ruffled her feathers then settled down again.

"Okay, but if you're going to be my familiar then we have to get a few things settled. You can't peck me anymore. And you have to act like a normal chicken whenever another nonmagical person is around. That especially means no popping up wherever you want."

"*I'll agree as long as you agree to a couple things for me. You can't leave me; if you leave, then I go with you. And you'll never ever put me in a cage.*"

"When you say leave, you don't mean for a couple of hours to visit someone or go to work or shopping?"

"*No, I mean long term.*"

"The cage thing...how can you live in an apartment without making a complete mess?"

The hen squeezed Alex's shoulder with her foot. "*I'm not stupid, you know. I can use kitty litter, but I prefer to use the toilet. It's a lot neater. I don't like all those granules sticking to my feet. It's uncomfortable.*"

"Okay," Alex said, "but we have to tell Steve. I don't want him to accuse me of stealing one of his chickens."

"Deal," the hen answered. *"I need a name. You can't keep calling me demon hen or Houdini hen."*

"I'll think about it."

"Good, now get your wand out, and get your chores done."

The hen sat on Alex's shoulder and watched her do all the chores. When Alex milked Anna Belle, the hen leaned forward to see what was going on. Alex filled the bucket with corn to feed the hens.

"Popcorn, make it popcorn. It tastes so good." The hen's head bobbed up and down.

"Okay, popcorn it is." Alex entered the henhouse and the hen jumped down to the floor. While the hen paced near her feet, the other hens hopped down and edged in closer. Alex pulled out her wand and turned the corn into popcorn. She dumped the fluffy kernels and collected the eggs. When Alex left, the hen stayed to eat.

Alex went back in the cabin and fixed breakfast. She'd only been reading for a half hour when Mandy started to bark. Alex looked out the front window and spotted Caroline riding her bike up the road. Mandy pawed at the door and they both went out to meet her. Caroline was breathless when she reached the porch.

"I wanted to come sooner, but Mom wouldn't let me," Caroline said. "I wanted to visit with you and see the animals, if that's okay."

"Sure, come on in. I let Anna Belle out in her pen, but if we head into the barn, I bet she'll come back in."

Caroline bounced up the steps and hugged Mandy. "One of these days I'm going to talk my parents into letting me get a pet. I'd like someone I could talk to. Tommy's a boy, he doesn't want to hang with a girl any more than he has to."

"I know what you mean, my younger brother and I were like that too." Alex showed Caroline into the cabin.

"Wow, he sure doesn't have much, does he?" Caroline scanned the room. "How can you spend the whole summer here?"

"I like it. It's more comfortable than it seems." Alex showed Caroline to the barn door. "Let's go see Anna Belle."

They entered the barn and Alex called Anna Belle. The cow came back in and wandered up to Alex.

"You mean he just lets the cow walk around?"

"Sure." Alex stroked the cow's neck. "She's part of the family." Anna Belle leaned against her.

Caroline reached out tentatively and touched the cow's neck. When Anna Belle didn't move, Caroline slid her hand down. "I've never petted a cow before."

"Haven't you ever come here before?"

"Nah, Mom won't let me. Somethin' about being alone with a single man. I've only stopped by with Mom to pick up eggs." She continued to pet the cow.

"Well, while I'm here, you can come visit occasionally. But call me before you come, so I can be sure you get here safely."

"That'd be great, I could play with Mandy."

"Do you want to see one of the hens?"

"Ooooh, could I?"

"Wait here a minute and I'll go get one."

Caroline nodded.

Alex went into the henhouse and looked at the Houdini hen. "You need to behave. There's a little girl here who wants to see a hen. She's never seen one before, so be nice, no pecking." Alex held out her arm and the hen jumped on.

The hen shuffled her feet. "*I've never seen a little girl before.*"

"Be good," Alex whispered as she headed back into the barn.

"Can I pet her?" Caroline asked.

"Just be sure to pet her down her feathers. They don't like having their feathers ruffled up."

The hen squeezed its feet. "*You bet your sweet booty.*"

"Wow," Caroline said. "This is so much fun. When can I come again?" Caroline continued to pet the hen.

"Why don't you come back in three days. I have a lot of work to catch up on."

"Okay. Oh...I'm supposed to pick up a dozen eggs while I'm here. Usually we get them from Mr. Robertson, but since I'm here, Mom said to ask."

"Do you have a way of getting them home?"

"Yeah, I rigged up my basket so they won't break." Caroline looked at the hen intently. "You look like a Ginny to me. Like in the book." She looked up to Alex. "Is it okay if I name her?"

"*I like Ginny,*" the hen said to Alex.

"Ginny she is," Alex said. "Let me put her back then I'll get the eggs for you." Alex put the hen back and could swear Ginny was primping. Caroline left and Alex sat down with her book. One day off to read, then she'd get back to reviewing the manuscripts. After an hour, the hen, Ginny, popped into the cabin and settled down at Alex's feet next to Mandy. Alex muttered, "Of all animals, my familiar is a chicken."

Chapter 32

By using magic, it was a lot easier to get the chores done, even with Ginny sitting on her shoulder. Alex was able to get a lot of work done during the day without any distractions. She'd play with Mandy after breakfast and at lunch to give herself a break. When she finished the late afternoon chores, she'd go over to Peter's. She'd use the Internet, they'd eat dinner, watch some TV, and she'd return. She borrowed Peter's ATV so she could get hay and oats out to the unicorn. Her excuse had been that she wanted to explore the valley.

By the second week, she'd caught up on all her work. She'd finished ahead of schedule. It was time to celebrate. She started a small fire and pulled out three candles from the storage room, then fixed herself a juicy steak, potato, and salad. The light had already gone behind the mountains by the time she finished. She poured a glass of wine and sat down at the candlelit table so she could see the fire. But it wasn't the same.

She missed seeing Steve sprawled out in his favorite chair reading with Mandy at his feet, especially his smiling face from across the table.

She went to take another drink to find the glass empty. She refilled the glass. There wasn't anything she could do until he got back in September. Worrying about it now wouldn't help. She sighed, then lifted her glass. "To getting done early and best of luck to Steve."

Mandy's tail thumped on the wooden planks.

Alex reached down to ruffle the dog's head. "I know. You want me to hurry up and eat so you can have some fat scraps."

Mandy's tail thumped faster.

Alex cut off a small bite from the outer edge and handed it to Mandy. She was glad she'd stayed home tonight to get finished. Tomorrow she'd have to go over to Peter's earlier so she would have enough time to get all her e-mail done. She'd avoided it for the last few days so she could concentrate on work.

Now she'd have a week to explore the valley some more. She needed to deliver eggs to the neighbors, and maybe see if she could collect a few crystals. She couldn't use as much power as she'd done in the spring. She couldn't risk not functioning for several days. There were animals who depended on her. Who would have thought she'd ever be the sole support for others? Not her. Maybe she was ready to settle down. One bright point in her week was when Steve would call on Saturdays, but he kept the calls short.

The third week she was there, Principal Vale arranged to bring some of the teachers out to collect the eggs. They pulled up late one morning in two four-wheel-drive trucks, one towing a three-horse trailer. Alex recognized the teachers: Mr. Richardson, Transfiguration; Mr. Norman, Charms; and Mr. Sheppard, Animal Husbandry. They all got out and shook hands.

Vale asked, "Any problems?"

"No. I take him hay and oats each week and go see him every couple of days to make sure he's okay. He's always glad to see me. After I give him food, I brush him down. He seems to really enjoy it," Alex told them.

Sheppard said, "He actually lets you brush him down. Our group at school won't let me. I'm amazed."

Alex nodded.

"I will do a couple of spells so everyone will take a nap so we can work without being seen," Vale said. He, Richardson, and Norman pulled their wands out and chanted some type of spell. The whole valley went silent. Not a single bird chirped or bug buzzed.

"What'd you do?" Alex asked Vale.

"Anything that is not magical is sleeping. They will stay asleep until we counter the spell," Vale said. "We should get moving."

Alex and the others climbed in the trucks. She headed them over to the path that led to the cave. They parked at the edge of the trees and walked in. The unicorn was waiting, as usual, at the crevice's mouth. Sheppard let out a quiet whistle. "What a beautiful creature."

Vale nudged him, and the three teachers and Vale approached him. They all bowed. The unicorn approached each one in turn, sniffed him then went on to the next. Once he'd finished his inspection, he pawed the ground and nodded his head. They rose and the unicorn approached Alex. He shoved her with his shoulder then pranced around in a circle, kicking up his heels and shaking his head.

"I told you he liked me," she said. She touched his shoulder to get his attention.

He turned his head toward her.

"We've come to move the eggs to a safer location."

He nodded and pawed the ground.

"They wanted me to ask you if you wanted to go

with them so you could stay with the eggs. They're taking them to the wizarding school. It's a really safe spot. We talked about this. Do you want to go?" Alex asked the unicorn.

He nodded his head several times, nudged her in the chest, and nodded his head again.

"I won't be going, but I could visit if you want me to. Steve will be there for a couple of months. And there are other unicorns there," Alex told him.

"Some really good-looking females," Sheppard added.

The unicorn nodded, turned, and pranced into the crevice. They all followed him, using his light to illuminate the passage. When they entered the chamber, the unicorn stepped over to the side so the others could approach the eggs. Alex lit the lantern and helped Vale brush the dirt and leaves away to expose the eggs.

Richardson whistled. "I never thought I'd ever see one."

Alex and Vale moved away so the others could get a better look. Richardson then Norman knelt down, ran a hand over the eggs, then stepped back. Sheppard approached doing the same and said, "It's obvious which is the male and which is the female." He looked at the unicorn. "A pair. We're so lucky you found them. Who knows how long they've been here."

"And how much longer it would have been if not for Alex," Vale added. The others nodded, looked at her, then looked back at the eggs. "We had better get busy so we can wake everyone up," Vale said. They nodded and slowly slid their wands out.

Alex whispered to the unicorn, "I know you don't like this part, but we can't move them without using wands."

Vale and Norman used their wands to lift the larger red egg, while Richardson and Sheppard lifted the blue egg. They ever so slowly followed the unicorn out. They maneuvered the two eggs into the front of the horse trailer and secured them with blankets and ropes. They stepped out and stood back. The unicorn laid its head against Alex's chest. She gave him a hug then walked over to the ramp with him. He stepped in and she patted his rump. Alex handed Sheppard his brush and Sheppard closed the tailgate. They climbed back in the vehicles and drove back to the cabin.

When they were almost there, Vale said, "I almost forgot. I have arranged for a dozen students to take care of mowing the hay. I will call you so we can set up the dates."

They got out and had their wands out to perform the awakening spell when they spotted a little girl on her bike headed their way.

Alex said to Vale, "I thought you said everyone would be asleep?"

"Everyone nonmagical; she must have magic. Who is it?"

"That's Caroline. She's the one who spotted the unicorn and told me about him. Go ahead and do the spell, I'll take care of her."

"I will have to meet her," Vale said.

"Another time. You'd better leave before she spots the unicorn and asks questions."

They performed the spell, climbed in the trucks, and eased back out onto the road. They'd pulled out and had gotten a little ways down the road when Caroline finally approached. Alex waited for her in front of the cabin. Caroline skidded her bike to a stop right in front of Alex, gasping.

"I didn't know what to do. Dad went into town and Mom and Tommy are sound asleep. I couldn't get them to wake up. I called you but you didn't answer," Caroline blurted out. "I called everyone and no one answered." Her eyes were puffy and tears continued to run down her cheeks.

Alex laid a hand on her shoulder. "It's okay. I'm sure they were really tired and were taking a nap. Why don't we go inside and you can call them? I bet they're awake by now."

Caroline propped her bike up against the porch, and Alex draped an arm around her as they went inside. Caroline picked up the phone and called home. Her mom answered and they talked for a couple of minutes.

"Why don't I drive you home? You and your mom can stop by tomorrow for a visit and get your bike then," Alex said.

Caroline relayed the information and her mom agreed. She hung up.

Alex fixed her a glass of water. "Better drink this." While Caroline gulped the water down, Alex said, "Remember how we talked about the unicorn and no one else believed you?"

Caroline nodded and continued to drink.

"This is another one of those things. You don't want to worry your mom, do you?"

Caroline shook her head.

"She was taking a nap and you got upset. You came down here to talk to me and wanted to see Mandy. Okay?"

"Okay," Caroline whispered.

Alex knelt down. "Do you feel better now?"

Caroline nodded.

"Let's take Mandy with us; she'll enjoy the short ride." Alex called Mandy and they all got in her car. She drove Caroline home then headed back. "That was a close one," she said to Mandy. Mandy thumped her tail and continued to hold her muzzle up to the partially open window as they headed back up to the cabin.

Alex had settled into a comfortable routine as the days passed. One cooler evening, Alex carried her hot chocolate out onto the back porch and flopped down in the chair. She blew on the steaming liquid as Mandy wandered over to the screened-in windows, stopped, raised her head, and sniffed the air. Sunset had already arrived with the skies starting to shift into violets and midnight blues.

Mandy's ears perked up.

Some animal must be moving around out in the meadow. It had to be pretty far out or in the trees on the far side. If it was closer, Mandy would be barking. It was so different from when she'd been here in the winter. Chickadees and even some hummingbirds could be seen during the day. The faint breeze brought the scent of hay and pine with it. Now she could understand why Steve enjoyed it out here. With only the few residents, you rarely heard a car, so the wildlife wandered around undisturbed. Peter had sighted a couple of female elk, but she hadn't seen them yet. She'd only seen elk by going to one of the state parks during mating season when they congregated in herds.

All the years she'd spent in Colorado, and she'd seen deer but rarely anything else. Every day she would take time to try and spot something. There were a lot of deer, and farther down in the valley, there was a pair of beavers in the small lake. She knew there wouldn't be any bears in the area, but Steve had mentioned that an occasional mountain lion might enter the valley. Of course, he would chase the mountain lion away before it had a chance to settle in...if he was here.

Mandy strolled over to her chair and plopped down with a grunt.

Alex reached over and scratched her ears while she sipped her drink, savoring the rich chocolate. It was so peaceful out here. Before she'd always enjoyed the museums, concerts, movie theaters, and restaurants a big city could offer. Now, whenever she returned to Denver she found the constant noise a major irritation. Spending a month here had changed her perspective. She'd even learned to love the peaceful winter.

Summer here was like heaven. Her soul was at peace. She no longer regretted being a wizard, and she'd never try to deny her magic again. She could be a part of both worlds; she'd finally found a balance. And then there was Steve.

He was always on her mind. Was he enjoying Aspen Glen? Did he like the classes? Were they able to help him control his shifting? Would he continue next year? Did he resent her for thrusting him into this new world? Had he accepted the fact that he was a wizard? If he didn't, would security erase his memories?

He'd become so distant the last couple of months. Now he only called to check up on how everything was going. He'd ask about Mandy, Anna Belle, the hens, and even how the hay was coming along. Of course, he'd be concerned about all this, but he never asked how she was doing. She'd have to sit him down and find out how he felt about her when he got back. Maybe once he got used to the magical world, he'd enjoy being a part of it, including her. Until then, she'd have to wait. And wait.

****

The cooler days moved into the hotter ones of summer. The day was stagnant. Moisture hung in the air from the rains the night before. A cricket chorus was already in full swing, but the birds were quiet. They were probably conserving their energy for hunting food. Heat waves emanated from her little car and the rocks shimmered under the sun's rays.

It was definitely hotter outside than it was in the cabin. Alex wandered back inside and spread a towel over the leather chair. Between her iced drink and fan, she should be able to cool down. She snapped the oriental fan open and fanned herself. Mandy wandered over and plopped down against Alex's legs, leaning her head back to take advantage of the moving air.

"You're too hot, girl." She shoved Mandy away. "Maybe when the sun goes down, it'll be cooler."

Alex tried to read for a while but couldn't concentrate. It was too hot. She peeled off her clothes on the way to the bathroom, filled the tub with cool water, and sank her body down into the refreshing liquid. Now this was what she needed. She soaked until the water felt tepid, then dried off and dressed. One advantage Steve had when he shifted, he would wander around when it was cooler at night and sleep during the day's heat. How would he like being awake during the hot day?

If she lived here, she'd make sure she had more electric appliances. A couple of fans would go a long way to make the cabin more comfortable, as well as a microwave. It was too hot to have to be turning stove burners on. Next time she went to town she'd definitely pick up a couple of fans and a long extension cord. July was just starting. August would be even hotter.

Chapter 33

The fourth of July arrived and Peter was throwing a party for everyone. No potluck this time, he was providing everything, all they had to do was show up. Alex finished her chores early with magic but waited until enough time had passed to have been able to do part of them the normal way. She used the time to get gussied up, something she hadn't done since she'd been here. She drove over to Peter's and paused before heading up to the door. This would be so different without Steve; she felt so alone without him by her side. Peter answered the door.

"One minute, I know it's in here." Peter rooted through a box that was next to the door. "Ah-ha, here it is." He handed her a piece of metal filigree.

Alex took the object and inspected it. "I loved the dragon. He was unique." Once she orientated the piece of metal she could tell it was an openwork design that had swirling tendrils and crystals. "So why the masks?" She tied the mask on.

"I thought a masquerade would be fun. It's too hot for heavy costumes, so we have masks."

"But you have AC? Just set it a little cooler."

"No, we're going to have a cook-out with fireworks once it gets dark enough."

"I'll have to go back for a while to take care of Anna Belle."

"I know, we'll wait. If you go before dinner it should all work out." He headed her into the living room where most of the other residents were. "Once everyone gets here we're going to have a short game."

Alex picked up a glass of water and looked around the room. There were all kinds of masks, some made from metal or feathers, heavily adorned with various colored rhinestones. Some were papier-maché animal masks. Everything from fancy and elaborate to simple bands with eye cutouts like Zorro or the Lone Ranger. It was hard to figure out who the men were with their masks covering most of their faces. She sipped the water while she figured everyone out. One man's eyes struck her for some reason. She knew him, but who was he? She edged closer and closer until she could hear him speak. The laugh and joking didn't ring any bells, but the authority in his mannerisms did. "Principal Vale," she whispered and clamped a hand over her mouth. He was probably using another name, but why was he here?

She maneuvered through the crowd to join his group. She extended her hand. "I'm Alex."

"Derek." He shook her hand. "It is a pleasure."

Peter joined them. "Ah, I see you've met Derek. He's been giving me some great input on one of my games."

"Which one?" Alex took another drink.

"The one about wizards and magic."

Alex spit some of the water out. She grabbed a napkin off a table and wiped the water off. "Wizards and magic?"

"Yeah, Derek here has been giving me some great ideas. I'm so glad we met." Peter placed a hand on

322

Vale's shoulder.

Alex stifled a laugh. "Where did you meet?"

Peter patted Vale's shoulder. "We met at Comic-Con. I was there watching some of the wizard characters when Derek here introduced himself." Peter looked at Vale. "I loved your wizarding outfit, I'm going to have to get one. You'll have to let me know where you got it."

Blue Columbine she bet. "Where did you get it?"

Vale smiled at her then looked at Peter. "I will get one for you."

"You don't need to do that." Peter tipped his face down and shuffled a foot.

"It would be my pleasure. You invited me to this wonderful party," Vale answered.

The doorbell rang and Peter hurried off to answer it.

"Where did I get my robes, good one," Vale said.

Alex looked around to see if anyone else was close. "So why are you here?"

Vale moved closer and whispered, "I need to meet the little girl."

"Caroline?"

He nodded.

Alex looked over at the door and saw the Gibsons. She nodded her head that way. "That's Caroline by the door. Are you going to ask about the unicorn?"

"If I get a chance."

"We made a promise to not tell anyone else. I'll let her know that it's okay to tell you."

Vale nodded and moved off to mingle. Alex followed his cue and went to talk with Daniel and Henri. Moments later, Caroline came bouncing over wearing a mask made out of peacock feathers.

"Look which mask I get to wear," she said to Alex.

Alex touched one of the feathers, "It's really beautiful. It's perfect."

Caroline grinned from ear to ear. "I like yours too, but it doesn't have any feathers."

Alex pulled Caroline a few feet away and knelt down to her level. She nodded over to Vale. "You see that stranger over there?"

Caroline nodded.

Alex leaned closer and whispered into Caroline's ear. "He also believes in unicorns."

Caroline looked over at Vale, her eyes wide and mouth gaping. "No kidding?"

"No kidding, we were just talking about them. I bet he'd love to hear about what you saw."

"But we promised not to tell anyone."

"I know, but I think he'd be okay." Alex straightened up.

"If you say so, I'll let him in on the secret."

Alex nodded. "But make him swear to keep it a secret."

"Of course…"

"If I can have everyone's attention," Peter said. "Now that everyone is here we can start the game. I've hidden strands of Mardi Gras beads around this room. Whoever finds the most will be crowned king or queen of the party and will win a special gift." Peter held up a fist. "On the count of three." He counted to three raising one finger each time and everyone started searching.

Alex located a bunch of strands hidden behind the DVDs and games, then a clump under the sofa cushions. As the minutes passed, it became harder and harder to find any beads. Any time Alex passed Caroline, she'd hand the girl all the beads she'd found.

After a half hour, Peter shook a cow bell interrupting the search. "Everyone count how many strands they found and pick up a glass so we can toast the winner." The kids were all given a small black cow for their drink. The adults were given a small tumbler that contained an amber liquid that smoked over the top, curling down the sides.

Peter stepped forward and lifted his glass. "Three cheers for our queen. To Queen Caroline."

Everyone lifted their glass and chanted, "Long live the queen."

Caroline turned to face the others. "Thanks," she whispered.

Peter handed her a bag that exploded with ribbons and beads. "The rest of the prize is that one of the women in my next game will be named after you."

"Me? Wow!" Caroline looked at her feet, then sat down on the sofa, and dug into the bag. She pulled out one of his game packages and looked up at him. "Is this the new one?"

Peter nodded. "It will be in the stores in another month. You get the first copy, signed by me."

"Wow! Look, Tommy." She rushed over to Tommy to show him.

"The lunch buffet is open, so feel free to make a sandwich whenever you want," Peter said.

After getting some lunch Alex introduced Caroline to Vale. "You gotta see this," Caroline grasped Vale's hand and pulled him to the bedroom. Once inside, she dropped his hand and started rooting through the jackets that had been laid on the bed. She yanked her backpack out along with a couple of jackets and flung the coats back on the bed. Setting the backpack down, she plopped down next to it and started to pull items out. A scarf, a zebra striped box, and a pencil case.

"This is my favorite," she said and pulled out a stuffed unicorn. "I saw one, you know."

"You saw one?" Vale asked.

"Yeah, but nobody believed me." She handed the unicorn to Vale. "Except Alex."

"What did Alex say?"

"She thought it should be a secret. But that I should tell you."

"Did you want to keep it a secret?"

Caroline shrugged. "Might as well. Everyone laughs at me when I tell them."

"Why don't you tell me," Vale said.

Caroline repeated her tale of seeing the unicorn wandering around the valley.

"Do you like stories about unicorns, dragons, and wizards?"

Caroline touched the unicorn's horn. "They're my favorite, especially the ones about the boy wizard."

"Would you like to go to a magic school like he did?"

"I don't know. I wouldn't want to fight an evil wizard."

"But would you like to go to a school like that without the evil wizard?"

"Oh yeah." Caroline beamed up at Vale. "That would be so great. But I'd have to have magic to go, wouldn't I?"

Vale nodded, "What if you had magic and you did not know, like the other kids that got their letters?"

"That'd be like a movie. Nothing that good ever happens to me." Caroline looked down at the stuffed animal.

"Let me see if I can do something, but until then…"

Caroline looked up.

"You have to make a pledge. You have to keep this just between the two of us until I tell you otherwise." He looked straight into her eyes. "Deal?"

Caroline nodded.

Vale spit on his palm and held it out.

Caroline looked at his hand for a moment before spitting into hers and shook his hand with a single pump. "Deal!" She stuffed everything back in her backpack, zipped it shut, and tossed it on top of the coats. They headed back out to rejoin the party.

When Alex got a chance to be alone with Vale, she whispered, "Is she?"

Vale nodded. "As well as her father. I cannot quite tell with her brother, he is still young. He might not have come into his power yet."

"What are you going to do?"

"See if I can convince her parents to let her come to school."

Alex nodded. She looked at her watch then headed back to the cabin to get the evening chores done. She returned as soon as she could. Peter was grilling up some steaks and hamburgers. A long table was set up on his back porch so everyone could eat together. They enjoyed the food and company, talking well past sunset. The candles flickered, lighting up everyone's faces. After dessert, Peter gave all the adults a glass of champagne. He lifted his glass. "To the best friends a man can ever have."

"Hear! Hear!" everyone answered and drank the delightful liquid.

Peter got up again, "If you'll all stay seated, my new friend, Derek, is going to give us a short fireworks display." Peter sat and a few minutes later several balls lit up the night sky. It only lasted a minute when there was a pause and then the whoosh of a firework shot echoed. They watched it travel up then expand into a dragon. Everyone gasped. The dragon spread its wings and circled the sky three times. It disappeared with a pop. They sat there for a moment then started clapping. Shortly after, the partygoers collected their jackets and started to wander back home, Alex being one of the earliest. She didn't have the luxury of sleeping in. Anna Belle and Mandy would be wanting attention.

****

A dozen students from Aspen Glen arrived in three trucks a week later. They cast an ignore spell so no one would watch what they were doing. They magically cut the hay, dried it, and moved it from the field to hay stacks closer to the barn. After they finished that step, they baled it and moved the bales next to the barn. It took all day, but by sunset they were finished. They piled up a ring of stones and started a bonfire. Then they sat around the ring and roasted hot dogs. As they fixed and ate their dinner, they told stories about school—especially those involving the various magical creatures that resided on the school grounds. A mean nanny goat took center stage in a lot of their tales. As Alex listened, she stroked a finger down Ginny's chest. How similar the stories sounded to hers with the hen. They partied until late in the evening. Alex had them bunk in the barn and cabin so they could leave the next morning after breakfast. The whole time Ginny rode around on Alex's shoulder. The students teased her mercilessly about having a chicken for a familiar. For the first time she didn't mind being teased. Over the winter and summer, she'd finally become comfortable with who she was. She no longer minded that her magic wasn't as strong as a lot of the other wizards. It was enough for her.

In August, a series of storms passed through bringing the stifling temperatures down to comfortable levels. Each afternoon, she'd take a book and drink out to the back porch. Sometimes she'd simply sit and watch. The wildlife would scatter as a storm approached and then gradually reappear after everything was over. The birds bathed in the short-lived puddles before searching for their evening meal. She sighed; it was so peaceful and quiet. If anyone would have asked her if she would ever live in the mountains, she'd have told them they were crazy. Not now. She'd changed. Denver's hustle and bustle had now become a pain. She wanted this quiet life. Or did she want this because she wanted Steve? To be with him the rest of her life.

The summer was winding down. Steve would get back in a few weeks. She shut the lid on her laptop. All morning she'd tried to get some work done, but she couldn't focus. Her thoughts kept turning back to the previous day's phone call from Steve. He asked about Mandy, Anna Belle, and the chickens, if they were all healthy and managing. He asked if she was having any problems with taking care of everything. How often she was going over to Peter's. He was business, all business. He never asked about her. Then he found an excuse to end the call after only a few minutes. She knew school would be hard for him, but this?

"Why? Why is he doing this?" Alex said.

Ginny was on her shoulder as usual. *"Maybe he isn't interested. Maybe he can't stop shifting and doesn't want to risk having you around. Maybe he's found someone else and is afraid to tell you."*

Alex shooed the hen away. She picked up her iced tea and wandered out onto the back porch.

Mandy shuffled out after her and approached the screen windows.

Alex settled into the chair and looked out across the valley.

Mandy sniffed the air and carefully scanned the area, then plopped down next to her feet.

Alex sipped her tea as she watched the evening fall. The birds were stilling as the sun set behind the mountains. Only the robins called out as darkness claimed the valley. She spent the time going over possible scenarios. She knew he'd be worried about his animals, his family, his home. He would be curious about his friend, Peter. She knew he hated going to school, dealing with the new magical subjects, and learning about the magical world. Would he continue on with the schooling? He probably didn't even realize he'd been abrupt.

If she hadn't shown up, he wouldn't know about magic. She was responsible for all this. She'd thrown his life into disarray. He could blame her for all these changes. Was he trying to distance himself? Did he want to end their relationship?

Now that was the problem. Her future hinged on

what he wanted, and it would be weeks before she could find out. Mañana. Why was everything important always mañana? The cow might jump over the moon before then. Alex kept going over the possible scenarios. Of all the possibilities, the most likely was that he was trying to distance himself. She'd been responsible for all the changes he'd been forced to make ever since she'd shown up on his doorstep. Was he blaming her for everything? She had thrown his peaceful life into chaos.

Mandy picked up her head and nudged Alex's leg.

"I know, girl." She stroked Mandy's head. "Everyone is waiting for dinner."

Chapter 34

The day Steve was finally coming home had arrived. Alex looked at her list again. The steaks were seasoned, ready to be cooked, and the vegetables were almost finished, needing only a couple of minutes more. She set the dishes and wine glasses on the table. One last look around and she was satisfied that everything was ready. They could have an early meal and spend some time together well before sunset. Maybe she'd get some answers to her many questions over a relaxing dinner and a glass of wine. Now she only had to wait for Steve to get back home.

Alex paced the room and Mandy watched from her spot at the window next to the front door. Alex fussed with the wildflowers on the kitchen table, rearranging them again. She couldn't stand this not knowing.

Alex and Mandy rushed out onto the front porch when Steve's truck pulled up. He greeted and wrestled with Mandy. When he'd finished, he reached in his truck and pulled out two of his bags. He strode to the porch, and Alex opened the door for him. He nodded and walked in.

"Would you like me to help get the rest of your stuff in?"

"No." He set the bags down near the table. "I think you should go ahead and head home."

"I still have to finish packing." She shut the front

door. "I could finish and we could talk over dinner."

"You have to be gone before sunset...remember."

Alex nodded.

"Hurry up and pack while I unload my truck. You need to leave." He headed back out the door.

Alex rushed into the bedroom and finished throwing her clothes in her suitcase. At least she'd already packed up everything else. She tossed the last item in and zipped the bag. She grabbed the bag off the bedspread, scattering the rose petals she'd tossed there this morning. She carried the bag to the door next to some of her other things. Steve had already carried half her things out to her car. She paused when he came back in and picked up some more of her items.

"There's still a couple of hours before the sun sets," Alex said.

He hesitated then walked back out.

She watched him go and carried her suitcase out. Steve had set everything down near her trunk. She placed everything in the trunk as he finished carrying out the rest. She set her computer bag on the back seat and walked over to him.

"I need some time alone," he said.

She reached up and gently stroked his cheek. "Give me a call so we can talk." She walked back to her car and got in. He didn't even watch her leave but went straight back inside and shut the door.

She'd just backed out and put the car in gear when she remembered her promise. "Ginny," she yelled. "Ginny. You have to come right now."

The hen popped onto her shoulder. *What's so urgent. I was enjoying some more of that popcorn.*

"We have to leave." She started driving out.

"*I thought you'd be staying.*"

"Steve wants me to leave."

"*Oh.*"

Alex pulled out onto the road and looked back at the cabin. Mandy's nose was pressed against the front window and Anna Belle was watching her from the pasture. Alex gently lifted the hen down to the front seat then drove on. Before she even reached the highway, she had to pull over because she couldn't see the road anymore. She sat there and cried until her tears slowed down. She pulled a wad of tissues out of the box she kept in the car. After several minutes she had calmed down enough to drive on. She took one of the exits and picked up a greasy burger, large pack of fries, and a chocolate shake. She nibbled on the food as she headed back to Denver.

Alex moped around for a week before her brother cornered her. "Sit," Joe said. He pulled out a chair at the table and went to the kitchen.

"Why?" Alex asked, taking the offered chair.

"You need to unwind."

She could hear ice cubes hitting the metal shaker. "I have too much to get done."

"Not tonight." He walked back out carrying two martinis. "Drink this and we'll talk." He sat down across from her.

"About what?" Alex savored the cold liquid and the sharp bite. "You do make a good Sour Apple Martini."

He held up his glass to make a toast. "Here's to getting your love life settled."

Alex paused then touched her glass to his. "I wish I could, but I haven't heard a word from Steve. I'm afraid

I've forced too many changes on him." She gazed into the clear green liquid.

"Who wouldn't want to use magic?"

Alex looked up at him.

"I know, you thought you could be normal. And how did that work out for you?"

"It didn't." She took a drink.

"Of course not. You can't deny who you are. You're a wizard and you should marry a wizard. You can't be normal even if you want to be."

"But that didn't work for me. I never got along with any of the wizards I know. They're all so full of themselves, and they make me feel like a failure." She took another good drink.

Joe got up and topped off her glass. "Then maybe you should move. Find some new men. There has to be one out there you'll fall in love with." He placed the shaker on the table and sat back down.

"That's the problem. I did fall in love."

"Does Steve feel the same way?"

"I thought so…but now…I don't know."

"How long are you going to wait for him?"

Alex shrugged. "I have to give him a chance. He put up with me for months, never once complaining. I can be patient and give him some time. He needs time to settle into his new life. Maybe then he can decide about us."

"And what are you going to do until he makes up his mind?"

"Wait. I want to be with him."

"Then do something. Give him a call, stop by to drop something off, anything but just sitting here worrying."

Alex sipped some more of her drink.

"Whatever you decide, I'll take your side. Don't let Mom influence your decision. We have to stick together." He clinked glasses with her again. "It's us against the world. We can do this."

A week later, Alex got a box from Steve. Alex grabbed the box, but Ginny dug her claws into the cardboard and started flapping her wings. "This is not for you, let go," Alex said.

Ginny dug her beak in the ripped slot and pulled another piece of cardboard away. She snatched at the edge for another hunk.

"Don't you dare eat any of that cardboard." Alex stared into the hen's eyes. "The last time you ate too much, you had trouble laying any eggs for days."

Ginny paused with a large hunk of brown paper still sticking out of her beak. She jostled the paper so it stuck out of both sides of her beak.

"Drop it," Alex repeated.

Ginny dropped the piece. She snatched three more hunks away before stopping. Brown paper floated to the floor.

"Are you done yet?"

Ginny ripped off a couple more pieces with her feet. She stuck her head in the hole.

"Don't you dare eat anything that's in there."

Ginny pulled her head out and shook her feathers. She let go and hopped onto Alex's shoulder.

"Satisfied?"

"*Yep. I wanted to find out what was inside.*"

"If you'd waited a couple of minutes I'd have had it open.

Ginny shuffled her feet, "*Just wanted to see first.*"

Alex quickly finished opening the box. What did he send? She pulled out the article inside; the sweater she'd left behind. She turned the box over and shook; he hadn't even included a note. Would he ever talk to her?

****

A month passed before Alex got a call from Steve. All he said was that he wanted to come to Denver to see her. He gave her a date and time and hung up. The day of the date finally arrived. Alex would pick out an outfit, hold it up so she could see it in the mirror, then toss it on the bed. Nothing seemed to be just right. She tried outfit after outfit.

Ginny hopped up on her shoulder, *"Wear the black one. Black always works for everything."*

"Think so? I don't know. I want to look…"

"Sexy, so he can't turn you down."

Alex nodded. She slipped the black dress on and looked at it in the mirror. "Good call." Ginny hopped down.

A knock on her door brought her running.

She looked out the peephole and saw Steve. Her fingers fumbled with the keyed deadbolt. The stupid key just didn't want to turn. She took a couple of deep breaths, touched the thin metal, it turned, and the lock tumbled open. She yanked the door open and jumped up on him, wrapping her legs and arms around him, burying her face in his neck.

He staggered into her apartment with her entwined in his arms. He kicked the door and fell against it, clicking it shut. She unwrapped her legs and slid them back to the floor; and he was finally able to push her away to arm's length.

"We need to talk," he said.

"Okay." She took his hand and led him over to sit down on the sofa. He wore a black suit and tie with a white shirt. "Why the suit?" she asked looking him over. He looked great in the suit, but so unusual. She'd never seen him in anything other than jeans and flannel shirts. It had to be serious for him to put a suit on.

He straightened his tie and fussed with the jacket. "It's important."

Important bad? Was he going to tell her he didn't want to see her anymore? She'd thrown his life in chaos and he wanted to go back to his old life. Could he still be worried about her safety? She dropped into the nearest chair and buried her face in her hands.

Steve rushed over, knelt down in front of her, and pulled her hands away from her face. "No, Alex. You were right. In another year I'll have my shape-shifting completely under control."

Alex looked up but couldn't focus through her tears. She pulled a hand out of his and swiped at her eyes. "I was right," she managed to get out.

He nodded and squeezed her other hand. "Hurry up and finish getting dressed. I want to take you out to celebrate." He pulled out his pocket watch to check the time. "I've got a half hour to get there. You have to hurry."

She fussed with a lock of hair near her face. "But I'm such a mess."

"You're beautiful." He pulled her up and gently touched her damp cheek. "I want to tell you the great news with some champagne."

"Champagne." Great. Here he was and all she could do was parrot him. She looked down at her bare feet. "I'll be ready in five minutes," she said and dashed off.

Steve watched the way she moved as she walked out of the room.

Ginny strutted out into the living room. Steve looked at her. "Why's my chicken here?"

"You didn't give me a chance to tell you," Alex said from the bedroom as she put her jewelry on. "You just pushed me out the door."

"Sorry about that. I was strung out after exams. I didn't mean to be so abrupt."

"But you had to be sure I left before sunset?"

"Yeah, it was a full moon that night," he said. Ginny jumped up on the chair and eyed him. "What's the deal with the hen?"

"Apparently she's my familiar." She could hear Steve laughing. "When I came back for the summer, she introduced herself."

"All the shit she put you through."

"She said she was finding out if I was worthy." Alex brushed her hair. "By the way, she's Ginny now. Caroline named her."

"Did Caroline name all the other hens?" He stared at the hen.

"I think so, but I can't remember all the names."

"I leave for the summer and all my livestock gets named or becomes a pet."

Alex slipped her shoes on and walked out. "She's not a pet. She's my familiar."

Steve looked at Alex from her feet to her head. He rose up.

Alex stepped closer and touched his lapel. "What's with the black suit, it looks like you're going to a funeral."

He touched the neckline of her dress. "It's the only suit I own. I guess I'll have to get another one so we can go out. I like how you look all dressed up."

She smoothed the front of his jacket. "You look good in a suit. It's so different from how I'm used to seeing you."

He took her arm and headed for the door. They went to a nice upscale restaurant. The waiter seated them and he ordered some champagne. "I can't wait to tell you all about school. It was great there. Nothing like I'd ever been to before."

The waiter poured the champagne and Steve held up his glass. "To Alex. You changed my life."

Alex hesitated. "For the better or the worse?"

"Definitely for the better."

Alex lifted her glass and clinked it with his. They both drank and she held up her glass. "To Steve. Who convinced me I hadn't found the right man until him." They touched glasses and drank again.

Steve picked up his menu. "You know, I think I'll have chicken tonight."

Alex giggled. "Ginny is going to hate you."

Steve smiled. "I hope so. That's what she gets for deserting me. I looked for that hen for a week. I was afraid she'd gotten eaten."

"You could have called me to ask."

He looked down. "I know. I didn't know what to do."

Alex watched him. "Do you now?"

Steve looked up and looked directly into her eyes. "Definitely." He reached over and took her hand in his. "I want to talk about that after dinner." He released her hand and concentrated on his menu.

They ordered and talked about how everyone in the valley was doing while they ate. Alex hardly touched her food. He was avoiding talking about them. After they'd finished, they headed back to her apartment. She opened the door and went in.

"I'll be right back. I left something in the truck," he said and strode back down the hall.

Alex went inside and closed the door. She waited against the door for him to return. Within a few minutes he tapped on the door. She opened it and let him in. He didn't say a word but took her hand and led her into the bedroom. He stopped and she ran into him. She edged sideways to see why he'd stopped.

His eyes remained glued to her bed. "What the hell is that?"

She dropped his hand, maneuvered around him, and placed her hand on one of the four knobby bed posts. "My bed."

"It's so…so…ornate."

She slid her hand down the post and trailed her finger over the intricate turnings that formed the footboard. "It's a family heirloom. My great-great-grandmother got this as a wedding present. It's been passed down through the generations."

He walked over to inspect it more closely. He ran his hand down one of the six-foot-tall posts that was covered in knobs with turnings at the top and bottom. "And you plan on keeping it for future generations."

"Of course."

He touched the footboard that was made up of more knobby spindles that connected a straight board on the bottom to a turned board on top. He moved up to the headboard and ran his fingers over the intricate leaf scroll-work. "How long does it take you to dust it?"

"A while," she answered.

He pressed down on the mattress. "Is it safe?"

"Of course it is. I sleep on it every night."

"But is it strong enough to hold both of us?"

She giggled. "It was strong enough for my parents."

He flung his body onto the mattress. He bounced on his back once, but the bed-frame remained silent. "Remember when you collected the crystals for me and you passed out in the hotel?"

She nodded.

"I didn't tell you, but I called Principal Vale. He mentioned a way to get your power back faster."

She approached the bed and reached out to hold a post near him.

Steve watched her every move. "He said that by having unprotected sex I could transfer some of my power to you."

"But you didn't do it."

"No, because he mentioned two side-effects of doing this." He clasped his hands together on his stomach. "The first part is that by doing this, it will bond two wizards together."

"And the second?"

"That you might get pregnant." He sat up. "That was a risk I didn't want to take."

Alex moved to the edge of the bed, positioning herself in front of him.

Steve placed a hand on her leg and eased it up along her thigh.

Her skin felt alive wherever his fingers touched

her.

He kept looking into her eyes. "But I'm really interested in the first side-effect. I was thinking we might want to evoke that type of bond tonight."

"Why?"

"Because I love you. I've loved you for months now. I want you to be mine forever. I was afraid of putting you in danger."

"What about now? Is the bear still awake?"

"I took my potion. It allows me to shift only if I want to. If you haven't noticed…it's night and I'm still human."

"Sorry, I was distracted by your call. I'm not used to worrying about you shifting. We spent most of our time together in the winter when it wasn't a problem."

"Are you using your magic again?" he asked.

Alex nodded. "I no longer have to choose only one world. I can be a part of both. I've finally found a balance."

"Not still searching for someone normal?"

"No. I want to be with you." She took his face in her hands. "I love you."

"Then bond with me tonight."

She released her hands and let them fall to her side. "What if I get pregnant?"

"It won't matter. We're getting married next week during the full moon."

"What?"

"Oh yeah, I forgot." He reached in his pants pocket and worked a ring box free. He held it out to her.

Alex took the box and cracked it open, almost afraid of what was inside. She took a deep breath, closed her eyes, and opened the box all the way.

Ginny popped onto Alex's shoulder. *"Oh, how pretty. You gotta see this."*

Alex shooed Ginny away and opened her eyes. A large emerald-cut aquamarine stone sat in the middle of the setting with swirls of small diamonds outlining it. She reached out and touched the stone. "Is this from your claim?"

He nodded. "It's a stone that I collected last year. I held on to it as my best specimen." He pulled the ring out and slid it on her trembling finger. "I know it's not the traditional diamond..." Steve paused, "but I thought this might mean more to you."

"I love it." She held up her hand to look at it more closely. The light danced among the facets. "This means so much more. It's special."

"Will you marry me?"

Alex nodded. "Yes, oh yes."

"Will you do me the honor of becoming my mate, for life?" He held out his hand to her.

She wrapped her left hand around his and he pulled her down onto the bed next to him.

He wrapped his arms around her.

"Are you sure?" Alex asked.

"I've never been so sure about anything in my life. I want to have a whole pack with you. They won't have to suffer through their adolescence like I did."

"But what about the full moons. The neighbors might begin to ask questions if they see a pack of bears wandering around."

"I'll just take them up into the mountains on those nights."

"And I'll be alone in the cabin?"

"I'll make it up to you." He pulled her closer. "Are

344

you up to the challenge?"

"I can't wait." She placed a hand along his cheek.

"I want to be bonded to you from this night until forever. I love you," he whispered.

"I love you," she answered.

A word about the author...

Donna Kunkel is a paranormal romance author. Within the pages of her tales you can visit with witches, wizards, shape-shifters, and other fantasy creatures. Figurines of the magic realm surround her computer for inspiration. She lives at the edge of the Colorado mountains with her husband of many years and her two dogs. When not writing, you can find her browsing the fabric shops for her next quilt, stitching Japanese embroidery, or curled up with a good book. She enjoys spending time in the mountains, at Lake Tahoe, or relaxing on a beach in Hawaii.